THE TEXAS VAMPIRE

WILLIAM HATCHETT

A Wild Wolf Publication

Published by Wild Wolf Publishing in 2023

Copyright © 2023 William Hatchett

All rights reserved. No part of this book may be reproduced, stored in a retrieval system or transmitted in any form or by any means without the prior written permission of the publishers, except by a reviewer who may quote brief passages in a review to be printed by a newspaper, magazine or journal.

First print

ISBN: 979 8869766458
Also available as an E-book

www.wildwolfpublishing.com

1

Dorset Street

Task: Jack The Ripper

You know who he is (I hope) the Victorian slasher. There are various theories as to his identity. Well, I'm sending you into the heart of the East End of London, to find out the truth. I want you to make sure that the guilty party is apprehended and safely delivered into the hands of the authorities. Be careful, won't you. Life was cheap in those days.

Time: 1888
Lives remaining: 7
Special powers: 0

The sky is grey, the weather nondescript. A slight mist or fog hangs in the air from thousands of smoking chimneys. The streets are animated by a strange vitality. Horse-drawn vehicles dominate – tottering trams, cabs and piled-up carts. The pavements, and the roads too, are full of people: women in long dresses, some with shawls and bonnets; men in dark coats, all wearing hats, and children dressed in torn and filthy clothes.

Flower sellers, bootblacks and board carriers are plying their trades, some making strange cries. The overloaded carts threat to topple their wares onto the road.

Almost everyone here is puffing the noxious weed – even children. The old ladies who sit on the pavement like bundles of rags suck on clay pipes. Those who do not favour clays have briar pipes or cigarettes. There's an unholy racket – wheels on cobbles, street cries, bells – all subsumed into a general murmur of humanity going about its business.

What the hell am I supposed to do? I have no idea. I obviously look unexceptional, because no-one is noticing me. Don't panic, I tell myself.

I'm dressed in a suit – for once in my life – and a dull thin tie. Oxblood red. I hate ties. I touch my face. Jesus, I have a moustache! I'm taller than most of the people around me. Some of them are ruins. They look as if they're rotting from the inside.

•••

The road is the width of a couple of carriages. It leads to another broader, more prosperous thoroughfare. I step from the kerb and I'm almost obliterated by a speeding four-wheeled carriage. It is being driven by a man wearing a silk top hat and white cravat. As he flicks his whip, his gaze falls on mine. His hard white face views mine with indifference.

Across the street is something I recognise – the handsome spire and portico of Nicholas Hawksmoor's Christ Church, the pride of Spitalfields. Perfectly symmetrical, the church looms over the smoking rooftops, like a proud grey heron.

I'm about to take on the challenge of crossing the road again when I feel a tap on my shoulder. I turn round. In front of me is a lady. She is tall, with a pale complexion and blue eyes; blonde hair spills from her bonnet. She is wearing a red shawl and white apron over her black dress.

Is she...a prostitute? Could be. This is one of those apparently random encounters that's going to be significant. I know that from the countless hours I've spent in dark rooms with a hand controller, staring at a screen. Hours not wasted.

'Good day, sir.'

I detect a faint Irish lilt in her greeting.

'Good day.'

'Would you like some company?' she asks, innocently.

I'm a lonely man, wandering around the East End. Why not?

'Do you know these parts, sir?'

'I've been here a few times. And I've read about them – Nicholas Hawksmoor.'

She looks at me blankly.

'Read about them? You mean in books?'

'Yes, books.'

'I live close by, sir,' she says. Her hand is on her hip, her head tilted to one side. 'In Dorset Street.'

'Would you like to see?'

Jesus Christ. She's a hooker. A Victorian hooker.

'I would love to. I mean, if it is not too much trouble'.

She laughs.

'Come,' she says, 'It is very near,' and then, strangely, 'everything will be all right.'

She takes my hand and leads me down this road, Commercial Street.

We could be a well-matched couple out on a stroll, I tell myself. She informs me that her name is Marie Jeanette. I ask her if she is French. No, she is from Limerick, in Ireland, she says. When she first came to London, she lodged with a French woman in Kensington, in a large house. She liked her new name and decided to keep it.

Detecting an unfamiliar accent, she asks me where I'm from. Am I a yank – a seafarer perhaps? I say that I am, indeed, an American seafarer – no, even better! – a ship's captain. I've just arrived in the docks after a long voyage. I am anxious, I say, to see the famous sights of London.

The sights of London. I'm getting the hang of this. It's amazingly realistic. It's immersive, augmented, the real deal. I'm walking around the streets talking to people in my own voice, and I can go anywhere. It's like a lucid dream – a dream I can control.

Dorset Street is so narrow that you can almost touch its walls of soot-blackened houses with outstretched arms. As we walk down the street, matriarchs eye us through grimy windows. Bare-footed urchins tussle with stray dogs for scraps of food in the gutter. A grim tunnel leads us to a dismal space, enclosed by the neighbouring properties. I look up at a sign on the soot-blackened wall: Miller's Court.

She hums a sentimental song, A Violet From a Mother's Grave, as she fumbles for her keys. She seems proud that she has her own front door.

Illuminated by a guttering gaslight, the hallway is dark. Strips of brown paper hang from the wall, like forlorn banners.

'Nice, ain't it,' she says, as we stand outside her room. This is not Marie Jeanette but Mary Jane, a woman of the slums making the best of her miserable life.

And she, in one way or another, is going to lead me to The Ripper and to the end of the first level. Seven lives left. No special powers accessed. It's looking good. But am I actually going to have to…you know? My stomach is tightening. What if The Ripper is in her room? Jesus.

'We shall be warm inside,' she assures me. 'I 'as a cosy fire and a bottle of Madeira.'

'Thank you,' I reply.

She opens the door. Revealed by the fitful light that struggles into the room is her hopeless life – a stained, dark green coverlet on the bed, two chairs, a table with a crust of bread upon it, a small cold grate. A cheap print on the wall depicts a fishing boat bobbing on a spray-capped sea. *It's like a student's bedsit.*

'Don't be shy.' She leads me into the room. 'You 'as some coppers, I suppose?'

That's cheap. Fortunately, there's some spare change in my pocket.

'If you wouldn't mind, sir?' She looks at me hopefully. 'It's fourpence.'

Well, this is weird. I place the agreed sum on the bare wooden table. She lays back on the bed and its springs creak. She lifts her cream dress to above her garters.

Am I supposed to...?

'Listen,' I say, 'I…'

Suddenly there's a crash and the flimsy door splinters open.

The man who enters is more canine than human. He is shorter than Mary Jane and powerfully built. A bulldog. He wears a bowler.

His face is blotched with rage.

'Oh Christ,' I hear from the bed, 'it's Joseph!' She brushes down her linen.

'You f–ing whore!' he growls.

I freeze with terror.

One of Joseph's hands has been hidden behind his back. Not anymore. There is a hammer in it. I cower.

'Joseph, no!' She looks at him, pleadingly.

He lifts his arm. *Show's over, Chris.* With all his strength, he lands the hammer on my head. There is a vast, shuddering concussion as my skull shatters. I see stars. The impact leaves me in the middle of a black hole as a galaxy ends, or begins.

2

The Ten Bells

Dead in the game, an important lesson learned, but not in life. Here I am, back at base camp. My legs are stretched out on the bed in front of me. On the bedside cabinet is a tumbler of rum and coke from the minibar, untouched. I hook the controller back on the wall. I leave the TV on, with the volume down. It looks like it's having an epileptic seizure of pulsating light cells.

CloudCorp, the creators of Get The Bad Guys, have done me proud. Let me explain: they're putting me up at no expense in a luxury hotel at a secret location (not very secret, it's close to Eastbourne) while I try out their newest console game.

They're offering a prize for the first tester to complete the final level. It's supposed to be a million dollars. Yeh, right. I don't believe it – must be a catch – but I'm not complaining. It's a free holiday doing something I enjoy – or, rather, used to enjoy. A lot. I spent far too much time in my twenties sitting in the dark blasting zombies, aliens and strange slithery things that dropped from the ceiling, often while mildly stoned. My carbs came exclusively from Doritos. The soundtrack was provided by Metallica. I played and re-played my favourite games. As with most hollow-eyed, sleep-deprived addicts, I eventually wrestled back some semblance of a normal (i.e. non-gaming) life. But I still feel nostalgic for those years. Gaming is immersive, not passive like cinema, because you are interacting with a story, nuancing your progress scene by scene like a rock climber, perfecting a difficult route. In real life, you can't say 'whoops I fucked up – can we do it again?' The fact that you can in a video game helps to explain its addictive nature. It's about perfectibility, the primary human aspiration.

The Get The Bad Guys prize is obviously a scam, but who cares? CloudCorp are paying for hotel, etc., so they seem to have money to splash around. I mean, look at this place! Technically, it's The White Lodge Hotel, that's the name picked out in gold letters above the entrance, but everyone just calls it The White Lodge.

It's a modernist, flat-roofed, architectural icon – South Downs Le Corbusier, cocaine white and with many balconies, shadowed by enormous fir trees. Expensive vehicles in the car park disgorge relaxed, well-dressed guests with designer luggage and tennis rackets. Their skins glow with health.

My room on the fourth floor benefits from a highly-prized feature – a view of the sea. One can glimpse a delightful beach-fringed bay from the balcony. The room is luxurious but functional – no tacky abstract art. Its main elements are white walls, glass and chrome.

It is afternoon. Wafted by a sea breeze, the bedroom is pleasantly cool. I know that the hotel has a convivial bar, a pool, spa and other delights. But they can wait. I'm in a hurry to get back to Spitalfields. That moron with the hammer has just deprived me of one of my precious seven lives. The drill is, I get to return to a point before I died and have another go.

I re-arrange myself on the bed, turn on the TV and unhook the controller.

Don't mess it up, Chris, think big. There's a reward if you get to the last level. Has to be. Come on chap!

Task: Jack The Ripper
Time: 1888
Lives remaining: 6
Special powers: 0

Smoke, noise. Old ladies begging for coppers. Kids in bare feet. *How utterly tragic.* I walk jauntily along this road, Brushfield Street. I know who I am – an American sea captain who has just arrived at the docks with a pocketful of money. *Let's be efficient this time.* I turn right into Commercial Street. Christ Church is still doing its baroque magic, towering over the neighbouring slum. I stand at the kerbside waiting for the hansom to rush past me and then the tap on my shoulder. *Here we go.*

'Good day, sir.'

It's my good friend Mary Jane who calls herself Marie Jeanette.

'Good day.'

'Would you like some company?'

Now, let me see.
I said I would.
'Do you know these parts, sir?'
I say no, not very well, I have merely studied them.
'Studied them? You mean from books?'
'Yes, from books. Do you live round here?'
'I do,' she says, 'in Dorset Street. Would you like to see?'
Not really. I know what's waiting for me there – sudden death.
'No,' I say, 'but thank you. I'd like to go for a drink.'
She looks puzzled.
'In a public house?'
'Yes, I fancy a pint. Would you like to join me?'

She smiles and takes my hand, as if we are already sweethearts. Her apron is not perfectly white, I notice. It is grey from frequent washing and spotted with holes.

'Well, there's The Ten Bells', she says, 'but Joseph may be there.'

'Joseph?'

'My er...cousin.'

Christ, that brute with the hammer. Still, at least we'll be in a public place.

'The Ten Bells it is then,' I nod. 'Good plan.'

Keeping a weather eye open for constables (to a casual eye we could look like an innocent couple), we stroll along Commercial Street.

We begin to converse. *Here comes the spiel.* Her name is Mary Jane but she likes to be known as Marie Jeanette, the new moniker she adopted when she lodged with a French woman in the West End. *Was that in a brothel perhaps? Blah blah blah.* I tell her I'm an American sea captain. I have recently concluded a long voyage and I'm anxious to explore this famous city.

'I bet you ain't seen nothing like this,' she says, indicating a luminous palace of pleasure on the corner of Fournier Street. *The Ten Bells!*

Fixed to a wall nearby is a handbill. I read it carefully:

IMPORTANT NOTICE

To the Tradesmen, Ratepayers and Inhabitants Generally of Whitechapel and District. Finding that in spite of the Murders being committed in our midst, and that the Murderer or Murderers are still at large, we the undersigned have formed ourselves into a Committee and intend offering a substantial REWARD to anyone...

Mary Jane clutches my arm and shudders:
'It's 'im what done in Mary Nicholls and Dark Annie. They call him Leather Apron, The Whitechapel Murderer.'
I say I have no idea what she's talking about.

3

To Bow Street

Midway through a November afternoon, the establishment is heaving. Many dialects and languages are being spoken here in The Ten Bells, often slurred by inebriation.

The exterior – primarily glazed bricks and frosted glass – glows like a crystal cathedral. The purple of broken veins has darkened the faces of the most regular customers. Gin is the drink of choice here, especially for women. The pub is clearly popular with the criminal fraternity.

Between the door and the bar, Mary Jane is greeted by a gaudily-dressed woman who evidently knows her.

'Who's your sweetheart, deary?' says the dark-eyed, plump girl with the auburn curls.

'This is my friend,' Mary Jane replies. 'He's a yank.'

'Is he now?' says the girl, with a smile.

'What's 'is name?'

'What *is* your name?' Mary Jane asks me.

'Billy,' I say, thinking quickly. 'Billy Wilkins.'

'Is Joseph in?' my companion enquires of her friend, with a trace of anxiety in her voice.

'Nah, he's been taken sick I 'eard, from a mussel. I ain't seen 'im.'

'Is that so?'

Thank Christ for that. I hope he's laid low for days.

Mary Jane's mood lightens.

'Ain't you going to offer a girl a port and lemon, Billy boy? I'll be sitting over there.'

She indicates a partitioned booth in the corner. I make my way to the bar.

Outside, a dusky twilight has cloaked the sky. On a winter's evening, one can easily see the attraction of the warmth, light and vitality of a place like this.

Okay, a port and lemon for the lady (*nothing changes*) but what should I drink? A man standing next to me at the bar offers a solution – a pint of pale and mild, known as a 'half and half'.

Most of the customers in the saloon bar are well-dressed – clerks and the superior kind of artisan. I understand why Mary Jane has scuttled to a seat at the back. Professional ladies would be conspicuous.

Waiting to be served, I pick up some intelligence about the recent murders. *That's what I'm here for.* The victims' internal organs, it appears, have been removed in a gruesome, quasi-surgical manner and arranged around their cadavers. *Sounds like The Ripper.*

The whole pub is agog with speculation:

'He must have a job, cos all the murders is at the end of the week…'

'He must be a doctor…'

'He wears a leather apron, so 'e must be a butcher…'

'Yeh, a Jewish butcher…'

'Nah, 'e's a Polish butcher…'

'No 'e ain't!'

•••

'Ah Billy boy!' says Mary Jane, as I place the drinks on the table. I like the name. It seems to suit me.

With its dark green walls and gloomy decorations, this part of the pub has the solemn, Sunday-like feel of a domestic parlour. The hubbub next door in the public bar is deafening. Here, it's possible to conduct a conversation.

After a while, itching to perform the transaction that will earn her fourpence, Mary Jane intimates as to the warmth and comfort of her luxurious apartment. Not wishing to risk another bang on the head, I encourage her to stay in The Ten Bells.

A solemn, respectably-dressed man joins a nearby table. His hair is thinning; by contrast, his moustache and side-whiskers form a hairy continuum, like a guardsman's chin strap. He pulls a copy of a newspaper, the Pall Mall Gazette, from his pocket and begins to read it.

'He's a bobby,' Mary Jane hisses under her breath, 'in plain clothes. Every pub is full of 'em – coppers, narks and rubberneckers what's come to gawk at us. The reporters is the worst. They just wants a good story for their rag. They don't care about nuffink else.'

I glance at the man. Absorbed with his paper, he appears to show no interest in his surroundings.

'So, you don't believe in Leather Apron?'

'What do you think?' She guffaws. 'It's a lot of nonsense. Do they think we 'is fools?'

She replaces her glass on the table. It's empty. I have scarcely touched my drink.

'So, Billy boy, 'as you got a missus in America?'

'Er…no.'

'Any nippers?'

'Not that I know of.'

'How old is you?'

'29.'

She looks puzzled.

'That's a bit young for a sea captain ain't it?'

Is it? I shrug.

Christ, I'm starting to find her attractive. Soon, she'll be like one of the broken down, gin-sodden creatures in the public bar. But for now…

Her eyes are sparkling.

'So, was you lying about being a captain?'

'Perhaps. Don't you lie sometimes?'

'But you is from California?'

'Oh yes.'

•••

I feel her body tense as a shadow crosses her face. Has someone she fears entered the bar? Is it Joseph? For that matter, is Joseph Leather Apron? I turn in my seat. Who has she seen?

I spy a fellow whose black coat is trimmed with an astrakhan collar. He is wearing a cream fedora with a black band. He has a salt and pepper moustache that curls down at the ends. The spats buttoned over his shoes indicate a superior station in life, as do his cane and kid gloves. His expression is complacent.

What's a posh bloke doing in a dive like this?

'Do you know that man?'

'Nah, I ain't never seen 'im.'

Her reaction to his entrance has been instinctive, like that of a deer sensing danger. Her gaze flicks down to her glass, suggesting I should do the necessary and re-fill it.

I watch as Astrakhan settles himself. He carefully places an accountant's leather case next to his table before peeling off his gloves. *Well, that's a great big fat clue for you Chris. Bet there are knives in there, boy.*

He is only a few feet from the undercover bobby reading his paper. The detective studiously ignores him.

My trip to the bar yields no more information about the sadistic murderer. *Who is probably in here. Ironic.*

Mary Jane takes a gulp from her glass and leans across the table. Her breath is sweet.

'Ain't you going to be nice to me, Billy boy?' she asks suggestively. 'Why don't you come over this side?'

She pats the stained velvet bench. I transfer my position and she nestles against me. She fits comfortably into my side. This small intimacy makes me – *happy*. It seems right that we are together. We have largely exhausted our exploratory small talk. We're merry with drink.

A piano begins to knock up a tune in the public bar. Bacchus is smiling on this fuggy, tar-coated world with its polished wood and frosted glass, filling it with happiness.

She knows the song the pianist is playing – A Violet From a Mother's Grave. I hear her voice again, as I had in Miller's Court. *In my previous life. This one is so much better!* It is pure and crystalline.

'Why don't you come back to mine ducks?'

I glance over at Astrakhan. In front of him is a tiny glass of green liquid. Absinthe. His dark, reptilian eyes flicker round the room.

'I 'as a nice fire and a bottle of Madeira. It's waiting for us, all snug and warm like.'

Her voice is slurred. Astrakhan takes a sip from his drink. Through the glass door, I see the yellow glow of gas lamps. There will be fog now, thick and clinging. *Proper East End. They've done a good job.*

'Yes,' I say. 'Thank you.'

Unsteadily, I get to my feet and pull her up. She almost falls. Her laugh draws eyes toward us from all over the room.

Oh God, am I about to make the same mistake again, going back to hers? Trust me to let booze cloud my judgement.

•••

Outside, my head is spinning. The fog is thick and brown. It burns my throat. From inside the pub, we hear the sound of glass smashing and a crescendo of laughter.

'Listen, Mary Jane...'

My hand is around her slender waist. *I actually desire her.*

'Yes?'

'What if we go to a different place, a nicer place?' *Maybe one without a psycho. Can I find some kind of weapon?*

'You mean my place ain't nice?'

'I'm not saying that, I mean I haven't even seen it. I meant to a hotel.'

'A hotel?'

'I'll pay.' In truth, my supply of copper and silver isn't that generous. Still, I'll cross that bridge when we get to it.

'Look,' I say, 'we can get a cab. We can go to Piccadilly, or...Kensington.'

'Kensington? Ah...Billy,' she sighs.

My suggestion has perhaps reminded her of a time when she was happy. Before life turned sour and led her onto the streets.

I feel a hand on my shoulder. This is not like Mary Jane's delicate touch, but the steely grip of a pterodactyl.

'William Wilkins?'

'What?'

As I look round, my right arm is twisted behind my back. I cannot see who is addressing me.

'I am arresting you for the murders of Mary Ann Nichols, Annie Chapman, Elizabeth Stride and Catherine Eddowes. You do not have to say anything...'

'What?!' *Uh-oh.*

Brute force almost wrenches my arm from its shoulder.

'...unless you wish to do so...'

Mary Jane begins to howl.

I feel the sharp painful click of handcuffs. Two policemen bundle me towards a black, horse-drawn carriage. A third is watching.

History is in the making. Soon news of my capture will travel across Spitalfields and Whitechapel like a bushfire!

Mary Jane is standing beneath a gaslight, tears streaming down her face.

'Billy, Billy…'

That's the last thing I hear as they thrust me into the van. Inside, I am penned in a cubicle, like an animal. We jolt across the cobbles to the local police station in Whitechapel.

Later, I'm taken to Bow Street, where I'm charged with four counts of murder. I am sure the crowds here have been forewarned as I'm struck by a fusillade of saliva and abuse as police officers drag me, my head covered by a blanket, into the building.

4

The Drop

After my committal hearing, I am moved from Bow Street to London's model prison, Wandsworth, to be held on remand.

So here I sit, being peered at through a spy hole in the massive door; my meagre food slides through a hatch. The other prisoners know who I am, for my fame has been growing by the day. I am 'Bludgeon Billy' or 'The Beast of Flower and Dean Street'.

Some particularly sick and twisted inmates regard me as a kind of folk hero, but most stick to a simple repertoire of hatred.

My cell is close to the 'cold meat shed'. This is where condemned men are sent to the gallows, some reticent, some pleading for their lives.

In the exercise yard and at mealtimes, silence is strictly observed – a form of punishment – but at night in my cell as I drift in and out of sleep, I can hear the cries of my fellow prisoners, 'get ready to dangle, Billy!', 'they're gonna snap you!', and so on.

The saga of Whitechapel is running its course. The time has come for a sacrificial victim to be offered up to the shrine of sensation. Four witnesses have confirmed that I carried a bulging duffel bag into The Ten Bells – the kind of bag that sailors use. One has attested to a suspicious metallic clank from inside. The duffel bag and the surgical tools that it allegedly contained have been exploited enthusiastically in press reports.

In vain, I told the detective who interviewed me in Bow Street of other people in the pub who would have seen me – the man in the Astrakhan coat and the reader of the Pall Mall Gazette for example. Apparently, no-one else saw them. They do not exist.

I cannot call on Mary Jane as my star witness because, conveniently for the prosecution, she's disappeared. The story is that, traumatised by my behaviour, she fled the East End. Last seen in Ramsgate, she crossed the channel in a steam packet and has disappeared to the continent, leaving no further trace.

•••

In court at the Old Bailey, I have absolutely no defence against the mass of evidence assembled by King's Counsel, which he now rolls over me like a juggernaut. He's a slick, complacent creature who has greasily ingratiated himself to the jury, slavering over the details of my crimes.

I have no alibi and no alternative story to counter the prosecution's case or witness testimonies. The strange and vague explanations I've attempted to put forward have been interpreted as the ruse of a sly criminal mind. It seems obvious I'm pretending to be insane!

The trial is soon over. On a dreary November morning, verdict and sentence are announced. My face, blank and incredulous, is scrutinised intensely from the public gallery. It will be portrayed in pen and charcoal by court artists for the following day's press. I know these crude depictions will make me look evil.

The judge presents a detailed and lurid account of the murders. I have exploited the trust of the unfortunate fallen creatures who fell into my clutches – flowers of womanhood crushed in the gutter. My abominable crimes are 'beyond human depravity'.

The jury pronounces its unanimous verdict – guilty. A black silk cap is duly placed on the judge's head. He intones the litany that the public loves so much: 'The sentence of this court is that you shall be taken to the place from whence you came, and from there be taken to a place of execution. And there you shall be hung by the neck…until you are dead.'

The gallery erupts in jubilation.

The judge bangs his gavel.

'Take him down!'

•••

No-one visits me in the condemned cell, not even my barrister. Now that my appeal for clemency to the Home Secretary has inevitably failed, there is nothing between me and the rope.

On the eve of the execution, the prison chaplain makes a nocturnal visit to offer me solace. It's also an opportunity, he suggests, for me to confess my crimes and make my peace with The Almighty. I decline.

On the morning itself, I imagine that a small, ragged crowd has gathered at the gates of the prison before dawn – the usual salvationists and God botherers and bloodthirsty types who wish to send me to hell.

It's still dark outside.

The executioner is a thin, nervous man. He has the reek of stale spirits on his breath and adopts a crude bonhomie, designed to reassure me. It has the opposite effect.

'Come on, chin up. It's nearly time.'

One door and a short corridor separate me from extinction. In the execution chamber are the governor, the prison chaplain and two other formally dressed men. Standing on the trapdoor, I stare defiantly ahead. My legs aren't shaking, I'm merely curious as to what an execution will feel like.

'I think we'd better 'ave this on, don't you...'

The executioner thrusts a canvas hood over my head. His hands are trembling. A moment later, he wrenches on a lever.

The trapdoor opens and I drop into space. There's a loud crack as my spinal cord snaps.

5

Back In The USSR

Bummer. Back to base camp. Two lives gone – five left. The million dollars is slipping away. In my room is a message – a piece of paper that's been slid under the door: 'Please report to reception.' I expect some bad news. *You're so crap at this that we want you to leave. Bye Chris.*

'Hello.'

The receptionist of The White Lodge seems pleased to see me. There's a lilt to her voice. Is she from the Caribbean?

'What have you been up to?' she asks me.

'Not much, just hanging around.'

'Oh.'

'We've had to put you in a different room, I'm afraid.'

That's a relief. They're not throwing me out. My mood lifts.

'Really?'

'Yes, we're very busy.'

I glance outside through the open door. It's a bright day, late afternoon. Where are the other guests? On long walks or playing tennis?

'This room doesn't overlook the sea, but it's just as nice as your last one', the receptionist assures me.

'That's fine.'

'First floor.' She hands me the door swipe. 'Would you like a newspaper?'

I pause.

'A newspaper?'

'Yes,' she says. 'It's a special service. We can provide you with a copy of virtually every newspaper ever printed in English that exists online.'

Wow, that's impressive.

'OK. How about The Times from 10th November 1888?'

'That shouldn't be a problem,' the woman replies, without pausing. 'It will be delivered to your room. Or would you like us to e-mail it to you?'

'A paper copy would be great.'
'Anything else?'
'No, thanks.'
Her eyes lock onto mine for a fraction too long.

•••

It's almost four o'clock. Those strolling or exercising outside in the perfect golden light can observe the shadows lengthening, their stomachs tightening in anticipation of dinner.

From inside my room, I can hear the thwack of tennis balls from the court, but there's another sound thrumming through the floor: the muffled repetitive figures of a bass line. There are odd stops, starts and repetitions. I recognise the unmistakable sound of a function band rehearsing. Beyond the glass balcony doors, which I slide open, is a vista of smooth emerald lawns nibbled by deer. Beyond this is a belt of trees, through which I can glimpse a river. Truly this is a perfect place.

I touch my neck. There's no trace of pain, but execution is not a trivial matter. It's a fairly definitive statement of being unwanted. I need a drink. The game can wait. But first, I need to check out the music.

The musicians are at the far end of the ballroom. There's a thin guy with hair that could do with a wash and some attention from a comb. He's wearing a suit jacket with silk lapels over a t-shirt and on his feet distinctive shoes with thick soles. He's a thrift shop dandy, clearly the guitarist. He seems exasperated, and I can see he's itching for a cigarette – which, of course, he's not allowed to smoke in the hotel.

Close to him is a smiling, blonde-haired girl in jeans and a silky, parchment-coloured shirt. The singer? There's a fellow dressed in combat trousers, probably the bass player. Bassists don't usually stand out. He offers no competition to the guitarist in the clothes department.

I almost turn away but I'm intrigued as I've noticed no-one's sitting behind the drumkit.

As I cross the room, the guitarist glares at me:
'Can we help you?'
'I just came to say hi.'

'Oh.' He looks away.

'I'm a drummer, actually.'

'Oh?'

Now he seems interested and we start chatting. He tells me his name is Simon Peaceful and his girlfriend, indeed the vocalist, is Anya. She is Polish. The bass player's name is Ben. All from London, they're here for the summer as the hotel's house band. They mainly perform covers, he explains, and they're playing a function here this evening, Saturday, but their drummer's disappeared.

Pulling a crumpled set list from his jacket pocket, he hands it to me. I study it: familiar, guitar-based wedding reception fare.

'Think you can handle those?'

'Yeh, I reckon.'

I've been playing most of these songs for years. I remove my jacket and sit on the drum stool. Two toms, bass drum, cymbals, snare, familiar set-up.

The first song is Back in the USSR. Luckily, I was once, briefly, in a Beatles tribute band.

Simon has already picked up his electric guitar – a Gibson SG.

'Ready?'

He glances at Anya, who's standing in front of the mic stand. Words aren't needed. They just want to get through this. There's an easy communication between them.

'1, 2, 3, 4!'

The first chords build up to a familiar crescendo. It's a smooth take-off.

•••

'That was good,' says Simon afterwards. 'I mean, you were okay.'

'Thanks.'

We've gone through the entire set easily, with few pauses. Now we're in the hotel bar, playing pool. The room is enclosed and illuminated primarily by neon, like an American bar, as if drinking is an illicit, sinful activity to be done shielded from daylight. Close to where we've been rehearsing is a large tank of brightly-coloured tropical fish. Above us hangs a portrait of a periwigged man – George Washington.

It's seven o'clock. We're on at eight. Anya and Ben are changing into their stage gear. Simon doesn't need to, his clothes are fine.

He plays pool with the fluidity of one who has honed his skills over many hours in the disreputable places in which the game is generally perfected. He's assertive and accurate. Polishing the cue tip, smoking, bending over the table, frowning as he concentrates on a difficult shot, his repertoire of movements flows seamlessly – the choreography of the pool hall.

He's not supposed to be smoking in the hotel of course, but he seems to me the kind of person who's always lighting up – the gestures of smoking punctuate his thoughts and his conversation. He is knowledgeable and easy to talk to, and we find ourselves chatting naturally, a camaraderie perhaps borne from being the same age. This first evening in the bar, drinking the hotel's pale, gassy lager, sets the pattern of our relationship. Every time we meet, we simply resume where we've left off.

One great thing about The White Lodge is that everything's free. Even tipping isn't allowed but this doesn't make the staff any less helpful.

There are lots of things to do. Apart from sporting and leisure activities, I've discovered there are talks by experts on topics including art, history and religion. They're streamed but, if you want to, you can also see the speakers in the flesh in one of the hotel's conference rooms.

It is only after an hour or so that Simon asks whether I'm a gamer. I say I am, so he asks me what task I'm on.

'Jack The Ripper,' I reply. 'It's not going well.'

'Really?'

'I'm already on my third life. I've been banged on the head and executed.'

'That's not good. Do you have any special powers?'

'What do you mean?'

'Did you find the gold sovereign?'

'What gold sovereign?'

'In your jacket. It's in one of the pockets. Press on it and see what happens.'

'Yeh, I will.'

•••

I don't have a chance to get back on the table for the rest of this game of pool, as Simon works his way through the yellow balls and clinically beats me. In the next game, he offers me some practical tips, but they make little difference and, again, he despatches me with mechanical efficiency.

It's quarter to eight and Anya and Ben appear in the bar in their stage clothes. She's wearing a clingy black dress showing lots of skin that glows with a tawny sheen. One can tell from their easy familiarity around each other that she and Simon are lovers. Ben's put on a shirt and tie. He looks uncomfortable.

After soundcheck, we play to a roomful of enthusiastic people. The news soon travels around that we have never played together before but the audience loves us, and we don't finish until after midnight.

As dawn rises, I wake up and notice that the TV is still on. *What was that Simon said about a gold sovereign?* I click on a page that explains the power-ups offered by CloudCorp's first-person walk through, Get The Bad Guys. To beat them, you need a little assistance. These ones are pretty weird – esoteric. That's good, in my eyes. Normally it's bigger guns and faster wheels. I'm interested in the occult and read about it a lot. It provides the imagery and ambience of my favourite music – metal. I know a lot more about it than the kind of people who flash devil's horns with their fingers. So:

1. Clairvoyance/sixth sense.
2. Ability to understand and speak in foreign languages.
3. Astral projection.
4. Full Ipsissimus. Includes extreme healing and endurance, expert proficiency on any musical instrument. Ability to assume another animal form and summon spirit helpers for assistance.

There's a note below:

'Watch out for bulb heads. If you see anyone in the game whose head is glowing yellow, it means that they've attained Level 4 powers. These are the Illuminati, so to speak. They're either going to help you or kill you.'

Hmm, that could be useful. Time to return to the streets of Victorian London. Go get 'em Chris! Come on. You can do it boy!

6

The Six-Pointed Star

Task: Jack The Ripper
Time: 1888
Lives remaining: 5
Special powers: Level 1

'Would you like a drink?'
'Sorry?'

Mary Jane was shocked. No sooner had she tapped me on the shoulder in Commercial Street, trawling for trade, than, reversing the normal procedure, I was propositioning her.

'You know, a port and lemon in The Ten Bells. That's what you like to drink isn't it?'

'Do I know you?' she said, looking perplexed.

'You don't,' I said.

'Are you an effing copper?'

'No.'

'Are you a poxy reporter then?'

'I'm not that either,' I said.

'Then 'ow d'you know my habits?'

Around us, the East End was going about its normal business on a November afternoon. The clouds over Christ Church were thickening. There was rain in the air. Soon, the gas lamps would be lit, adding their halos of light to the lurid melodrama of swirling brown fog and deep shadow.

'Look, all women like port and lemon don't they? And The Ten Bells is just up the road. It's not a time to be out on your own.'

'So, you wants to keep me company?'

She cocked her head to one side. Her blue eyes and fresh skin were striking. I knew, from our previous encounters, that she was sharp-witted and curious and that she liked to laugh.

'Yes.'

'And you're offering to buy me a drink?'

'Yes, more than a drink.'

'Oo-err!'

'I mean more than one drink.'

'You fancy your chances, do'ncher?' She laughed. 'You sure you're not one of them copper's narks?'

'I'm not. I'm just looking for some company.'

'Well, you seems like a gentleman. I'll be 'appy to walk out with you, sir.'

'Thank you.'

She offered me her arm and I took it. It was the third time. I hoped it would be the last. Keeping an eye open for constables, she led me up Commercial Street.

I remembered what Simon had told me about the gold sovereign in my jacket. Sure enough, there was a hard lump in my ticket pocket.

First, I touched the coin, then squeezed it between thumb and forefinger. As I squeezed harder, I felt energy, like a tingle of electricity, pass from the metal into my skin. The coin grew warm. My scalp felt tight. A tight band seemed to press against my eyes.

It was obvious that, once the coin had done its work of transferring its power to me, it would immediately cool down. And it did.

•••

I was now gifted with the first special power available to gamers – clairvoyance. Through the side of her body, I could feel Mary Jane's spirit. In my head, I heard the cry of a little girl sent to sleep with no supper, then another sound. She was pleading with a man not to beat her – Joseph.

It was odd being able to tell the true natures of people I passed in the street, behind the masks they presented to the world. The souls of some were dark and sinister. Others radiated joy and innocence. A few were merely blank.

I could tell Mary Jane's deepest thoughts from the touch of her body, as if I was reading a book.

I knew that if I looked into her face, I would see goodness shining out. Despite all her suffering, that innate quality had never been crushed. However, she was worried because she hadn't paid her rent for weeks. Tomorrow a fellow would come to her room in Dorset Street to collect it.

It wouldn't be the landlord, but his agent. He had pock-marked skin, this man, and cruel eyes. He went by a nickname – Indian something.

'How much do you owe, Mary?' I asked.

'What do you mean?'

'Your rent. You're behind with it, aren't you?'

'Twenty-nine shillings. So you are a copper!'

We had stopped walking. She looked anxious.

'I am not. Do I sound like a policeman?'

'No.'

'Do I look like one?'

'Not really. You ain't ugly enough.'

'The thing is, I have these special powers. I can tell things about people from their…vibrations. I could read your palm or your tea leaves or your Tarot cards. It comes to the same thing.'

'You're a clairvoyant.'

'If you like. That's one word for it.'

She beamed.

At some point, since the beginning of our walk, night had fallen. The sky was almost black. Ahead, on the other side of the road, warm, inviting and glowing like a tabernacle was The Ten Bells.

•••

I led her through the saloon bar, brushing past Lizzie's friendly greeting.

'You sit there. I'll get our drinks.'

The half and half that I had drunk here before was a little too sweet, so this time I ordered a pint of pale ale.

'Cheers,' she said, lifting her port and lemon. 'It's warm and cosy, you know, back at my place. Wouldn't you like to come and see it? It's much nicer than here.'

'Perhaps I will,' I said. 'You have a bottle of something back at home, don't you, Mary Jane? Don't tell me, it's…Madeira.'

'Gor blimey,' she said, 'you really are a mind reader.'

'Perhaps I should work for the police.'

'Or for a circus!'

I span her the usual line about being a man of the sea and not having a wife, or children. She talked of her Irish origins in Limerick, of the death of her first husband in a colliery explosion in Wales and of the happy time when she'd first come to London, lodging in Kensington. Perhaps she had been working in a high-class brothel there. I didn't inquire too deeply. Her eyes misted over at the memory of riding in carriages and accompanying a gentleman friend to Paris.

As we were talking, I anticipated a thin-faced man arriving to take his seat close to us. In he came, on cue, selecting his normal table and settling down to read his paper. Mary Jane had been correct in her previous assessment, he *was* a policeman. I could tell that now as plain as day.

The man buried his nose in the Pall Mall Gazette in an attempt to disguise his true purpose, but his senses were as acute as a bloodhound's. He was alert to everything going on around him. The Leather Apron business was of great importance to this individual. Why? Because he was a detective, an inspector, assigned to this celebrated case.

All of this I deduced from a brief glance at the unobtrusive man.

Perhaps intuition is merely a speeding up of the normal faculties? At any rate, I realised that I had previously been walking around half blind.

They say that being drunk exposes our true natures. In Mary Jane's case, even in mild doses, alcohol released the natural affection that welled up from inside her. An uncared-for plant will thrive in the right conditions. She had never been truly loved, nor allowed to love.

As she quizzed me about my life, I was only half listening. Soon, the man in the Astrakhan-collared coat and the cane and glove would come in. Now I would observe him with my new sixth sense.

•••

Mary Jane tensed. I turned in my seat. The blood froze in my veins.

Some individuals give off light. Astrakhan drew it in, like a universe approaching its dissolution, as time and matter are sucked into a black hole. There was an intense, impenetrable blackness at the core of his being. His lack of empathy was beyond cruelty. He was utterly insensitive to human feelings – humans did not exist for him. They were merely chaff.

I had a vision of the fellow at the centre of a dark chapel. The room was shaped like a basilica. I could hear a sound of intoning or moaning. There was an altar, but it was not a Christian altar where the Eucharist is observed. Light slanted diagonally into the room.

'Billy! Billy!'

Hearing my name brought me back into the room.

'I'm thirsty, Billy.'

'Oh, I'm sorry my love.'

As I walked to the bar, another image came into my head. It was that of a six-pointed star – the Star of David, the Masonic hexagram. Of course.

This was the key to the murders. The recorded victims, positioned on a map of the East End, corresponded to five of the six points of a hexagram. Annie Chapman was the top point of the star. The points to either side were Mary Jane Kelly (tonight's target, number five) and Mary Nicholls. Those at the base were Catherine Eddowes and Elizabeth Stride. That left a sixth point, at the base of the triangle.

The dates of the murders, if one looked into it, would undoubtedly match the days of some sacred or ritualistic calendar. There would be a sixth murder as sure as daylight after tonight's murder of Mary Jane, corresponding to the final point of the star.

I knew that the six-pointed star was not just a Judaic symbol but a more ancient Kabbalistic one, widely used by the Freemasons and Theosophists.

Perhaps the beast who had carried out these murders had conflated all these belief systems into one weird cult of evil – a cult involving human sacrifice.

Astrakhan placed the suspicious package on the table and slowly settled into his seat, kid gloves resting on his cane. He stared blankly ahead, with the cruel visage of a pagan god.

'I'm sorry, Mary Jane,' I said. 'I have to do something.'

I excused myself from our table.

•••

The detective looked up from his periodical, only a little surprised by my interruption, and invited me to sit at his table.

'Sir,' I said, 'we need somewhere more private for what I'm about to tell you.'

He studied my face. Then he nodded.

There was a place in the pub that fitted the bill perfectly. Furnished with gleaming mirrors and marble like a royal palace, it was conveniently empty.

Standing next to the gurgling urinals, Inspector Abberline said that Astrakhan had already attracted his attention as someone who did not normally drink in The Ten Bells.

As I elaborated upon my theory (I didn't say that it was based upon pure intuition), he nodded gravely.

'A Masonic cult, ritual magic…I see.'

I told him that, if he did not prevent tonight's murder, there would inevitably be a sixth one. I added that, using a map of the East End, I could pinpoint its location (the missing point of the hexagram) to within a few feet. I could even predict its day and time. However, that did not need to happen.

I persuaded Abberline to send a messenger over from The Ten Bells to Spitalfields police station with clear written instructions, which must be followed to the letter. A life was at stake.

The plan was simple: I would leave the pub and, soon afterwards, Mary Jane would follow me. Falling into her old habits, she would take up her familiar spot outside, asking male passers-by if they wanted some company.

Astrakhan would have already spotted her, like an octopus hiding in a reef eyeing its prey. He would surely pick up his package of surgeon's knives and take the bait.

Abberline and the constable who had been called out from the station (at my suggestion) had merely to follow Astrakhan and Mary Jane down to Miller's Court. They should wait for a carefully judged period of time and burst in, praying that her throat had not already been slashed.

Abberline was keen to adopt my plan for his detective's instincts matched mine. He had pretty much identified Astrakhan as The Ripper when he'd first walked into the pub. My story merely confirmed his suspicions.

He left the gents first. I followed after a respectable interval.

Mary Jane was disappointed that our time in The Ten Bells was coming to an end.

A piano was banging out a tune in the public bar. The night was getting into full swing.

She pleaded with me to stay, but I was adamant.

'Why? We're having a nice time ain't we?' she said.

'I know, that's why I have to leave.'

'That don't make sense.'

I reached into my pocket.

'Here, have this.'

I placed the sovereign on the table.

'What's that for?'

'It's to pay your rent – but be careful. Don't flash it about.'

'I ain't stupid.'

She secreted the coin in the pocket in her apron, then smiled at me and clutched my hand.

'Don't go.'

'I'm sorry, I have to.'

Abberline was talking to the pub's potman as I passed his table. Soon, this fellow would pass a folded scrap of paper with pencilled instructions to a constable outside. With many similar documents, this grubby souvenir would enter Jack The Ripper folklore.

The inspector did not acknowledge my glance. Astrakhan was openly staring at Mary Jane now – the pretty woman in the corner in a red shawl. Briefly, I looked back at her table. She stared at me imploringly across the noisy room.

I pushed open the glazed door and stepped into the thick, rasping fog.

•••

I did not wish to step on the police's toes as they set their trap so, leaving the pub, I turned left into Fournier Street and walked towards Brick Lane. The mean, shadowy houses were overhung by the pale stone of Christ Church. The street was eerily deserted.

I was in another pub, The Frying Pan, on the corner of Thrawl Street, when it happened. The door was flung open and a shaved head poked into the noisy, smoke-filled room.

'They've nabbed The Ripper, in Dorset Street!'

The news flew round the pub like a shuttle. There was little more to go on for now, other than that a foreign gentleman had been caught red-handed by the police, moments before despatching and eviscerating a new victim.

The following day more information would be forthcoming as the first printed accounts of the arrest would appear, padded out by speculation.

I was waiting to be served amidst a crowd of roughly-dressed men. Stimulated by the excitement of the news, they crushed and jostled me. The till was rattling like a machine gun.

I felt dizzy. Was hunger the cause, or perhaps elation from my success?

There was a hole in my stomach. It rose up to my chest, then to my head, which seemed to fill with light. This was not like dying, it was like waking up in a bright room.

7

The Black Locust Tree

Task: Jack The Ripper
Mission completed

Well done, you have succeeded! Jack has been caught. Be proud of yourself, you are a true hero. You may now proceed to the next task.

I rub my temples. I turn off the TV. *This room is becoming familiar now.*

It is the end of another perfect day. The sun is dipping into the trees and wood pigeons coo across the lawns. A faint impression of wood smoke in the air combines deliciously with the cooking smells rising from the hotel kitchen. I like this room, although it can be somewhat noisy and lacks direct morning sun.

Two copies of The Times, both published on Monday 10th November 1888, have been slid under my door. There were no headlines clammering for attention in broadsheet newspapers in those days, nor pictures. The news filled seven narrow columns crammed to the edges of pages.

The front pages look identical until you study them closely and realise that, actually, the story in the left-hand column of each newspaper is different.

In the first newspaper, the story reads:

'Sailor is Whitechapel murderer
An American seafarer named William Wilkins, lately arrived at the West India Docks, has been apprehended in Spitalfields, following the ghastly murders of Catherine Eddowes and Elizabeth Stride. Mr Wilkins…'

And in the second:

'Ukrainian priest apprehended

Isaiah Brodsky, a former Orthodox priest of Ukrainian nationality has been charged in Bow Street and named as the perpetrator of the Whitechapel murders. Scotland Yard…'

Congratulations Chris! Or is it Billy? At last, some success in your life.

I should frame these stories and keep them as souvenirs. I recall Mary Jane's face in The Ten Bells on the night The Ripper was caught. She had looked at me pleadingly, begging me to stay. What will become of her? I'm going to miss her. I realise how hungry I am. I need a drink.

•••

Simon, Ben and Anya are in the George Washington bar, wearing their normal clothes. They're drinking lager. Music is playing faintly in the background. It's jazz – the unobtrusive kind that I find annoying.

The guitarist rises to greet me. He's smiling.

'How's it going?'

'Brilliant,' I say.

'Did you nail The Ripper?'

'I did, thanks to your help.'

'My pleasure.'

He touches the pocket of his embroidered western shirt, where his cigarettes are.

'Smoke?'

'You don't vape then?'

He grins.

'Tried it. Didn't like it.'

From the dining room next to the bar, glass doors open onto a terrace. We sit on a stone wall, observing the hotel's well-manicured lawns. The first lawn is dominated by a magnificent golden-leaved tree. I later learn that it is a black locust tree, or false acacia.

A group of people, male and female, are sitting in its shade, listening to a man talking. They have the smooth skin and clear-eyed smiles of those who eat healthy food and live without too much stress.

The women are wearing tight clothing – leggings and yoga pants. The man is dressed in a white t-shirt and faded jeans. His long grey hair and beard make him look like a prophet. Simon points at him with his cigarette:

'That's the tantra guy,' he says. 'He's called Bernard.'

'He looks happy,' I say.

'It's his job.'

He breathes out a stream of smoke.

'The gig went well,' he says.

'Yeh, I thought so too.'

'Didn't see you afterwards.'

'I went to bed,' I say. 'I was knackered. Do you have any more coming up?'

'There's one on Saturday. It's a big one. The owner of the hotel is coming for the weekend.'

Simon explains that a man called Strobe Kitson invented the technology that made this game, Get The Bad Guys, so immersive and realistic. He likes to say that his reality is the best kind. His favourite outfit is a white suit and Stetson. He is immensely rich. This is only one of his many properties.

'Would you like to play the party with us?'

'Are you sure you want me to?'

'Yeh, we've talked about it. Our regular drummer's gone back to London. You're a lot more experienced than he is. And you're better. I mean, you can count to four. That's a bonus.'

He looks up and gestures with his cigarette: 'Ah, here he is.'

'Who?'

'Kitson.'

8

The All-Seeing Eye

At first, he was just a white shape seen through a glass door. Then a man a few feet away.

'Can I help you?'

'Are you Strobe Kitson?'

'I am.'

'My name is Chris,' I introduce myself. 'I'm playing Get The Bad Guys.'

He nods: 'How are you doing, dude?'

'Quite well. I caught Jack The Ripper.'

'That's good, not many get that far. Anita says that you're settling in very well.'

'Who's Anita?'

'The receptionist.'

Well, that's interesting.

Soon, we're drinking together in the bar.

'I guess you were thinking I might be a Freemason,' he says.

'No, why would I think that?'

'Well, the name of this bar, the George Washington, should be a clue.'

I don't respond.

'He, one the founding fathers of America, being a well-known member of the craft.'

'I know,' I concur.

I'm familiar with the litany of the American dollar bill, popular with crackpot conspiracy theorists everywhere who like to recite the whole nine yards. Which I do now, for Kitson's benefit. On the front face of the note, as well as Washington's image, is a thirteen-stepped pyramid topped with an all-seeing eye. The date shown, 1776, was the year of the founding of the United States – and there is a Latin motto from the Roman poet, Virgil, 'Novus ordo seclorum', meaning 'A new order of the ages'.

The founding fathers, I continue, intended to build a perfect civil society from scratch, starting from the base. That's why the pyramid was unfinished. They had been heavily influenced by the English political philosopher John Locke. Their wish was to progress human affairs towards a state of perfection – the golden age of Saturn, as predicted by Virgil. Yada yada yada.

Kitson smiles.

'Very good. Ah, here's my wife, Tammy.'

A tall, blonde smiling woman joins us, a vision in white, with perfect teeth. Kitson introduces us and I suddenly realise, from her blue eyes and high cheekbones, that I've met her before. She's extremely familiar. This woman, despite her American accent, is an exact match for Jack The Ripper's final victim, Mary Jane Kelly.

He senses my confusion.

'Don't worry,' he says, with a half-smile. 'You are going to be seeing a lot of Tammy. We've used real people as models for the avatars in the game.'

'I see,' I nod.

'Some people who play get to be characters. It's a form of recycling.'

'Really?'

'It says so in the terms and conditions. You didn't read them did you?'

'Of course not.'

'No-one does, luckily for me. Think of the game, Chris, as an infinite number of alternative universes. Or as an aquarium, like that one.' He points across the bar.

'What do you mean?'

'The fish have volition. They respond to food and light and they swim around. They see our silhouettes on the other side of the glass. Their lives are totally dependent on ours but they don't know it or, even, that they're alive. What if humans were like that?'

'I...'

'Humans *are* like that, Chris.'

He puts his arm around Tammy.

'By the way, only a very, very few people will reach the end of the game – it's that difficult – possibly only one person. It could be you. In case you were thinking of leaving, consider that there's a really good reason why you should carry on playing.'

'What's that?'

'As well as the million bucks, there will be more benefits to come for the winner.'

'More benefits?'

Tammy smiles more intently. My question goes unanswered.

'Look, it's good to meet you. We have to go now.'

He turns away, but then looks back. He's obviously just remembered something:

'Did Simon tell you about the party on Saturday?'

'He did.'

'Fantastic, well I guess we'll see you there then... By the way, did he also tell you about my birthday party? I'd like you to play for that too. It will be at my place, in Brazil.'

'In Brazil?!'

Fuck. I nearly drop my drink.

'I think you'll like it there, Chris, *we* do.'

Tammy turns up the volume on her smile.

'We'll see you there, dude.'

Her cornflower eyes are peering into my soul – the eyes of Mary Jane Kelly. In a blur of white, they're gone.

•••

The gig on Saturday went well. Better than well. We played through our crowd-pleasing set without incident and the audience loved us. They didn't want us to stop. We gave them one more song at the end – 'always leave the crowd asking for more', Simon's always saying.

A few days later, as promised, a white CloudCorp helicopter landed in front of the hotel. It carried us to Northolt Airport and, from there, we flew across the Atlantic in the kind of aircraft that doesn't have normal seats but comfortable leather armchairs, white carpets, a seemingly limitless bar and attentive staff who are not too fussy.

The gig was in the grounds of Kitson's hacienda close to Cape Kitson, his rocket launch pad. His colourfully dressed party guests formed a phalanx in front of the stage. We'd got to know some of the English contingent on the plane. They werer an interesting bunch – executives from Kitson's company and the kind of hedonists and chancers who congregate around rock bands. Their tans showed that this kind of jolly was normal for them.

The band was augmented by a conga player who rehearsed using videos. Simon played his guitar as if possessed by a magical spirit. We played two sets. As evening fell, the humidity that was pressing down on us intensified. Dark clouds gathered over the pampas and tongues of lightning flickered from the sky. Fortunately, there was a canopy over us. It didn't start to rain until we were halfway through our last song.

The big fat drops were soft and warm. The guests welcomed them with upturned faces, entranced by our music. I saw Kitson point to me as he said something to Tammy, bending to talk in her ear.

That gig was the best I'd ever played. But now I was looking forward to returning to the hotel in England and getting back to the game. A million dollars was at stake!

9

Colebrooke Row

Task: Joseph Stalin

Nasty dude, this one. One of the top three genocidal dictators of the 20th Century. Not many people know this, but he visited London in 1907 for a historic political congress, before he acquired his nickname 'man of steel'. That's your opportunity. You are going to be working for the Secret Service, in an unofficial capacity, to 'take him out', as those folks like to say. The powers that be are anxious to nip Bolshevism in the bud before it takes root in Britain. Remember, those Bolshies are handy with coshes and knives! Be careful hombre.

Time: 1907
Lives remaining: 5
Special powers: Level 1

I was in London again. This affluent neighbourhood was far removed, both socially and geographically, from the crowded and noisy streets of Whitechapel. I was standing in a wide road lined by Georgian terraces, with half-basements and iron railings.

I was wearing the same clothes as on my previous task but, this time, I was carrying a small leather suitcase. I searched my jacket pocket for a gold sovereign. There wasn't one.

One could tell that these houses weren't sub-divided into miserable dwellings for the poor; they were homes for prosperous individuals and families. Their servants lived in the claustrophobic rooms squeezed beneath the roofs.

There was an interesting vehicle in this road. Adapted from a horse-drawn carriage, it was a curious contraption with brass coaching lamps and running boards. Apart from this motor car (another sign of affluence), the street was empty. The day was pleasantly warm and I was sweating in my jacket. I divined a hint of spring in the air, confirmed by the pale green buds sprouting from the London plane trees.

A young lady in a pale dress and bonnet was pushing a large black perambulator towards me.

'Good morning,' I said to the woman, moving aside for her to pass.

'Good morning,' she echoed, with a nervous smile.

Hearing a noise, I turned my head to the left.

A door opened. It was set in an imposing entrance, framed by a Grecian porch.

A lady with piercing blue eyes looked out. I could see that she was wearing the black dress of a maid, with a white apron and bonnet.

'Oh, you're here,' she said, with a tone of exasperation. 'You're late!'

Was I? I glanced at my watch. It was ten past eight.

'I'm sorry,' I replied.

'Well, come in.'

I surmounted the steps to the threshold. Looking down into a narrow, gloomy yard beneath the level of the road, I surmised that this would be where the servants worked – the kitchen, pantry, scullery and coal store.

I offered my hand for her to shake. She stood aside.

'The master is in his study.'

'Thank you,' I said, still confused.

•••

The master was in a bad mood. He glanced ostentatiously at his pocket watch as I entered the room. He must've been in his sixties, I estimated. He wore a black morning coat and pale grey trousers – the uniform of the important.

The study was lined with books and furnished with a large desk. A small fire burned in the grate, although today's weather hardly made it necessary.

'Take a seat,' he gestured towards an uncomfortable looking chair.

He paced the room impatiently as he talked. I remained in the chair, my gaze shifting between his face, the leather-spined books and the glowing crust of coal in the grate.

'We've lost time,' he said, 'so let me briefly outline the position. My name is Fulsome, Sir Thomas Fulsome. You are probably unaware that I work for the Government. My duties are of an unusual and unofficial nature and are divided between the Home Office, the Board of Trade and...er...Special Branch. I report directly to the Privy Council through the Home Secretary. Are you following?'

My attention had strayed to a photograph of a solemn Victorian family hanging over the mantelpiece. There were also some hunting prints and political cartoons on the walls.

'Yes, sir,' I replied.

'Good.' He turned away. 'To specifics. You have been selected for this role for two principal reasons. Firstly, because you are unattached – a bachelor. Secondly, your proficiency in Russian and German will be invaluable.'

'Sir, I...'

I did not know a single word of Russian and what I knew of German could be written on the back of a postage stamp. His frown cut short my interruption.

'We know that you are of a sound and sober temperament and that we can rely upon your honesty. Your references have been thoroughly checked and have proved satisfactory. This is a post that requires intelligence and good judgement but, above all, discretion. Your job, essentially, is to watch and listen, not to participate. It will be essential to keep a cool head at all times, even in the presence of grave danger. Do you understand?'

I said that I did.

'Good. Right. Now, let's cut to the chase. In a nutshell, the Prime Minister, the Home Secretary and I are extremely worried about the increasing number of foreign revolutionaries coming to London and spreading their malign influence. The problem is particularly acute in the East End, but it is not just there. It is also found in the drawing rooms of Fitzrovia and Bloomsbury and, even,' he paused, 'in the reading room of The British Museum.

'These people are from many countries, including Russia, Poland, Latvia and Lithuania. Many of them are of the...er...Hebrew faith. Some of their ideas, I'm afraid, are already taking root here like an insidious disease. The spectre of radicalism is not to be taken lightly, Mr Wilkins, especially when it enters the House of Commons in a deerstalker.'

I knew he was referring to the leader of the British Labour party, Keir Hardie, elected to the House of Commons in 1892.

I did not respond.

'Your job is to be my eyes and ears, for I cannot be everywhere. I want you to go into the slums and cellars where these noxious ideas fester and find out what harm is planned. Then I want you to report back to me so that the necessary action can be taken. Do you follow?'

'Of course.'

'Initially, you must make your way to the Whitechapel area. Find out what you can, particularly of the foreign revolutionaries arriving in London for congresses. I want their names, although many of them use aliases unfortunately.'

I sensed that he was coming to a conclusion.

'My maid will furnish you with appropriate clothes so that you'll fit into your surroundings. A room is available for you in this house and you can come and go as you please.'

'I see.'

'I am not often in this residence,' he added, self-importantly. 'I'm usually at my country house or in my office in Whitehall. Sometimes my wife will come here when she's in town, but you must never speak to her. You will enter and leave by the tradesmen's entrance and you will take all of your meals with the servants. Officially, we have never met and your appointment does not exist. Do you understand?'

I nodded.

'Before you ask, the salary is £100 a year. All of your expenses, including travel and clothing, will be fully reimbursed. I trust this is satisfactory?'

'I...'

'You will report to me in three days' time, at eleven o'clock in the morning, not before nor after. You will have noticed that I cannot abide unpunctuality.'

He consulted his watch.

'I must go now, I have a pressing appointment. Miss Brundle will attend to you. Our meeting is concluded.'

I began to speak but he waved me towards the door.

•••

The housemaid was standing in the hallway.

'Did you take the position, sir?' she asked.

'I think so,' I replied hesitantly. I'd been given no choice in the matter.

Her voice seemed familiar. I studied her face – pale skin, clear eyes, strands of hair falling across her brow. It was Tammy Kitson aka Mary Jane!

'It's you,' I said, 'isn't it?'

She did not respond.

'Mary Jane Kelly from Commercial Street.'

'Mary Jane? I believe you are mistaken, sir. My name is Phoebe, Phoebe Brundle. It always has been.'

Her accent was less Cockney than Mary Jane's but her face, mannerisms and way of speaking were identical. I made the point again, but she was adamant that she was not this person and that she had no idea what I was talking about.

'Shall I carry your case, sir? Joseph is driving the master down to Whitehall.'

Joseph, was he here too? Oh, dear.

'Don't be silly,' I said. 'Chivalry is not dead you know.'

She smiled for the first time.

'I'll show you to your room.'

•••

The staircase grew narrower the higher one climbed. On the first floor were the living and drawing rooms, on the second the principal bedrooms. The stairs ascending to the third floor were almost as steep as a ladder. The room was wedge-shaped, its sloping ceiling matching the angle of the roof. One could barely stand up in it. It was good enough for servants, I supposed.

A metal bedstead, a chest of drawers and a washstand had been squeezed into the room like the final pieces of a jigsaw. There was a gas mantle here. The rest of the house, I'd noted, was illuminated by electricity.

Phoebe stood outside the door as I placed my case on the bed:

'You'll find your clothes in the trunk.'

It had been slid under the bed. Inside was a faded black jacket, its elbows and cuffs threadbare. There were trousers that didn't match, a stained shirt with no collar, some braces and a moth-eaten cardigan. To complete the outfit were a cotton muffler and workman's cap.

Is this what I was supposed to wear? Perhaps Sir Thomas had never been to the East End, merely read about it in condescending articles which warned of the moral abyss that existed to the east of Bishopsgate.

'Quite the thing to catch a lady's eye,' I said.

She laughed: 'We, the servants that is, fetches our water from the pump in the yard. You must not use the bathroom, sir.'

'I understand.'

'Will that be all?'

'Yes, thank you.'

I sighed. *Was I really going to have to put on these old clothes?*

'Very good.'

She looked into my face and her blue eyes locked onto mine.

'My room is next door,' she paused, '...if you want me'.

Her eyes held fast.

'I see. Does Joseph sleep up here?'

'No, he has his own quarters in the coach house.'

'Oh.'

'I'm going down to the scullery, sir. If you needs a set of house keys before you leave, let me know.'

'I shall.'

She added as an afterthought, 'usually, Joseph and I has our supper at about seven when the master is away, as he will be tonight. You are most welcome to join us.'

'Do you think Joseph will mind?' I asked. 'I wouldn't like to intrude.'

'On no sir, Joseph will be pleased with the company.'

'Well, I may take you up on your kind offer,' I said.

She smoothed the coverlet. Before leaving, she turned and smiled at me sweetly again, then she was gone.

I squinted down at the street far below through a window coated with grime.

Reluctantly, I donned the ragged clothing. So, I was to be a tramp. Great. My mum would have been proud. There was nothing to keep me in this dreary room. It was actually smaller than my cell in Wandsworth Prison.

I walked down through the house, resisting the temptation to peer into empty rooms. From the clammy feeling in the air, the place was unaccustomed to people and warmth.

I collected my house keys from Phoebe, whose hands were wet with suds. I did as I had been instructed by Sir Thomas and left through the back door, which led down a narrow passage. The day was warming up nicely. Next stop, Whitechapel. My task? To protect England from foreign revolutionaries.

10

The Socialist Club

I walked down the road, which I discovered to be Colebrooke Row in Islington. I entered Upper Street and walked to where it terminated at the junction that is celebrated on the Monopoly board as the Angel Islington. Clanking cars and motor vans weaved around horse-drawn buses and carriages honking their horns. Most of the hansom cabs were still of the equine variety – the traditional four-wheelers known as growlers.

The sun was shining. The sulphurous hell of the new underground station held little attraction, so I ventured a halfpenny fare on an electric tram to take me down City Road. It was open-topped and emblazoned with the legend 'Lipton's Tea'.

In Great Eastern Street, I sensed the East End was beginning to assert itself, as foreign accents and rag trade emporia appeared. Here, caps outnumbered bowlers and top hats –porters and costermongers rather than office workers. There were bare-armed women, some smoking pipes.

I entered Commercial Street on the upper deck of a swaying horse-drawn bus. It was cramped and uncomfortable but at least I was in the open and able to look about. Mary Jane would always be associated in my mind with this road now. I alighted in front of Christ Church.

William Wilkins, secret agent. I had no gift for languages to help me nor knowledge of weapons or ciphers; my street level familiarity with this part of London had been recently acquired. It could be useful. Millions of people lived in this great city – the hub of the world-spanning British Empire. One particular person was my quarry.

When the rich man shuts his door at night, he seals himself off behind his fence or privet hedge. He may be friendly to his immediate neighbours, but the people who live beyond these barriers are normally a mystery.

Not so, the poor man. There are threats and opportunities all around him. Coleman's Row would be silent after dark but, in this part of the London, scavengers pored over scraps of rancid meat and costermongers sold their stale greens from flare-lit stalls from dawn until far into the night.

•••

To fill my stomach, I had a pint of porter and a satisfying meal in a chop house.

I simply wandered around afterwards, so it was purely by chance that I discovered the International Working Men's Educational Club in Berner Street, Stepney.

It was a plain building – narrow and flat-roofed, with a ground floor like a shop front. A sign over the front door proclaimed its name proudly to the world. Many men, who appeared largely foreign, were milling around inside. I sensed immediately that I was on the right track – revolution was in the air.

The club was a hive of activity. Inside was a printing press which produced an anarchist newspaper, Worker's Friend. The lecture hall on the first floor had long benches, like the stalls of a church. There was a stage on which plays were performed and from which the catechisms of revolution were delivered. This room was not decorated with images of martyrs and apostles but, instead, pictures of the heroes of anarchism and socialism.

On the ground floor was a working man's café. It was packed. The air was fuggy with smoke and unwashed bodies and the babble of many languages was almost deafening. Men of multiple nationalities were drinking tea and eating penny buns. Some were playing chess, others reading pamphlets and newspapers. They were of a type, I noticed – lean-faced men with sunken eyes and hungry looks.

I realised that these fellows were animated by something far more powerful than mere food and drink. It was the force of an idea that had propelled them across Europe to London – the idea being that the tyrannies of class and religion needed to be overthrown. Such men, as Sir Thomas suspected, did indeed pose a considerable threat to the established order.

With a mug of tea in my hand, I crossed the crowded room. Dressed in these clothes, I could almost have been one of the revolutionaries. I attracted only the odd curious glance, perhaps to establish my nationality or to which creed I belonged.

It was by chance that I stumbled upon a man who spoke English. In fact, he *was* English. It was Simon Peaceful from The White Lodge!

•••

'Jesus Christ,' I said, 'what are you doing here?'

He returned the same blank stare as Mary Jane had done.

'Mind if I join you?'

He shrugged.

We began to talk. He explained that most of the people in the club were delegates of the fifth congress of the Russian Social Democratic Labour Party. They had come from many countries. Some were Bolsheviks – Marxist hard-liners believing in armed revolution. Others were Mensheviks, Bundists and Social Democrats who favoured a more gradual approach. Their common interest in a fairer world had drawn them to Berner Street.

'Where is the congress being held?' I asked.

'At the Brotherhood Church in Hackney.'

'When?'

'It starts tomorrow.'

'What will they do there?'

'Make speeches, vote on motions, the usual. I've a feeling the Bolsheviks are going to win. They have the wind in their sails.'

The man had no objection to my asking him questions. I could easily have been a spy for the Russian Tzar.

'Do you mind if I take some notes?'

From my pocket I pulled a notebook and pencil I had purchased en route, anticipating that I would need them.

'Of course not.'

He pushed aside the English paper he was reading – Justice, the organ of England's leading socialist organisation, the Social Democratic Federation. The paper was the usual mixture of constipated terminology, vituperation of erring comrades and rosy promises of the dawn of socialism.

'Oh, I'm William Wilkins by the way,' I explained. 'I'm a reporter for an American paper you won't have heard of. I'm trying to capture some local colour.'

'In the land of Jack The Ripper...'

'Exactly. And your name, sir?'

He offered his hand. *Why do the best guitarists have long, thin fingers?*

'My name is Peter.'

'Peter what?'

'Just Peter. You can call me Peter The Anarchist if you like.'

He laughed.

'That's a good name. Are you attending the congress?'

'Only if they'll let me in. I don't have the credentials. I'm just interested.'

He offered me a cigarette – I accepted – and lit his own.

11

Koba The Great

He (Stalin) was of very small stature and ungainly build. His torso was short and narrow, legs and arms too long and his left arm and shoulder seemed rather stiff. He had quite a large paunch, and his hair was sparse although the scalp was not completely bald. His face was white, with ruddy cheeks.

The teeth were black and irregular, turned inward. Not even the moustache was thick or firm. Still, the head was not a bad one; it had something of the common people, the peasants, the father of a great family about it, with those yellow eyes and a mixture of sternness and mischief.

Milovan Djilas quoted in The Deal: Churchill, Truman, and Stalin Remake the World by Charles L Mee Jnr

For a minute or two, Peter and I did not talk, but merely absorbed the sights and sounds of the room. The men around us were noisily disputing points of principle or engaging in the complex and murderous game of chess. Many of the chess players wore the kippahs, or caps, of Orthodox Jews.

Those who were here for the congress clustered in groups according to their nationality, gesticulating and emitting clouds of smoke. I needed some intelligence to take back to Sir Thomas – some exotic-sounding names – but it was complicated. Peter explained that Bolsheviks liked to use *noms de plume* or nicknames like 'iron man' or 'hammer', never 'fork' or 'fly whisk'. It was partly for practical reasons (they were often in hiding) and partly to increase their revolutionary kudos. Having a pseudonym was a plus point for a revolutionary, like being sent into exile.

However, Peter did furnish some useful specifics on the congress. Some of the participants were famous, leading lights of the revolutionary movement that Marx and Engels had sent running across the world. The Bolsheviks and Mensheviks, he continued, couldn't even decide on a suitable description for the event. Was it the fifth congress or the third? This important topic alone was likely to involve many hours of debate.

Vladimir Ulyanov, also known as Lenin, was the most prominent Bolshevik (and he was staying in Bloomsbury). He, Peter said, had visited London twice before and, in fact, had lived in the city for a whole year in 1902. He liked to travel around on buses and visit the hallowed reading room of The British Museum where Karl Marx had sat in the 1850s, making notes for Das Kapital, the bible of Bolshevism. He had edited the Bolshevik newspaper, The Spark, from offices in Clerkenwell Green.

'So, who else is here for the congress?' I enquired.

'Let me see. There's Gorky, the writer, and Lev Bronstein, known as Trotsky. He's Jewish. He fell out with Ulyanov at the last congress. There is a female revolutionary – Rosa Luxemburg, the leader of the German Social Democrats. Julius Martov is here too – he's the leading light of the Mensheviks. He's sitting over there.'

I saw a stooped man with sunken cheeks, whose clothes hung off him like those of a scarecrow. He looked as if a strong wind would blow him over. His pockets were bulging with papers.

'He's known for his brilliant oratory,' Peter explained.

'Is there anyone here from Georgia?'

I'd remembered from somewhere in a dusty corner of my brain that Georgia had been Stalin's homeland.

'Yeh, Joseph **Dzhugashvili**. Most people know him by his childhood nickname, Koba. He's staying at the same lodgings as me. The place is infested with bed bugs.'

'Where is he?'

'There.'

The man was standing in the middle of a group of comrades. There seemed to be something magnetic about him. I observed that his audience was following every word and gesture. They looked as if they'd been hypnotised.

Dzhugashvili or Koba, who would later become known as Stalin, was short and stockily built. He had a good head of thick black hair but an ill-defined beard and moustache. His eyes were strange, almost like a cat's. His face was pockmarked.

My intense scrutiny was ill-advised. Noticing me and my notebook, he stopped talking and leaned over towards a comrade, muttering something in his ear.

Oh dear. Arousing Koba's suspicions – not a good idea.

•••

It was a long afternoon and night. Peter 'The Anarchist' loved to drink and talk in equal measure. There were two pubs in Berner Street. The closest, The Nelson, was next to the socialist club so was inevitably filled with non-English voices as evening arrived and the thirsty revolutionaries made their first acquaintance with English beer.

Koba's eyes had spooked me. With my newly-acquired sixth sense, I divined that his character was complicated and that he had no compunction about killing anyone who got in his way.

Wishing to steer clear of the Bolsheviks, we chose the George IV pub at the end of the road. I continued to question my new acquaintance and my notebook was soon filled to the brim. All this information would be grist to Sir Thomas' mill.

At eleven o'clock, Peter said he was going to return to his digs at Rowton House, Fieldgate Street, and turn in for the night. It had a smoking room and even a library, he said. The sleeping facilities were communal – nothing more than beds in cubicles. The sound of snoring must've been phenomenal! I didn't fancy that but I also didn't want to go back to Islington now that I was hot on the trail of the revolutionaries. In the end, I decided to seek a furnished room in Spitalfields that I would not have to share with strangers.

•••

We said our good nights and Peter vanished into the darkness. We had agreed to meet early the next morning. In an act of brotherly solidarity, we would walk with the delegates from the socialist club, where they would assemble, to the Brotherhood Church in Hackney for the first morning of the congress.

Ambling around in the middle of the night in the East End – what the hell was I thinking? Compounding my idiocy, I attempted a short cut. Heading north from the busy artery of Whitechapel Road, I wandered into an ill-lit region – meaning that it was as dangerous as a tropical jungle.

I was halfway down Osborn Street when I felt a blow to my skull. Perhaps my assailant hadn't meant to kill me but it was a powerful crack to the head, obviously from a heavy implement. My body crumpled to the pavement. Stupid! I had just lost my third life. At this rate, I would soon be out of the game.

•••

My fellow band member is in the bar, naturally. He rises to greet me.

'Hi, Simon. Or should I say Peter?'

'Sorry, what do you mean?'

'Peter The Anarchist.'

'Is that a band name idea?'

'No. Whitechapel, remember? The club in Berner Street?'

He looks blank. He has no idea what I'm talking about and I can tell he's being sincere.

He's played the game but doesn't know he's become a part of it. *That's odd.*

However, he's happy to give me tips, as ever.

'Did one of Stalin's guys do you in?' he asks.

'Yeh, I got coshed.'

'That's nice. I was strangled. Then they pushed me into a canal.'

'Any advice?'

'You need to find Culadar.'

'Who?'

'Culadar. He's the Chinese guy.'

'How do I do that?'

'Well, you're gonna run into him at some point. Follow your nose.'

'Follow my nose?'

He offered no further explanation.

'Would you like a drink?'

'Yes, if you're paying.'

This has become one of our jokes because we don't have to pay for anything.

12

Culadar

Task: Joseph Stalin
Time: 1907
Lives remaining: 4
Special powers: Level 1

I stood in a prosperous road in Islington, lined with London plane trees and Georgian houses. I ignored the pram pusher in the blue dress – she didn't bat an eyelid.

A door opened. I apologised for being late. I went into the house and endured my interview with the pompous man in the morning jacket, murmuring appropriate noises in the right places.

After that, I followed Phoebe upstairs. I stooped to enter my room in the servant's quarters and placed my suitcase on the bed. She was standing outside the door, watching me intently. Why was she still here?

'There is no wardrobe for your suit, sir, I'm afraid.'

'That's OK.'

'You'll find your clothes in the trunk.'

The trunk was under the bed. It contained the dirty and stained clothing. They were probably taken from paupers who had died in a workhouse infirmary. *Do I really have to wear these?*

'Quite the thing to catch a lady's eye,' I said with a slight smile.

She laughed.

'We – the servants that is – fetches our water from the pump in the yard.'

God, she was beautiful. I was falling in love with her. It was good that she would never recognise me, however many times I returned. Each time I met her, I would discover her afresh.

'Will that be all, sir?'

'Yes, thank you.'

Oh God, please don't go. Let me look at your delicious face for a little longer. Those eyes...

A faint smile played on her lips. This was the coquettish Mary Jane.

'My room is next door, sir.'
Is it now? Really?
'Does Joseph sleep up here?'
'No, he has his own quarters in the coach house.'
How terribly convenient.
'I'm going down to the scullery, sir. If you needs a set of house keys before you leave, just let me know.'
'I shall.'
She paused, adding an afterthought:
'Usually, Joseph and I 'as our supper at about seven when the master is away, as he will be tonight. You are most welcome to join us.'
Is Joseph by any chance a jealous lunatic with a hammer?
'Well, I may take you up on your kind offer,' I said politely. 'Thank you.'
She smiled sweetly and left with a slight curtsy.
For a moment, I am tempted to spear myself with a shard of glass, so that my game self will die and I can re-replay this scene with its significant glances and undercurrents. Phoebe is an ingénue. She does not actually know how beautiful she is. She is like a moth drawn to the flame of love. But I have already lost three of my seven lives. I can't afford to sacrifice another one.

Next task – put on shabby clothes, go downstairs and take keys from my new below-stairs friend. She will be doing the washing in the scullery.

•••

As ever, Christ Church was my lodestar. I fancied that in Wilkes Street, which is nearby, I would find what I was looking for, a furnished room which could be rented by the night.

I had to knock on four doors before I found a place that would take me. At the fifth attempt, a large lady with plump arms appraised me from her front door. She was blocking the way like a gorgon.

She assured me that this was a respectable house and that she did not welcome 'professional' women or members of the criminal fraternity. Visitors, in general it seemed, were not allowed – the room was for me alone. She required payment in advance – sixpence. If I liked the room, it could be let by the week, providing that my behaviour was acceptable. Did I play a musical instrument by any chance? I assured her that I did not. She let me in.

It was a miserable hovel. Attempts to disguise this fact were poignant. Wallpaper with a pattern of delicate flowers was peeling away from the damp plaster to which it had been attached on a wing and a prayer. The floorboards creaked. Built on mean foundations, the house was sinking into the London clay, like a leaking ship.

There was a noticeboard in the hallway. A paper pinned to it repeated the rules solemnly explained to me on the doorstep and announced that guests could order meals in advance from the proprietor.

What kind of transient or desperate souls would stay here? What circumstances or volition would bring one to such a place? My room at least overlooked the road, not the backyard. I lit the gas and settled on the bed. There was a cacophony of shifting springs as it gave way beneath me. Soon, exploratory bed bugs would find their way into the folds of my flannel underclothing.

Half hidden in the shadows of the room were a broken-down wardrobe and a miserable dressing table and washstand. The gas mantle hissed faintly, making a sound that evoked carnivorous insects in some hideous jungle.

I had no wish to go out, there was no need to. I knew tomorrow's destination – the socialist club in Berner Street. I sat upright on the bed and drifted into a daydream. The sky turned black as smoke from East End chimneys slithered into the dismal room. I heard someone opening a door upstairs. They clumped across the floorboards and, from what I could hear, sank into their antique bed.

There was a constant murmur from the road; occasionally the sound of raised voices. Mainly, I was thinking about Phoebe, imagining conversations that I might have with her. I also thought of Koba – his harsh accent, short, thickset body and yellow eyes. How could such an ordinary man have done so much evil?

I must have fallen into a fitful sleep because, after several hours, I woke up. It was around the middle of the night. I had been roused from sleep by a peculiar smell.

•••

It was sickly and cloying – an aroma that I half recognised. There were notes of sandalwood and juniper in it but also a trace of ambergris, the enticing perfume of the blue whale. Follow your nose, Simon had said. The source of the smell was a room across the gas-lit landing. I tapped tentatively on the door.

A faint but distinct voice, like the crackle of a phonograph, beckoned me inside.

'Come in.'

I turned the doorknob and entered. The room was dark, apart from the light of a small candle placed in the centre of a low table, whose surface was coated with black Japanese lacquer. Within its aura, I could make out a man sitting in an armchair. His hands rested comfortably upon his abdomen.

Straggly black hair framed his sallow, angular face. He was looking down. In the poor light, I could not see his eyes. One could sense from his composure that he'd been sitting in this posture for a long time.

Next to the candle was a small silver pipe and ashtray. Opium. I wondered how the man's smoking habits had not been found out by the lady who ran the house.

I edged forwards.

'Come in, my friend. Don't be shy.'

'Who are you?'

'All in good time.'

Languidly, he reached to shake my hand. His fingers felt like ice. After this small formality, he took his pipe and lit it. I looked around the room. Like mine, it bore the hallmarks of neglect – liver-spotted wallpaper and ugly, ill-used furniture.

'Please, be seated.'

There was nothing else for it – I must sit on the bed. He re-lit his pipe, tugging on it before offering the implement to me. I declined.

'My name is Culadar. That, in itself, is an enigma. You are probably also wondering where I am from?'

The smoke had evidently reached the depth of his lungs. He made a strange sound, like a death rattle. His dark eyes widened and a broad smile of contentment crossed his face.

'Am I a Chinaman, a Lascar, a Malay, or possibly an Indo-European? It is hard to tell from my accent, is it not? Many races commingle in my veins.'

A wheezing laugh issued from his throat.

He moved forwards. His huge pupils focused lazily on mine.

'Let us proceed to business, Christopher. May I call you that?'

'As you please,' I said. *How did he know my real name?*

'Have you heard of The Ancient Order of The Sons of The Dragon?'

'No, I can't say I have.'

'It is a venerable order, far older than any such fraternities that exist in Europe or the Americas. For millennia, its adherents have devoted their lives to a single objective…'

He drew again on his pipe and breathed out slowly. I was feeling light-headed.

'… the elimination of evil. And that is your purpose, is it not?'

'Is it?'

'I believe so.'

The rattling laugh came from his chest.

'I am a Master of The Order. You have already achieved the first stage of the second degree, I am happy to say. Your fame precedes you, sir. Well done!'

'Thank you.'

'Now you have a man called Koba in your sights, do you not?'

I nodded.

'He is a nasty specimen, but do not judge him too harshly. He was schooled by a Jesuitical order and beaten mercilessly by his drunken brute of a father. Those are the two forces that shaped his character. He took to Bolshevism like a duck to water. It offered a rigid system of beliefs and tests of adherence, backed by the promise of a better life to come. It demanded absolute loyalty, with the threat of violence, or death, for those who strayed from the path. That was perfect for young Koba.'

He knitted his fingers so that his arms were arranged in a triangle.

'The psychologist would call him a sociopath and say that he is punishing others in order to compensate for his lack of paternal affection. That is certainly true, but he also has a charming side. You have seen his charisma, have you not? This is what makes our Koba so dangerous; it explains his rise to the very top of the tree and why even people who he starved and persecuted retain an affection for the man.'

The opium I was passively inhaling was performing its alchemy deep in my brain. There was a yellow halo around Culadar's head. His eyes were blazing like suns.

'Here's the thing.'

His words brought me back to earth.

'Our Koba has a weakness. Two weaknesses, actually.'

'What are they?'

'One is his sentimentality – it is often a bedfellow of brutality. Is it not strange that a man can spend his day murdering his fellow humans and cry at the sight of a wounded deer? But it is so.'

'And the other weakness?'

'Carnality. I will not term it 'love'. It has something to do with his relationship with his mother Keke, of course.'

More amateur psychology. I sighed. He sensed my impatience.

'Earlier today, the comrades saw a playbill. Printed on it was a picture of the female music hall artiste Vesta Victoria. She is a beguiling, sloe-eyed creature with plump thighs. Koba is fascinated with her, far more than he is with the dry theorems of Marxism. He wishes to possess her. Accordingly, he and a group of Bolshevik comrades are to attend the Scala Music Hall in Charlotte Street. Lenin will be there too.'

'Lenin?!'

'You may know him as Vladimir Ulyanov. I don't think Lenin will enjoy the spectacle at all. He is a cold, passionless creature.'

He shifted in his seat.

'Why are you telling me this?' I asked.

'The reason will soon become clear.'

'I am very tired.'

'Of course, you must be. I am so sorry. I am detaining you from your bed, Mr Wilkins.'

'It's not very comfortable.'

'Indeed.' He laughed again.

I stood up.

'Before you go?' he enquired.

'Yes?'

'I have a gift for you. It's a small thing, but it may prove useful.'

He reached beneath the table. In his palm, gleaming in the candlelight, was a gold sovereign.

I took it.

'Thank you, sir.'

'No, thank *you*. Take your sweetheart for a nice dinner.'

He winked.

'I don't have a…'

'Don't you?'

'Good night to you, sir.'

'Good night.'

I weaved my way across the poorly lit room and back to my own lodging. Burrowing into my clammy sheets fully clothed, I was rewarded by a brief, fitful slumber.

•••

In the morning, there was no trace of opium fumes. I tried Culadar's door, but he was apparently not there. I left the house without telling the landlady, leaving my key in a box in the hall.

It was already almost seven o'clock. The delegates would have begun their expedition, marching from Whitechapel to Hackney for the congress. I hurried to Berner Street on foot, hoping that I wouldn't be too late to catch the stragglers.

13

The Brotherhood Church

Task: Joseph Stalin
Time: 1907
Lives remaining: 4
Special powers: Level 2

The party congress of 1907 held its meetings in a socialist church in London. It was a protracted, crowded, stormy, and chaotic congress.
The second Duma was still alive in St Petersburg. The revolution was subsiding but still arousing great interest, even in English political circles. Prominent liberals invited the better-known delegates to their houses to show them off to their guests.

Leon Trotsky, My Life, Chapter XVI

The Party will henceforth pursue the strict class policy of the socialist proletariat. The red flag of the proletariat will no longer be hauled down before the spell-binders of liberalism. A mortal blow has been struck at the vacillation characteristic of intellectuals, which is unbecoming to the proletariat.

J V Stalin, Works Vol 2, Notes of a Delegate

In front of the socialist club was a large group of jostling men. Happily for me, the bulk of delegates had yet to begin their long march from Stepney to Hackney.

Dressed in a black coat and worker's cap, Peter The Anarchist was hard to distinguish in this group – which is what he wanted of course. This time, I didn't make contact with him.

Earlier, I had gripped the sovereign that Culadar had given me and absorbed its properties, hence the power-up. The effect was extraordinary. It had given me the gift of tongues. I could now understand what the delegates were saying!

My brain, amazingly, could distinguish meaning from the stream of mixed languages that was issuing from the incredible coin – Latvian, Lithuanian, Russian, Polish and Yiddish. I sought Koba amongst the Russian Bolsheviks but I couldn't see him. Perhaps he had already set off for Hackney.

At some point, as if by a spontaneous decision, we moved off. A crowd creates a collective energy that is greater than the sum of its parts. We were a shuffling mass motivated by a common, powerful will. As I joined the group, I imagined that the spirit of revolution had entered me. I could feel it coursing through my veins, like the music of Rimsky Korsakov.

The delegates were far better dressed than I had expected and some were even wearing bowler hats. Peter had explained to me that both the Bolsheviks and Mensheviks crossed the social spectrum, from bourgeoisie to office worker to labourer.

Regardless of their class, I could see that the marching participants had worn their Sunday best. Travelling to London had been a huge enterprise for most, never to be repeated. This meeting was an important and formal occasion.

The English 'fellow travellers', including Peter and myself, had dressed down. A raggle taggle of English socialists and anarchists and the merely curious formed a small group at the back of the march. It was odd: at the front of the group, smartly tailored and splendidly whiskered, were the professional revolutionaries. But, for the most part, we were following a procession of men in bowlers, like a group of clerks on a Sunday morning outing.

The majority of the march was to take us through working class districts. We didn't enter the City and trouble its temples of mammon, the stone-clad fortresses of capitalism.

•••

Up Commercial Road we trudged, then on to Commercial Street. We glimpsed shoeless urchins in backstreets and passed streets like dark canyons in which banners of washing hung forlornly between rows of houses.

In City Road we came across the imposing Alexander Trust Dining Room, a spacious establishment spread over several floors offering cheap meals for the working class. A three-course banquet for fourpence was a tempting proposition but we solemnly filed past, our stomachs rumbling.

We had already walked across Shoreditch High Street, where the houses became less shabby and the streets wider, when we encountered our first hostile reaction – a shopkeeper in Great Eastern Street enraged by the invasion of London by foreigners. And in New North Road when we were nearing our goal, another surprise – not Cossacks or Tzarist soldiers but a group of boys, loyal to the forces of capitalism, jeering and hurling racial abuse at us before running away.

As if on cue, policemen suddenly appeared and started to escort us, some riding on chestnut horses. The delegates were hugely amused by these London bobbies with their tall helmets and chinstraps. They were genial men; it was noted that they were not here to attack us with sabres, but to ensure we could walk along freely without being molested. Amazing!

In this country, a sense of tolerance was apparent – one could move around freely without the need for identity papers; moreover, England had offered a home to the fifth congress following its rejection by Denmark, Sweden and Norway. In London, there were even churches modelled on the writings of Tolstoy, which welcomed pacifists and vegetarians and where socialism could be preached from the pulpit. The city also held other attractions for these visitors. The wondrous British Museum and its superb library (which had been of great use to Marx and Ulyanov) and its public reading rooms in which working men could consult newspapers, albeit standing up.

For relaxation, even in the most densely populated parts of the city, the countryside in the form of the royal parks, open to all, could be reached by tram or bicycle. And, of course, the comfortable public houses, with their flocked wallpaper and frosted glass, offering cheerful forgetfulness courtesy England's favourite beverage, beer.

•••

I had not met Lenin until that year, nor even read him as much as I should have done. I was strongly drawn to him, however, by what I had read of his writings and, particularly, by the enthusiastic accounts of people who were personally acquainted with him. When we were introduced, he gripped my hand firmly, probing me with his penetrating eyes, before saying in the humorous tone of an old friend: 'I'm glad you came. You like a fight, don't you? Well, there's going to be a big scrap here'.

Maxim Gorky on the fifth congress, quoted in Lenin Mausoleum

Once we crossed the Regents Canal, we entered a different world. The Georgian villas in Baring Street exuded the calm complacency of the bourgeoisie. At the end of the street was a warehouse brandished with the name Thomas Biggs of London Ltd, and a pub, the Rosemary Branch. It was a good bet that many of the delegates would return here later to slake their thirst.

A group of protestors was waiting for us in front of the Brotherhood Church. The jeering group carried home-made banners: 'Hurrah for the Tzar' and 'Bolshies go home!'. As they goaded us, press photographers clicked their shutters. Horses became agitated and policemen moved their hands to their truncheons.

Most of the delegates remained impassive. They did not wish to abuse the hospitality of their hosts; in any case, this was small beer compared to the treatment served up in their own countries.

Outraged newspaper headlines about Russian revolutionaries meeting 'secretly' in a London church would appear over the next few days (it would be hard to imagine anything less secretive than this congress). It was amusing to see some delegates hiding their faces behind their hats. Could the eyes of the Tzar and his secret police, the dreaded Okhrana, peer as far as the streets of Hackney?

The English fellow travellers held back as the delegates filed into the church in a dignified fashion. Their behaviour was less restrained than that of their foreign comrades. I observed that Peter was having an argument with an angry protestor who was jabbing the air with his finger, spittle flying from his lips. Soon, they were trading blows and Peter was dragged, arms flailing, into a police van.

I had not seen Koba all day. It would take a long time for the delegates to have their credentials checked. The long-winded proceedings that would follow – the interminable speeches, motions and votes – held little attraction for me. I remained outside as the protestors dispersed, reporters pocketed their notebooks and photographers packed up their equipment. Soon one could hear the murmur of debate, punctuated by laughter, jeers and applause, from the interior of the gloomy Victorian building. History was being made.

Southgate Road was quiet now. Small and claustrophobic as it was, my room in Colebrooke Row seemed enticing. It was not far from here; I could walk all the way along Regent's Canal.

I set off on foot, leaving the Bolsheviks and Mensheviks to their eternal argument – should they seize power from the Tzar by force in a bloody revolution, or work more gradually through bourgeois institutions?

14

Tea At The Angel

Walking along the canal with its oily water, coal wharves and gloomy warehouses gave me some time to think. God knows what was in that water – dead cats and half the filth and slime of London, one would imagine.

The following morning, I would provide my first report on alien revolutionaries and domestic agitators to Sir Thomas Fulsome. I had managed to scribble down some names in my notebook and Peter's background knowledge would be invaluable.

But what of Koba? My task in the game was to remove his evil influence from history. Could I reason with him, convince him to abandon Bolshevism? After all, I spoke his language now. Still, it was not very likely. Koba was firmly committed to his path. Even the strongest allures of sex or money paled into insignificance compared to the power that was potentially within his grasp – ruling over a vast country spanning two continents.

No, I concluded, it would be better if Sir Thomas dealt with the problem through the offices of Britain's security service (Britain had no secret police, the closest institution was Special Branch).

For this to work - removing Koba permanently from the scene - I would need to implicate him in a plot of heinous nature, and there was only one such plot of sufficient magnitude. Continuing along the canal, I decided I would tell Sir Thomas that Koba was the ringleader in a plan to assassinate the British Royal Family!

I would tell him that to achieve his wicked purpose, Koba and other Bolsheviks were negotiating with Irish Fenians for supplies of guns and explosives; that this was the main purpose of their visit to London and that they'd been meeting secretly with a Fenian agent in...Whitechapel. Of course!

What was the Irishman's name? 'Thomas O'Rourke': a tall character with black hair, long side whiskers and striking blue eyes. I would elaborate by saying I had seen O'Rourke with my own eyes talking to Koba in a pub in Stepney.

Continuing this fiction, I would elaborate that in The Nelson public house in Berner Street, I had overheard the Bolsheviks' terrifying plan to kill the King and Queen! Sir Thomas would love this. He would lap it up like a thirsty Labrador. If my plan worked, Koba would inevitably be removed from the scene by Special Branch. As far as the rest of the world was concerned, he was just a tourist from Georgia. The event would attract little attention.

•••

I'd been pontificating so intently I scarcely noticed that I'd arrived at Colebrooke Row. I let myself in the servant's back door entrance, as requested.

The house seemed deserted. I borrowed some sheets of paper and a pencil and, sitting upright on my bed, made notes about the Russian plan to strike at the heart of Britain – names, plans, snatches of conversation. The newspapers would take to the story with gusto – 'Bolshevik plot to kill King foiled'. Of course, my heroic role in preventing the assassination would never be revealed.

By three o'clock, after a nap, I had virtually finished. The notes were in such a form that they could be typed up and given to the necessary authorities.

There was a tap on the door. My nerves were keen – my senses had been sharpened by the last power-up. I looked round the room for something I could protect myself with. The jug on the washstand?

'Billy?'

It was a quiet feminine voice. I relaxed.

'Mary Jane,' I said, then corrected myself. 'I mean – Phoebe.'

I opened the door.

'I heard you go into your room,' she said. 'I wondered if you would like a cup of tea?'

Who could refuse such an offer?

'I'd love one,' I said. 'I didn't see you when I came in.'

'Tuesday is my day off, sir,' she explained.

'That's nice.'

I saw that she was not dressed for work but wearing a delightful green dress. It was nipped in at the waist, showing off her figure.

'Do you have any plans for this afternoon?' I asked.

She appeared unsure.

'Not really. I might see my friend Betty.'

'How about going out for some tea?' I suggested.

She smiled.

'Oh…yes, I should like that.'

'That's excellent. Let me change first.'

My original clothes were folded neatly. My hat was hanging on the back of the door. I soon felt like a new man.

•••

We strolled down Upper Street to the imposing Angel Café Restaurant. It was a splendid terracotta building of four storeys on the corner of Pentonville Road.

The sovereign that Culadar had given me in Wilkes Street could have bought us literally anything on the menu – probably all of it. We sat before a spotless white tablecloth arrayed with gleaming cutlery and a bone china tea service.

Astonishing confections were offered to us on towering trolleys. Coloured light filtered into the room through stained glass.

Phoebe explained that normally she had her afternoon tea in the kitchen in Colebrooke Row, adding, 'it ain't like this though. I feel like a queen! I really do, Mr Wilkins!'

The staff here, impeccably dressed in formal black and white, were attentive to our every wish. Between mouthfuls of tea and cake, Phoebe told me the story of her early life in Ireland, her time in Wales where her husband had died tragically in a colliery explosion, and her arrival in London. I listened intently.

In London, she had encountered good fortune. She had been offered a parlour maid's post by a well-to-do family in Kensington. They had treated her well, giving her an excellent grounding in domestic service.

'I don't know what would have happened to me but for that, Mr Wilkins,' she said. 'There is plenty of women like me. I would probably have ended up on the streets.'

Her pause indicated the dreadfulness of such a fate. I assured her that she was a remarkable and talented individual. And beautiful. She blushed.

She explained to me that her present position, working for Sir Thomas Fulsome in Islington, had been advertised in The Lady. She and Joseph were the only full-time servants employed in the house.

So, what of me? What had brought William Wilkins to London?

I improvised, embellishing upon my previous stories.

'I grew up by the sea,' I said. 'The Pacific Ocean. Have you heard of San Francisco?'

'I think so.'

'I was a fisherman, like my father. We went out into the bay to catch lobsters and oysters.'

'Oysters?'

'Oh yes, sometimes they had pearls in them. Once, I found a huge one the size of a marble. It was worth a fortune. With that money, I bought a yacht and sailed to Tahiti.'

'Really, Mr Wilkins? What was it like there?'

'It was very nice, but I got bored after a while so sailed back to San Francisco. It was hard going back to simple fishing after that.'

'It must have been.'

'So I went up to the Klondyke to do some gold prospecting.'

'Did you? What was that like?'

'It was very cold,' I replied. 'And the Klondyke is ruled by the law of the gun. There were lots of fights. I made a fortune.'

'Another fortune.' Her eyes widened. 'How much?'

'It was a great deal. Unfortunately, I lost it at the gaming tables.'

'Oh.' She seemed disappointed.

'I still have some money though.'

'That's good.'

I carried on in this vein, talking about the team of huskies that had pulled my sled through the Alaskan tundra, the wild west-style saloons, the prowling wolves, the epic poker games and knife fights – all of this taken from a novel I'd once read. Phoebe smiled admiringly.

Anything seemed possible. The tea, cakes and stained glass were working their magic; we were cocooned in a golden glow of intimacy.

We strolled back to Colebrooke Row arm in arm, studying the shop window displays in Upper Street, comparing notes on the things that pleased us.

15

The Honey Trap

After Phoebe and I returned to Colebrooke Row, we spent a couple of hours in the warm, cosy and compact basement kitchen chatting and drinking tea. There was a coal-fired range, above which a row of shining copper pans hung from a rail; a battered black kettle lived permanently upon it.

Phoebe had made a sponge cake and told me how proud she was of her baking skills, which she'd learned from the cook at her last place in Kensington. It was a pleasure to watch her neat, economical movements as she attended to her duties. Every so often, she'd turn from her task to ask me another question.

Finally, I could no longer resist it. Under the pretext of helping her with the recipe, I stood behind her, placed my arms around her waist, spun her round and pulled her towards me. Her mouth found mine and we were hungrily kissing each other when there was a tap on the window. It was Joseph.

•••

'It's good to meet you, Mr Wilkins,' said Joseph, offering his hand as he entered the kitchen. 'Phoebe has told me a lot about you.'

'Likewise,' I said.

'Sorry about my hands,' he commented.

Was he holding a weapon behind his back to bludgeon me with?

I'd been apprehensive about meeting Joseph. After all, in one version of the game, he'd murdered me by means of a blow to the head; in another, his damning evidence had helped lead to my hanging at Wandsworth Prison. But this man here in the kitchen was not what I'd expected. He was certainly as powerfully built and stocky as the man who had killed me, but this Joseph was a genial and cheerful soul.

'I've been working on the car,' he explained.

'Oh, I see.' I breathed a sigh of relief.

I saw that his cuffs and sleeves were coated with grime. He was evidently the kind of man who loved to tinker with engines to make them run more sweetly and who is never happier than when he is lying beneath one with a smouldering cigarette protruding from his lips.

'Smoke?'

I accepted his offer from an oil-stained pack of Woodbines.

'So, what's on the menu?' he asked Phoebe.

'Suet pudding, your favourite. I used the beef what was left over from Sunday.'

Joseph seemed delighted. This man was a card, forever making humorous observations derived from his daily life. He had grown up in nearby Highbury, I learned, and, like Phoebe, came from a large Irish family. Joseph had begun his career in domestic service as a groom.

He was mechanically adept by nature. When motorcars had first appeared on the streets, he'd taken readily to the new machines and had obviously been delighted to accept a job that required servicing a Rolls Royce Silver Ghost and driving it around London for a wealthy, secretive man. The position, as Sir Thomas' chauffeur, also gave him a smart grey uniform with a peaked cap as well as comfortable accommodation.

Joseph's sister, Kathleen, he disclosed, worked in entertainment as front of house staff at the new Camden Hippodrome.

This amazing theatre, Joseph enthused, could hold more than 2,000 people. Built to the latest specifications in a Louis Quinze style, it towered over Camden High Street like a great white palace. The theatre had begun life showing straight plays, but that hadn't worked so it had switched to variety. According to Joseph, apart from the Alhambra in Leicester Square, The Hippodrome was the biggest and best music hall in London.

All the brightest stars appeared there, he explained, his eyes shining – Vesta Victoria, George Robey, Lottie Collins, even the famous singer Marie Lloyd, he added with lowered voice. And, as it happened, he continued, Miss Lloyd was appearing at The Hippodrome this very Saturday with the coster comedian Gus Elen.

He told us, proudly, that Kathleen was on first name terms with all these celebrated performers, for she'd booked them to appear. The salaries of those who were most famous were astonishing – Marie Lloyd earned a hundred pounds a week.

'A hundred pounds!' Phoebe repeated, incredulously. 'It don't seem right. What would you do with that money, Joe?'

'I'd buy a Rolls.'

'You could hire it out for weddings and the like.'

'I could.'

She opened the range and removed the pie she'd been cooking. Its warm, meaty aroma filled the kitchen.

'What about you, Mr Wilkins?'

'I'd buy us all a house,' I said, 'in Bloomsbury, close to The British Museum.'

'That's because you like books,' she said.

'I certainly do.'

We exchanged glances. Joseph looked at us in turn.

'You two is getting on well!'

Phoebe blushed. She tipped the pie from its bowl onto a plate. Its white suet gleamed enticingly in the dim light. Joseph went to the back door to finish his cigarette, blowing his smoke into the darkening yard.

I was watching Phoebe, but not seeing her. I was thinking about what Joseph had told me about Marie Lloyd and the Camden Hippodrome.

'Billy!' she said.

'Pardon?' I hadn't been listening.

'There's a bottle of stout if you'd like one in the pantry. Get one for Joe, too.'

'Yes, sure.'

She took off her apron. All was ready.

Three white plates, the plain tableware reserved for servants, awaited the delicious meal that she had prepared.

She smiled sweetly.

'Tuck in boys. Dinner's served.'

Joseph left soon after we had finished the meal. It was too early to go to bed, so I watched Phoebe as she did some darning. The kitchen clock had a loud tick. But the gaps in our conversations were not awkward. I was just as happy to watch

Phoebe working as to listen to her stories of growing up in Limerick or her descriptions of the amazing biscope pictures she'd seen in Upper Street.

I glanced at the clock. It was nine o'clock. She'd already told me this was her bedtime. Neither of us said anything. It was by an unspoken agreement that we climbed the stairs together and spent the night in her room, in her small creaking bed.

•••

I tapped on the door of Sir Thomas' study at precisely one minute to eleven on Wednesday morning. I was shaved and beautifully presented. The night that I had spent with Phoebe had filled me with a contentment that made me feel invincible.

Sir Thomas was standing in the same position as during our previous interview, in the centre of his Turkish rug. He consulted his pocket watch as I entered his study.

'Mr Wilkins, very good,' he said, simply. 'Now, what have you got for me, young man?'

'Quite a lot,' I replied. 'It is just as you said. The Bolsheviks are up to all kinds of mischief and London is infested with revolutionaries – at least in the East End. I cannot speak for the rest of the city.'

'Is that so?'

He peered at me over his spectacles.

'May I give you this, sir,' I said. 'I have made extensive notes, based on my observations.'

He did not say thank you but merely nodded as I handed over the document. I watched as he read it sitting at his desk. Ten minutes passed, then fifteen.

He looked up.

'Well, thank you, young man. I am indebted to you. You have far exceeded your brief. I'll have these notes typed up.'

He cleared his throat.

'So, let's be clear. The Bolsheviks plan to hold up the royal train in Norfolk in order to intercept the King and Queen on their way to the Sandringham Estate.'

'Yes, sir. They will block the track with sleepers.'

'They then intend to attack the royal party as they alight, killing as many people as possible.'

'Yes,' I said. 'Their original plan had been to use dynamite but apparently they have obtained, from the Fenian Mr O'Rourke, a Vickers machine gun. It will be a simple matter to rake its fire down the side of the train. The Bolsheviks have also obtained a supply of Mills bombs should their initial attack fail.'

'The fiends!' His eyes glowed with anger.

'It's the kind of thing they do, sir. Murder and robbery are specialities of the Bolsheviks. I believe that they intend to attack the train in a remote part of Cambridgeshire, somewhere in the marshes. But I have been unable to discover the precise location. They will then make their escape in fast vehicles back to London.'

'I see. Well, we will have to nip this in the bud, of course.'

Sir Thomas squinted at the loose-leaf sheets.

'I was intrigued by this passage, Mr Wilkins.'

'Sir?'

'You say that comrade Dzhugashvili, or Koba, is smitten with an English music hall singer by the name of Vesta Victoria. I have not heard of her, I must confess.'

'Yes, sir. He is a crude, lustful man. His passions are easily aroused.'

'Quite. You suggest on your concluding page that we tempt him, as it were, into a trap using a music hall as bait.'

'Yes. Miss Marie Lloyd is to appear at the Camden Hippodrome on Saturday. To use an aquatic analogy, Vesta Victoria, who Koba has his eyes on, is a mere minnow. Compared to her, Miss Lloyd is a…'

'Piranha fish?'

'Yes, or something equally deadly.'

'Indeed. Well, I like your plan. If you know where your enemy is and what he is doing, you have a huge advantage over him. My agents will handle our end of it, of course. We'll set him a trap.'

'Yes, sir. A honey trap?'

'A what? You must leave the details to us, Wilkins.'

Our business was concluded and Sir Thomas dismissed me. He told me to find as much additional detail as I could on the planned attack on the Royal Family between now and Saturday. I said that I would.

I had no intention of returning to the musty haunts of the East End anarchists. I would organise the next three days around Phoebe's domestic duties, strolling along Upper Street arm in arm with her and worshipping in the Temple of Love that her tiny bedroom had become.

16

The Palace of Pleasure

Saturday dawned. Sir Thomas must have telephoned the Home Secretary moments after our meeting on Wednesday. Since then, he had been quietly pulling strings at the highest levels.

A letter had recently been despatched by hand from an address in Victoria to Rowton House in Fieldgate Street, Stepney. It was written in Russian but I later saw an English translation. The letter read:

'To: The Comrades of The Russian Social Democratic Labour Party

Dear Sirs,

The Variety Artistes Federation extends fraternal greetings and welcomes you to London for your fifth congress.

We admire the successes that you have already achieved on behalf of the working people of Russia.

In relation to your heroic efforts, the success of our recent industrial action to secure better terms of employment for music hall artistes is a minor matter – a tiny spark compared to your revolutionary flame.

In admiration of your endeavours, we hereby extend an invitation to the members of your delegation to a special performance to be held in their honour at the Camden Hippodrome Theatre on Saturday.

The principal performer, Miss Marie Lloyd, will be happy to welcome you personally in her dressing room at the conclusion of the evening. We would be honoured if you will attend our little show as a small expression of our gratitude and admiration.

I should be grateful if you would acknowledge receipt of this letter.

Yours faithfully,

Gus Elen
On behalf of The Variety Artistes' Federation.'

Evening came and, not for the first time in my life, I was late. 'Doors 7.45pm. Performance 8.00pm', the Hippodrome's playbill announced. At the top of the bill, naturally, was Marie Lloyd, 'The Queen of The Music Hall', second was Gus Elen, 'The Coster Comedian'. Lower down, in ever-diminishing font sizes, were Colonel Jim Beam, 'Western Sharp Shooter', Kaufmann's Cycle Beauties, Miss Victorina 'The Human Light Bulb', Hatsley The Boy Wonder and Kelly and Collette, 'It's fun on a billiard table!'.

In theory, it was a short distance from the Angel Islington to Camden Town on the Northern Line tube, the underground railway. In practice, the clanking, smoky journey took an age, an experience I should never like to repeat. Shaken and almost suffocated, I arrived at Camden Town at a quarter past eight and hurried down the high street.

The magnificent building, as Joseph had said, glowed luminously against the sky like a sumptuous Renaissance palace. The building rose in four elaborate tiers faced in white stone to a copper-sheathed cupola. At its pinnacle, a gas flame flared into the sky.

Outside the theatre, the crowd's agitation indicated that the spectacle had already begun. The spacious ticket hall was a feast for the eyes – gleaming marble, play bills and more flames issuing from braziers. What ticket should I buy? The pit 4d, stalls 9d, dress circle 6d or gallery 2d? A little elevation would give me the best view of the audience, but I did not want to be jammed into a cattle pen. The dress circle would be best then, and I paid my sixpence.

A towering usher in a blue uniform inspected my ticket and I ascended a flight of marble steps to a carpeted vestibule known as The Crush Room. A few people were standing there and we were told to wait, because the onstage scenery was being changed.

I gazed at the auditorium from the doorway. Did St Petersburg have anything to match this? Its opera house would certainly be opulent, but The Hippodrome was a place of entertainment catering to all social classes. The huge, deep stage could have accommodated a battalion of soldiers. The pit was jammed with humanity; from there, sweeping back in waves, were the tiered seats of the stalls, scalloped balconies in cream and gold, the plush ruby seats of the dress circle and upper dress circle and, furthest from the stage, the gallery.

The theatre, from the stage to the far-distant cupola, its pale blue interior painted with allegorical scenes, was a palace of pleasure in which one could forget everyday woes.

At last, I was ushered in. A glorious assault of human warmth and noise hit me from the threshold – an eye-watering brightness, a murmur of voices that could rise in an instant from a whisper to a deafening crescendo, as if the minds of the audience were one single entity. This cream, gold and ruby palace of marvels was available to anyone for the modest price of twopence!

•••

I had arrived at the point at which Kelly and Collette's billiard table was being wheeled off the stage so I didn't get the chance to see what they did with it, or on it!

The houselights had been dimmed. I took my seat in the middle of the third row. A solemn attentiveness was not required here, as applied to more formal dramatic performances. The audience was restive, indeed many people didn't take their seats at all for the next couple of acts, remaining instead in the dress circle bar or smoking lounge.

The orchestra soon struck up a lively tune and Hatsley The Boy Wonder took to the stage. Once he'd demonstrated his competence at cycling along a wire and back again, his attraction waned and the crowd grew impatient. He was politely applauded and then disappeared into the wings to muted cheers.

Miss Victorina, who could swallow light bulbs so that they glowed through her skin, fared a little better, but only because of the body-hugging **crêpe** costume that could clearly be seen beneath her dress. She'd consumed enough light to fill a town hall before finally leaving the stage.

Things were looking up now. Kaufmann's Cycle Beauties rode onto the stage, their astonishingly tight pale green leotards and hats like bathing caps decorated with artificial roses. Their bicycles, equipped with the new pneumatic tyres, wove and circled in complex patterns until they culminated their act by creating a human pyramid. The whole routine was played out to a scherzo of lively violins. The six girls rode off triumphantly to whoops, cheers and cat calls.

Western Sharp Shooter Colonel Jim Beam won the crowd over but mainly because of his assistant. This dusky Red Indian maiden with the lively spring in her step was dressed in a tight buckskin costume the tantalising colour of human flesh. Her main function was to revolve on a wheel as the colonel took pot shots at her with his silver Winchester pistol, even shooting a pipe from her mouth at one point. It was hard to take one's eyes from Little Plum – her shapely thighs, tawny face and cantilevered eyebrows were magnetic. When I managed to turn my attention to the colonel, I was somewhat surprised. This tall man in a fringed jacket with two holstered six-guns and long blond hair was familiar. It was Strobe Kitson! I wondered if he had spotted me in the auditorium.

That shock of recognition sent me to the bar. When I returned to my seat, having consumed a double brandy, it was the intermission and the house lights were up. I chanced to look around at the boxes. These prominent viewing platforms to either side of the stage cost the astonishing sum of seven and sixpence! Reserved for wealthy and well-known spectators, they afforded an intimate connection between their occupants and the performers.

In the box closest to the stage, on the left-hand side, I saw them now – a group of Bolsheviks, dressed in sombre black. Foremost in the group were two people I recognised, the unmistakably prominent Ulyanov and Koba (respectively Lenin and Stalin). Koba's face was ruddy with pleasure – one could see that the entertainment had animated him. Ulyanov – distinguished by his goatee and domed brow – was placid and pale-faced. His command of English was better than Koba's and he occasionally bent his head to the latter's ear to explain something.

I don't think Hatsley The Boy Wonder or Miss Victorina would have been of much interest to the Bolsheviks. They were here for the main attraction.

•••

Gus Elen opened the second half of the show. He was dressed in a striped jersey and peaked cap turned rakishly to the side. A clay pipe, which was merely a prop, protruded from the side of his mouth. He seemed at odds with the world, in a permanent bad mood.

After his comic patter, which reminded me somewhat of Joseph's witticisms in the kitchen at Colebrooke Row, he sang a couple of songs and then delivered one of his standards, The Postman's Holiday, in a thin nasal voice. Elen's stringent social commentary may have appealed to those in the Bolshevik box had it crossed the language barrier. His main purpose, however, was to build anticipation for the celebrated soubrette who was about to take to the boards. 'You wants her don't yer?!,' he announced, cupping his hand to his ear. 'You is all a quiver! So am I!'

Marie Lloyd did not disappoint. She was a vision, wearing a white bonnet edged with artificial flowers and a white, lace-trimmed dress. During the orchestra's lively overture, the audience roared with delight, anticipating her famous and suggestive songs. She winked lasciviously, twirled her parasol and, with a wicked flourish of petticoats, gave them a taste of her famous skirt dance.

After this she performed Hello, Hello, Hello, Oh Mr Porter and She Has a Sailor for a Lover. It was said that Miss Lloyd could give the most innocent lyrics a sexual meaning, her capacity for innuendo was astonishing. One Thing Leads to Another and Whacky Whacky Whack! left little to the imagination.

There wasn't a man in the theatre who wasn't exercising his erotic imagination. Many people were crying with laughter, including the Bolsheviks. They'd abandoned their moral scruples and surrendered to the mood of the auditorium, helpless with mirth. Even Lenin was smiling.

Miss Lloyd approached the front of the stage, where the footlights gave her a numinous aspect. Her pale face fringed by adorable black ringlets, she looked up and spoke in Cockney – the voice of the streets:

'There is some very special people here tonight and they 'as come a long way to be here. So, let's give them a hearty London welcome, ladies and gentlemen – our good friends from Russia!'

She began the next number on one knee and, directly addressing the Bolsheviks' box, launched into her signature song, The Boy I Love is Up in The Gallery. The main recipient of her attention, Koba, glowed with pride, like a president pleased with his military parade.

She then sang a charming duet with Gus Elen, The Coster's Wedding.

To the scintillating backing of the orchestra, all performers returned to the stage for their curtain calls. Again, Miss Lloyd saluted the Russian comrades. The applause was rapturous. It would be hard for anyone to return to reality after such a memorable evening.

17

The Russian Delegate

Task: Joseph Stalin
Mission completed

Congratulations, you have taken that cruel son of a bitch out of history. Now he won't be able to starve millions of his people or cynically send Russian soldiers to their deaths. Well done, amigo! The world is a better place, so you should feel good about yourself. You can now move on to the next task!

I was puzzled by the message. How had I beaten Koba? In Room 107 at The White Lodge, it was mid-afternoon, a carbon copy of the previous time – the gorgeous light, the cooing purr of wood pigeons, grunts and thwacks from the tennis courts. I ignored all this, baffled as I was about the Koba message. Then I had an idea.

I headed to reception. The woman behind the desk, Anita, was my friend now. I established that she was of Jamaican origin and had been working in the hotel, a job she loved, for two years. She was in her mid-30s – one of those people whose positive outlook is an antidote to life's disappointments. She was delightful.

'Hi Chris,' she said, 'how's it going?'

'Fine,' I said, 'can you do me a favour?'

'Yes, of course. What is it?'

'Please could you print me off a copy of the front page of the London Times for Monday 3rd June 1907?'

'Shall I e-mail it to you?'

'Yes, please.'

She smiled.

'There are some talks today, if you're interested.'

'Oh yes.'

She read a list from her phone. Art for The People: The Life and Works of William Morris. Charles Babbage: Build your own Logic Engine. Nicholas Hawksmoor: Cosmic Draughtsman.

Her smile was delicious. The talks sounded fascinating but I was in a hurry to get to my room.

•••

I read the Times story onscreen:

'Murder in Camden. Man held.

A man was shot dead outside singer Marie Lloyd's dressing room at the Camden Hippodrome Theatre on the night of Saturday the last, following an evening performance. The victim is believed to be a delegate who had been attending the congress of the Russian Social Democratic Labour Party in Southgate Road. He has not been named.

The Times has learned that, five minutes after her curtain call, Miss Lloyd returned to her dressing room to find a gentleman waiting for her in an agitated condition. He told her, 'I'm going to kill you, damn your eyes' and drew a revolver from his pocket.

The man is believed to be Percival Charles Courtenay, Miss Lloyd's former husband, a commission agent of Streatham. A man of violent disposition, he had previously threatened her life following a performance at The Empire Theatre in Leicester Square and was subject to a restraining warrant.

A Russian delegate who had also come to meet Miss Lloyd came to her assistance. A shot was discharged by Mr Courtenay and it entered the Russian's head. He died instantly.

Mr Courtenay is being held on remand at Bow Street police station. The police are trying to trace the relatives of the dead man.'

Well done Sir Thomas, I thought. You managed to pop off Koba using the double of a known homicidal maniac who will now be hanged. This had all the hallmarks of a covert operation by the secret forces of the state. It would send a clear message to the Bolsheviks to back off, without alarming the public. It was the real

Percy who would pay the penalty, no doubt insisting upon his innocence to the last! One could understand him being filled with anger and jealousy over his former wife – flaunting her wealth and showing her underwear to the public. Now his life was forfeit.

•••

There was also an e-mail from Simon:

'Hi Chris,

If I'm not there, sorry. I'm writing this at the CloudCorp recording studio in Holland Park. Strobe asked Ben and me to help him with the soundtrack for a new game that the company is working on. It's set in ancient Egypt.

You'd love it here. There's more guitars and drums than in a Denmark Street music shop! That's the good news. The bad news is that Strobe's world has fallen apart. Yesterday, his prototype rocket blew up at Cape Kitson. Five people were killed. He's devastated, as you can imagine. The rocket was struck by lightning. Everybody told him not to build the launchpad there because of the weather, but he wasn't listening. Stupid fucker. He'll bounce back and make an even bigger rocket, of course. That's his nature. But not for a while. He's pretty down at the moment. Anyway, have fun and see you soonest. Hopefully we will gig again soon. Good luck with your next task dude. Hope you nailed Koba!

Peace 'n' love

Simon.'

I switched to the TV news. Halfway into a bulletin came images of an exploding rocket, then of Strobe Kitson disappearing into a white car in a hailstorm of camera flashes. A voice said: 'The beleaguered billionaire was not available for comment.'

Would I get my million bucks? Better hurry.
I turned on the game.

18

Cleveland Street

Task: Publius Ostorius Scapula

Get your toothbrush! You're going back a long way, to a remote part of Britain. You're joining a resistance movement – a band of mountain guerrillas. Your adversary? The most sophisticated and well-armed military force of the ancient world – the Roman army under a ruthless commander – a sadistic son of a bitch who loves to torture and humiliate his enemies, usually in public. By now, you should have access to some resources that they don't. You'll need them. If you succeed, it won't just be for yourself, but for your entire nation. Good luck!

Time: 55 CE
Lives remaining: 4
Special powers: Level 2

In all my life on this planet, I had never been to a brothel. (There was Mary Jane's place in Whitechapel but that was her room, not a house of ill repute.) From its exterior, the place I was standing in front of seemed innocuous enough – a plain brick dwelling, like thousands of others, in an ordinary London street; inside…but I'm jumping ahead.

To my surprise, this task had not begun in ancient times but, like the previous one, at Number 42 Colebrooke Row in the Victorian era. This time, it was a summer afternoon. It was not Phoebe who let me in but a different housemaid – a slight young girl with raven hair. Treating me with indifference, she admitted me for an interview with Sir Thomas.

The hallway was lined with packing crates. There were more unpacked boxes in the study and tottering piles of books and manila folders. As usual, Sir Thomas was impatient and distracted.

'Take a seat,' he said, barely looking at me. 'If you can find one. As you can see, I am in the process of moving in. It is most inconvenient.'

He looked at his watch. This indicated, to his disappointment I think, that I was on time for my appointment. He stood facing into the room with his back to the window. A quick glance verified that I was smartly dressed enough for his taste and that my shoes were polished. He began the interview.

The position he proposed was identical to the one he'd offered me before. I would be carrying out secret tasks for the state on his behalf, concerning matters of national security. Tact, good judgement and coolness of head were required. Naturally. The salary was a hundred pounds a year. I would live in the servants' quarters and I must enter and leave the house through the back door and never greet him if we should meet in public. Yeh, yeh.

Sir Thomas asked if these terms and conditions were acceptable, and I murmured that they were. The interview then took an unexpected turn. Seated at his desk, he had a strange look on his face. Was I aware, he asked me, of the so-called Jack The Ripper murders?

'Yes,' I began. 'I–.'

He cut me off.

'Dreadful business. You may or may not know that the police have made little or no progress in identifying the perpetrator. Inspector Abberline has made a complete pig's ear of the case. He is no closer to success than he was last year. Some strange rumours have been circulating. You may have heard them?'

Indeed. I recalled my night in The Ten Bells. The Ripper, it was speculated, was a Freemason, a butcher, a Jewish immigrant with a grudge, a foreign skipper, take your pick…

'We now come to the nub of the matter, Wilkins.'

'Yes, sir.'

He looked worried.

'Can I rely upon your complete discretion?'

'Of course.'

'Certain persons – crackpots of course – have concocted a theory as to the murderer's identity. It combines Freemasonry with the Royal Family which is, of course, absurd. To cut to the chase, this ludicrous theory involves Prince Albert Victor, the Queen's grandson, second in line to the throne.'

He looked uncomfortable.

'There is, in Cleveland Street, Wilkins, a notorious brothel – a male brothel. The establishment is used by some men of rank who should know better. It is a temple of Sodom, at the lowest depth of depravity. Boys may be procured there, I believe, their services hired for a few shillings. Many of them work for The London Central Telegraph Office in St Martin's Le Grand.'

'Does Prince Albert go there?'

His brow creased.

'Of course not. He has never been there. He is in no way linked to this establishment. But that has not stopped tongues wagging. Some people are saying that the Prince caused five women in Whitechapel to be murdered last year because they were cognisant of a secret.'

'A secret?'

'Yes. The story is that the Prince fathered an illegitimate child by a woman of ill repute. It is alleged that one of the women murdered in Whitechapel, Mary Jane Kelly, was the midwife at the confinement. It will all die down, of course. In a year's time, no-one will be talking about Jack The Ripper. But that does not solve our little problem.'

'Which is?'

'The alleged royal connection, Wilkins. Naturally, we have checked your credentials carefully. You are trustworthy and nobody in London knows you. But is your stomach strong enough to take on such a disgusting task?'

'What task, sir?'

'I want you to go over to Cleveland Street to see if you can find out who has been spreading these vile rumours. You will go there tonight. The address is 19 Cleveland Street in Fitzrovia. When you knock, you are to say one word – "Somerset". That will get you in.'

I nodded.

'You will report to me here in the morning at eight o'clock. Do not be late. I cannot abide unpunctuality.'

'No, sir,' I said.

'Miss Thomas will show you to your room. I suggest that you wait until well after dark before presenting yourself. The depraved catamites who frequent such establishments keep late hours I understand.'

'Yes sir.'

What on earth did this have to do with foiling a Roman invasion of Britain, I wondered? No doubt, a connection would duly appear.

With a curt movement of his hand, Sir Thomas dismissed me. He had never asked me if I wanted the job! Arrogant man.

•••

Cleveland Street was an unremarkable, narrow road in a well-off neighbourhood. Tonight it was wreathed in fog, punctured by sickly pools of yellow from the gas lamps. It was eleven o'clock and I was the only person about. From the outside, there was nothing to suggest anything other than banality to these modest houses – even Number 19.

With my heart in my mouth, I gave a tug on the bell. The young man who admitted me glanced up and down the road. I said 'Somerset' in a low voice and he ushered me in.

In the hallway, glowing dully through crimson shades, the gas mantles gave off a low light that flattered human skin. I saw that the boy's cheeks were rouged and there were dabs of kohl on his eyelids. I heard laughter from behind a door.

'Wait here please sir,' he said politely.

He directed me to a room even more dimly lit than the passage outside. The embossed papered walls were dark brown; thick velvet drapes eliminated any possibility of the ingress of natural light.

The young man bade me sit on an ottoman. It was large enough to serve as a bed and was faced by a large cheval glass, which could be tilted in its frame to give an optimum view. To one side of the room was a screen decorated with peacock feathers. In the corner was a table with a bowl and jug.

The young man inquired whether I would like to take some refreshment. I thanked him but declined. This was a functional as well as sensual room, I reflected after he had left. Had Albert Victor sat nervously at this very spot, observing his pale complexion in the glass as he waited...? But, waited for what? My sixth sense, the gift of Culadar, told me that he had been here.

There was a noise at the door. What now?

19

Amanita Muscaria

To my surprise, it was a lady who entered. She wore a dress of midnight blue and a turban the same colour, which was embellished with an ostrich feather and encrusted with rubies and sapphires. The woman's skin was dusky. The low-cut dress showed her bosom to its full effect and across her breasts hung a glittering crystal.

Her features were familiar – the warm brown eyes with their full lids, the smile that rarely left her face. It was Anita from The White Lodge! The strangest thing was that her whole head seemed to be glowing, as Culadar's had, in a corona of saffron light. This was a certain indication of a spiritually advanced being.

'Hello Mr Wilkins,' she said.

'So you know me?'

'I know who you are and who sent you and for what purpose.'

'You are very well-informed.'

'It's a small world, my dear. Culadar told me that you would be coming.'

Culadar? How could that be? I'd met him in 1907 during my pursuit of Joseph Stalin. This was a different part of London, at an earlier time.

She seated herself on a stool.

'Culadar said that you would come this way with your pencil and pad. Well, ask your questions since I am the Madam of the house.'

I decided to jump in with both feet.

'Prince Albert Victor.'

'You mean Eddy. Yes?'

'Does he come to this establishment?'

'He is here now, enjoying our celebrated *poses plastiques* – a tableau of male beauty.'

'Does he come here often?'

'Yes. Do you need proof? I can show you.'

She pulled back a drape on the wall behind me to reveal a two-way mirror. We could see clearly into the next room, where there was a man in a smart jacket and waistcoat sitting on a cane chair. He had a high collar and white buttonhole. I noted his unhealthy pallor and hooded eyes, and the neatly waxed black moustache.

'That's Eddy.'

The Prince's cobra-like gaze was fixed on a man who was standing perfectly still in front of him, like a statue. The man flexed his biceps, then moved his limbs into another athletic position. He was naked.

'Thank you,' I said.

She closed the curtains.

'Is it true that Prince Albert, or Eddy as you know him, is secretly married to someone who is not of royal blood?'

'It's hardly a secret, dear, at least round here. He keeps a house with his wife at Number 6. They are legally married. Walter Sickert, the artist, was their best man. His studio is down the road.'

'And they have a child?'

'Little Alice. She is four years old. I saw her yesterday, I took her for a walk in Regents Park to feed the ducks.'

'Is it possible that Prince Albert is…Jack The Ripper?'

'No, no, dear. He's far too fastidious. It wasn't Eddy who killed those five poor women.'

'Then who did?'

She spoke without pausing for breath.

'Sir William Gull, the Queen's surgeon. He's not a nice man. I would avoid him if you can. Gull is a leading Freemason, and Eddy joined the craft recently. They always protect their own, you know. I believe it was another high-ranking mason – the Prime Minister himself, Lord Salisbury – who ordered the killings of those women to protect Eddy's secret. The Freemasons like to do their deeds in a showy way. It gives people a message not to interfere with them. But they will always leave false trails to cover their traces. They're masters of deception.'

'So,' I said, 'let me get this clear. The Queen's physician murdered five women in Whitechapel on the instructions of the Prime Minister because the Freemasons knew about Prince Albert's love child.'

'You're catching on. Gull lured them into a carriage...' She paused as if to emphasise the horror inflicted on those poor women. 'Like I said, it's a small world. Alice and her mother are Catholics you know.'

'Oh?'

'It makes the scandal even worse, as far as the Royal Family is concerned. Poor Alice will be shut away in an asylum of course, or killed, and Eddy will be removed from the scene – on a long royal tour, something of that nature. The word is that our little cathouse is going to be raided soon. Inspector Abberline has been assigned to the case. He's desperate to grab a scalp after his failure in Whitechapel. There's far more to this place than meets the eye. Poor Abberline is far out of his depth.'

'What do you mean?'

'Well, to give you an example, Lord Somerset, equerry to the Prince of Wales, Eddy's father, is one of our customers. He is not very discreet. And then there's Lord Euston. He has a mouth like the Rotherhithe Tunnel.'

'I see. Well, I've got all that. But there's one thing I don't understand.'

'What's that?'

Her dark eyes widened.

'Culadar. How do you know him?' I asked.

'Think back, dear. He told you himself, didn't he? Culadar is a Master of The Ancient Wisdom, an immortal. He can serve our cause at all times and in all places.'

'"Our cause"? What do you mean?'

'The path that we're following – the path of light. I am also an immortal. Some people call me a priest or a witch. Some call me a...'

'Don't you work at The White Lodge Hotel as a receptionist?'

She looked surprised.

'I work here, dear, for Dr Ward, the owner. I am his black madam. He pays me well to look after his boys. I have Mondays and Tuesdays off and a comfortable bed. Why would I want another job? What's this hotel you are talking about?'

'Never mind. It doesn't matter.'

I shifted in my seat. I was ready to go now. What would Sir Thomas make of this information? Everything he had feared as tittle-tattle appeared to be true!

'Can't I tempt you to stay? We have plenty of toys, you know – switches, whips, dildos.'

'No, really,' I said, 'thanks for the offer but I must be getting along.'

'As you please.'

I stood up.

'Oh by the way,' I said, 'what's your name?'

She gave me her amazing smile.

'My name is Amanita. Amanita Muscaria.'

'Well, thank you for your help.'

'It was a pleasure, dear.'

As she guided me to the front door, our bodies touched. I felt a thrill of excitement pass through me.

20

Brightlands

My lack of sleep meant not a jot to Sir Thomas. I hadn't arrived back at Colebrooke Row until two o'clock in the morning and had risen at seven. He, of course, was neatly sprigged out in his morning jacket, waiting in his study for our eight o'clock appointment.

For the most part, he showed little interest as I recounted what I'd recently learned, merely nodding glumly and looking down at his papers.

It was a lurid story and I didn't pull my punches. Prince Albert Victor was a sensualist who frequented the Cleveland Street brothel. I had seen him myself enjoying the spectacle of the *poses plastiques*.

'What does that mean, Wilkins?' enquired Sir Thomas, looking over his spectacles.

'A naked man, sir, assuming different bodily positions.'

'Fully naked?'

'Yes...'

'Was the Prince...er...aroused?'

'From what I could see, he was sir, yes.'

He nodded. My answer had satisfied his curiosity. I told him about the Prince's love nest and the daughter who could often be seen in Regent's Park. Many people, I intimated (I did not say whom), thought the Whitechapel murders had been carried out by highly-placed Freemasons. I didn't mention the King's surgeon.

He didn't flinch.

'I see.'

That was all he said. One could guess that plans would soon be afoot to carry out an exercise in damage limitation. All evidence pointing to the Prince in relation to the murders would be erased; the hapless Abberline, aided by planted stories, would continue to be lampooned for his failure to find the Whitechapel killer. He'd merely be a scapegoat. Gull, meanwhile, would suffer a mysterious and convenient illness.

Sir Thomas was good at his job. He sighed, indicating that the matter was concluded. Then, unexpectedly, he slid a sheet of paper across the desk – a letter, composed in purple ink in peculiar handwriting that was all loops and curls.

'Read this, Wilkins.'

The letter, which bore an address in Sevenoaks, Kent, had been sent to the Home Secretary, The Right Honourable Henry Matthews QC. It had been posted the previous week. It carried a peculiar letterhead, which included a diagram depicting a serpent cradling a six-pointed star, with an Egyptian ankh at its centre. There was a motto beneath – 'Truth is our goal. Love is our way'.

I read the letter:

'Dear Sir,

I write on behalf of the London lodge of the Theosophical Society. Our society, as you will be aware, is devoted to human improvement, through study and spiritual practice. The basis of our beliefs is that the human race is evolving, through the actions of enlightened individuals, towards a state of perfection – a civilisation of light. We are also in frequent contact with souls who dwell beyond the veil, in the spirit realm…'

'Sir…?!'

I had no wish to read any more of this nonsense.

'Carry on, Wilkins.'

'Yes sir,' I sighed, then did as he asked.

'You will be aware that spiritualism is becoming a respected and effective weapon in the armour of the police. My colleague Mr Lee of Blackheath, for example, has recently been of assistance to Scotland Yard in their inquiries.

I am accordingly writing to offer you, Mr Home Secretary, the services of the society as a tool in counteracting alien forces that threaten our country.

I have recently become aware through a trusted spirit medium of a grave threat to Britain from foreign revolutionaries, which is what has prompted this communication.

At this point, I do not wish to disclose the precise nature of the threat but would be happy to provide more details, should you choose to send your representative to visit me at my house in Sevenoaks. My business card is attached. No appointment is necessary.

Yours faithfully,

Anya Petrovska'

'Well?' Sir Thomas inquired.

'The woman is clearly a crackpot,' I said. 'A resident of la la land.'

He looked at me sternly.

'It is not for us to judge, Wilkins. Often things are not what they seem. That is why I want you to visit her and find out what is at the bottom of this. I will reimburse you for a second-class railway ticket from London Bridge to Sevenoaks. You will go there today and report back to me tomorrow morning. Remember to bring your receipts.'

The matter was closed. He looked mournfully at the piles of books that lined the room. No more order had been established in his study since the previous day. I almost offered to help.

•••

Nothing suggested the presence of spirits when I approached the house, only the name perhaps – Brightlands. It was a recently built bay windowed villa with a small front yard, a short walk from Sevenoaks station.

I rapped on the door knocker and waited. The door was opened by a tall young woman with piercing blue eyes. Despite her extremely short hair, I recognised her immediately from her clear skin and intelligent expression – Mary Jane from Spitalfields! Of course she did not know me.

She was about to dismiss me as a door-to-door salesman when I pulled something from the pocket of my jacket. It was the card that had been enclosed with Anya Petrovska's letter which pronounced boldly, in capital letters, that she was a:

'PSYCHIC INVESTIGATOR & SPIRIT MEDIUM'

I explained that I had come from London in an official capacity. The servant let me in. Anya Petrovska's bulky form dominated the hallway. Her dress was of deep purple velvet, trimmed with lace. A string of amethyst beads lay around her neck; her plump white hands were festooned with silver rings, some with turquoise stones.

The woman's stern presence commanded respect. Her eyes were dark and deep-set, like points of jet. I divined that these hypnotic instruments were the principal tools of her trade. Her hair, although you could scarcely call it hair, was a helmet of close-cropped curls, glistening with sweet-smelling oil.

'Nuala, you stupid girl!'

The poor creature flinched.

'Why did you allow this interruption? We have already begun!'

'This man is from London madam, he…'

'Oh! Then he must join us! Come!'

Her black eyes bored into mine. Despite her exotic name, she spoke with an accent that occasionally betrayed a trace of London's East End. Anya Petrovska was a formidable person and evidently accustomed to being obeyed. I was barely able to get my name out and tell her who had sent me before she thrust me into her front room.

21

The Séance

To a more prosaic person, this part of the house would have been described as the parlour. To Madame Petrovska, it was The Temple of Horus. Thick damask curtains shut out the daylight; the room's illumination was provided by oil lamps and candles. In the centre of the room was a large circular table.

The timing of my visit had been propitious. Two people were already seated at the table and Madame Petrovska introduced them to me:

'Mr Wilkins, this gentleman is Mr Leonard Dawson Rogers of Hammersmith. He is a member of the London lodge of the Theosophical Society. Mr Dawson Rogers is the author of one of our most popular pamphlets, Scientific Evidence that The Dead Still Live. Have you read it?'

I said that I had not.

'Well you must.'

This solemn, self-important man was dressed in funereal black. He nodded.

'This is his wife, Mrs Dawson Rogers.'

She was a matronly lady with grey hair tied in a bun.

'I am pleased to meet you, Mr Wilkins,' she said.

'Let us begin!'

Madame Petrovska seated me to her right. Mr Dawson Rogers was to her left and his wife opposite her, so that men and women alternated around the table. She asked us to hold hands. Her plump fingers wrapped around mine like fat talons. The light dimmed theatrically.

Behind Mr Dawson Rogers, a large mirror hung on the wall. Could this be a two-way mirror, I wondered? Because of my recent experience in Cleveland Street, I was now knowledgeable in such matters.

Nothing happened for a couple of minutes. We could hear each other breathing. The silence was uncomfortable.

Suddenly, a peculiar sound came from Madame Petrovska's throat, like the rasp of a parrot. From my sixth sense, I could tell who was a psychic and who wasn't. Mr and Mrs Dawson Rogers displayed no affinity to the spirit realm. There was a faint white flicker around Madame Petrovska's head but, compared to the blazing saffron light that streamed from Culadar and Amanita Muscaria, it was insignificant.

'Argh...' The parrot's rasp startled us again. 'He is here!'

Who is here? Answering the question, Madame Petrovska spoke in a hoarse whisper:

'Ahmed, my Armenian spirit guide, has entered the room.'

Her posture stiffened. She closed her eyes. Her clasp tightened. The spirit medium's silver rings were cutting into my hand.

'Ahmed,' said Madame Petrovska. 'We are honoured by your presence. Speak to us if it is thy will...'

Ahmed was silent. But suddenly Madame Petrovska's body became rigid. The table started rising slowly. Were we imagining it? No... By degrees, the table reached chest height. Mr Dawson Rogers' complacent expression had not left his face. His wife, too, appeared to be unmoved.

Madame Petrovska's eyes stared fixedly ahead. Her aura had intensified. Now there was a faint glow around her head.

•••

A battering ram of air crashed against my face. When my senses returned, I experienced that ringing concussion in the ears that follows an explosion. Through the ruins of the wall, the shocked face of the servant Nuala was revealed, as white as a ghost. The control box with which she had levitated the table had been blown from the upturned table in front of her onto the floor. (I should mention, also, that the blast had torn off most of her clothes, leaving a few wisps of white linen.) She wasn't moving. Madame Petrovska and Mr and Mrs Dawson Rogers, too, were whitened by dust and frozen like statues.

The smoke cleared to reveal a chaotic scene of overturned chairs, scattered ornaments and a moraine of lath, plaster and rubble. The table upon which we had conducted the séance had been rent in two, as if struck by a giant hammer. I was alarmed when the figure of two men appeared through the swirling dust.

Both were filthy, their faces blackened with soot. One of them was wearing a stovepipe hat and black morning jacket. The end of his cigar had been blown off by the explosion. The other was a shorter, more thickset man.

'Damnation,' said stovepipe. 'Are you injured?'

The thickset man shook his head. I saw from his pug-like features that it was Joseph, Mary Jane's former tormentor and the card of Colebrooke Row.

Stovepipe stepped forwards.

'You are, sir?'

'My name is William Wilkins,' I said.

We shook hands. I noted that he had an intelligent face, defined by his dark eyebrows and side whiskers. His grip was firm.

'I am Kingdom, Derek Kingdom. This is my butler…'

'Joseph,' I said.

'How do you know his name?'

'Oh, just a guess.'

'Are you a spiritualist?'

'Good grief no,' I said.

Nuala murmured something as she came back to life. It was apparent that Madame Petrovska and her two acolytes were also waking from their suspended animation.

Joseph did the decent thing. In an attempt to protect Nuala's modesty, he placed his jacket around her shoulders.

Seeing the state of her room, Madame Petrovska let out a stifled cry.

'We must go,' Kingdom said. 'For this to work, we must form a circle.'

In a repetition of the séance, he took my left hand. My right hand held Joseph's left. It was by the purest chance (one that I later blessed him for) that Joseph was also holding Nuala's hand while she was leaning against Kingdom's leg, thereby completing the circle.

Kingdom frowned with concentration. He muttered a phrase under his breath. There was a blinding flash.

22

Caer Caradoc

I was in the entrance to a cave and a small fire was burning. I was bruised, hungry and exasperated. Nuala, perched on a turf seat next to me, trembled from cold and/or fear. Kingdom had removed his hat and brushed down his clothes. His face was still grimy from the explosion.

'Where are we?' I asked.

'That part is easy, my friend. We are in the Welsh border country in the territory of the Ordovices.'

'The what?'

'You mean the who. The Ordovices are the Celtic tribe that occupies this part of Britain. It is a beautiful spot, you will see for yourself at daybreak. Specifically, we are at the Iron Age hill fort of Caer Caradoc.'

'Where is that precisely?'

'I see that you are not an archaeologist.'

Kingdom noticed Nuala's embarrassment at her state of undress and that she was shivering.

'My dear, you are freezing. We can't have that. Do retire to the sleeping area if you are tired. You will find your bed to be at least warm, if not too comfortable. Tomorrow, we'll find some clothes for you and you'll be able to wash, and so forth. We might even rustle up some soap for you.'

'Joseph?'

Kingdom's servant emerged from the back of the cave.

'Please see that this lady has everything she needs.'

'Yes, sir.'

'Would you like a cigar?' he asked me.

He reached into his pocket and produced two Havanas. We lit them using a stick pulled from the fire. The sweet smoke was like a balm to me.

It was a mild night and the sky was filled with stars. I saw the Milky Way and the constellations Scorpius and Sagittarius, which meant that it was an early summer sky. The positions of the

Big Dipper and the pole star indicated that the cave entrance faced south.

'Not a bad place to spend one's time, is it?' commented Kingdom, reading my mind. He blew out a stream of smoke. 'Look, I owe you an explanation. Tomorrow, you will meet Brandon, the Chief Druid of the Ordovices. This is his cave by the way. It's kind of him to let us use it. It was his idea to pick you up from Sevenoaks, because he felt you may be able to help us.'

'Help?'

'Yes, my friend. He had been made aware of your presence in the psychic realm.' He paused and glanced thoughtfully at the fire. 'You see, delightful as this part of the world is, I have a problem.'

'What is that?'

His eyes engaged mine.

'My dear daughter has been kidnapped.'

He told me that he was a time traveller and inventor. A man of private means, he had become extremely wealthy from his manufacturing business and lived in a former manor house in Kent. This he shared with his beloved daughter, Georgina, and their domestic staff, including his butler Joseph and a groom, Snipe.

It had taken him ten years to perfect time travel. His first machine, known as a chronosphere, had been followed by a second. The two machines, the Daedalus and the Icarus, resembled large metal diving bells. They had been furnished in the Arts and Crafts style with the assistance of William Morris and Company's emporium, Liberty's of Regent Street. Equipped with comfortable sleeping partitions, they were able to accommodate up to four people. The devices were kept in his stables.

The Daedalus was being prepared for its first journey into the time stream, he explained. As a classical scholar, he was fascinated by the Roman period in British history; an autodidact, he had devoted much of his adult life to learning about Roman Britain.

Accordingly, the machine had been precisely calibrated to arrive in the year 50 CE at this exact location. The purpose of this sojourn into the past was, he explained, to witness a celebrated battle between the Romans and Celts – a battle that would decide the fate of Britain.

He continued:

'One morning, I went into the stables. To my horror, I saw that the door of the Daedalus was open. I mounted the steps and looked inside. Snipe was sitting at the control console. My beloved Georgina was inside too. She had been gagged and was tied to a chair. She must have seen Snipe enter the device when she was grooming her horse and tried to stop him. She's fearless, you see, as her dear mother was.

'Snipe saw me. He pushed the time lever forward to its full extent. I managed to jump backwards and save myself just in time. The machine faded from view as it entered the time stream. I felt terrible, as you can imagine. Georgina is my dearest treasure. Obviously, I entered the second machine, the Icarus, and set off in hot pursuit. Its controls were set so that it would arrive at the same place and time – or so I thought.'

'So, it didn't?'

'Not exactly. The first machine had preceded me by a few minutes. In that short interval, Georgina and Snipe had been captured by the Ordovices and taken to their chieftain Caractacus. They tried to grab me too, but I frightened them off with my revolver. That's when I met Brandon the Chief Druid. He tried to intercede on my behalf and negotiate with Caractacus for the return of Georgina. But herein lies my problem: Brandon and I don't speak the same language. That's where you come in.'

'I beg your pardon?'

'We need you to interpret for us.' A frown crossed Kingdom's brow. 'There aren't many people with your psychic powers and proficiency in multiple languages. Brandon was listening to the séance in Sevenoaks. He recognised you as an Englishman with the gift of tongues. Perceiving that you could be useful, he called in a favour from the Sun God Belenus to pick you up. Belenus gave the house a little tap with his war hammer.'

'It must be a large one.'

'Oh, it is,' Kingdom smiled. 'We didn't mean to bring the maidservant with us. The poor lady is an innocent victim in all this.'

'I see.'

I looked round. I'd heard a footfall close to the cave mouth. A man was illuminated by the glow of the fire, his ruddy skin glistening.

'Ah, here's Brandon.'

•••

The Ordovices' Chief Druid, their shaman, healer, bard and ceremonial officiate, was wearing his ceremonial cloak and headdress. He had a full grey beard. This man had a shimmering yellow aura – the strongest that I had seen. *Bulb head. Hey dude!*

He and Kingdom were able to converse now, with me interpreting. At first, they laughed about the damage to the house in Sevenoaks and how surprised the house's owner had been.

Kingdom asked Brandon if his daughter was safe.

'Oh yes,' said Brandon. 'She and the man Snipe are in the prison hut. They are being properly looked after.'

'Good.'

'However, it will soon be Beltane. The fires and wicker men are almost ready.'

'You mean…'

'Yes. I fear that Caractacus plans to sacrifice both of them as a special offering to the gods, to help him succeed in the coming battle.'

Kingdom's face turned pale.

'Oh dear.'

Brandon explained that he would be meeting Caractacus the following day but that, with my help, he was sure that his appeal to the leader would be successful.

The Chief Druid was a delightful man, cultured and learned. He explained to me that he had spent twelve years acquiring his Druidic craft, which included memorising long poems. Although the Celts used runes for magical and practical purposes, they had no written language. He was therefore the repository of the tribe's history and folklore.

He said he was supposed to know everything – what the gods were feeling, how to heal a wound, the next day's weather. It was an onerous responsibility. And his spiritual authority could be over-ruled by the temporal authority of Caractacus, who feared him and regarded him as a threat.

A battle was brewing. The Romans had conquered most of England. Caractacus had brought the remnants of his tribe, the Catuvellauni, from central England to here, the land of the Ordovices, to mount a last-ditch battle. Other clans would soon arrive from even further afield.

Two Roman legions, he explained, were on their way to this remote, mountainous country at the limits of their empire to crush the rebellion. It was rumoured that the Governor of Britain himself, Publius Ostorius Scapula, was in command of the Roman force. Hated by the Britons, he was an unpleasant character who inspired fear in his enemies through public torture and execution.

It must have been well after midnight when we finished talking. At the back of the cave was an area lit by tallow candles, where ferns and bracken were covered with sheepskin. Brandon said he and Kingdom would keep watch. I bid them both good night and found a place to sleep.

Joseph's snoring echoed around the stone walls. I chose a place close to Nuala, but not too close. The bed was deliciously soft. I settled into it feeling relatively safe but apprehensive as to what the following day may bring.

23

King Caractacus

'So, you're an inventor, Mr Kingdom?'

It was breakfast time. We were sitting in the cave entrance, in the same position as the previous night. The delicious oatcakes that Joseph had served us, sweetened with honey, had improved our moods.

'Yes, it is an interest of mine,' he said, modestly. 'Happily, I have enjoyed some success. Have you heard of my rocket pills?'

I said that I had not.

'They are the principal source of my financial success. It is these little pills that have brought me my worldly rewards – my manor house in the Weald of Kent, my servants. The public have gobbled them up, we can't make them fast enough! There's actually nothing to them, you know, they're primarily composed of sugar. There's also a secret ingredient – but I can't tell you what it is.'

'Of course not.'

'Would you like to try one?'

I held back.

'Please, my good fellow.'

He reached into his pocket and pulled something out. The paper packet was labelled 'Kingdom's Rocket Remedy'. It was illustrated with a picture of George Stephenson's celebrated steam locomotive.

Swallowing one of the small white pills had a pleasant effect. Within a couple of minutes, I experienced a sharpening of the senses and a mild sense of euphoria.

'We make a liquid tonic too,' said Kingdom. 'The pills can be kept in one's purse or pocket. Some people call them "pocket rockets", I believe.'

'I can see why,' I said. My nerve ends were tingling. The ferns and bracken on the hillside formed a magic carpet. The sky was an exquisite shade of blue.

Kingdom smiled.

'They have made me a very wealthy man, Mr Wilkins.'

My jaw was clenching. My thoughts were lucid, leading to words of marvellous acuity.

I didn't respond but merely nodded.

I glanced out from the cave entrance. Close by was a pool of sweet, crystalline water. It was here that we performed our ablutions. Nuala was sitting on the grass next to it, enjoying the spring sun. I saw that she was relishing her liberation from the tyranny of Madame Petrovska.

She was now wearing a woollen dress. Her face was already flushed from sun and fresh air. It appeared she had readily adapted to the life of her Celtic ancestors in the 1st Century.

•••

Daylight had revealed that the cave was enclosed within a stockade. Above, forming a jagged skyline, were the remains of the Caer Caradoc hill fort. A substantial settlement extended down the hillside. There was a cluster of circular huts with conical thatched roofs; beyond them were wooden ramparts and walkways with watchtowers protected by sharpened stakes. To the south was a broad valley through which looped a silver river.

I should add that three large bonfires had been built at the crest of the ridge next to the fort. Raised above each on long poles were the shapes of men made from wattles. Brandon explained that prisoners of the Celts previously captured in battle would be placed inside the hollow giants and burned alive. This would happen to mark the Beltane celebrations on the first full moon in Taurus, in a few days. Ash from the Beltane fires would be rubbed into their warriors' skin to make them braver in battle. After this explanation, he told me that it was time to leave. He had secured a special meeting with Caractacus.

Caractacus, son of Cunobelinus, King of the Ordovices, looked up as we entered his hut. His most recent concubine was just leaving. His blond hair was in ringlets. One could see from his fleshy, sensuous face that he enjoyed an ample diet. His eyes were a piercing shade of blue.

He yawned. The sight of my suit, tie and celluloid collar only briefly aroused his curiosity.

'Well?'

'I seek thy counsel on behalf of Tall Hat', said Brandon, referring to Kingdom. 'He is sorely grieving for the loss of his daughter, the flower of his life.'

'And who is this?' Caractacus waved his hand in my general direction.

'This is William, son of Ogma. He is a master of many tongues and has other powers too. He is prepared to help us in our great battle with the Romans – but only at a price.'

'And that is? Let me guess. Tall Hat wants his precious daughter back.'

'That is correct,' Brandon said.

'Well, he can have her. She is of no use to me.'

Presumably the chieftain's advances towards the girl had been spurned. We learned later that it was only his fear that Georgina was a witch that had saved her from his amorous intentions.

'I'm keeping the other one.'

Brandon seemed unconcerned about the appalling fate that was to befall Kingdom's groom, Snipe.

'The girl is yours. I'll send her up to your cave. Now go.'

'Yes, master.'

Brandon was pleased. Despite my alleged linguistic gifts, I had not said a single word, but perhaps my presence had helped. We left the hut and walked up the hill.

The giant wicker men formed a strange, unholy trinity on the skyline. How many people were to die in the flames to propitiate the Celtic gods before the battle?

24

Beltane

The sun had cleared the mists from the grass, rocks and gorse. Before dawn, Joseph had gone on a hunting expedition with his new friends from the Catuvellauni tribe. Kingdom left after breakfast to tinker with his time machine, which was hidden in a thicket of bushes nearby. Brandon accompanied him, saying that he had duties to attend to.

Nuala was washing clothes in the pool, wringing the wet garments and bashing them on a rock. Her keen eyes met mine as we talked.

'D'you know that old bat, Madame Petrovska, is not Russian at all. She's from Spitalfields. Her brother still lives there. He is a greengrocer.'

'It doesn't surprise me,' I said. 'How did you find yourself in Sevenoaks?'

'Ah well…'

She said she had arrived in London from Limerick, a county on the Emerald Isle. Arriving in London, she had obtained a position in a large house in Kensington. (*Sounds familiar, I thought.*)

'On my days off,' she continued, 'I used to walk in Hyde Park with the other maids and governesses. Well, one day I got talking to this man. He said he lived in the country. He travelled round the lanes of Kent in his caravan, following the harvests and the haymaking. That sounded grand. I gave up my job and went with him, didn't I?'

She raised her eyebrows and tutted.

'Was that a bad thing?' I asked.

'He didn't have a caravan at all, but a cart. He lived in a filthy old barn. It was full of rats. I only stayed for a week. One night when he was drunk he started abusing me. I waited until he was asleep and just started walking.'

'That was brave of you.'

'Oh, it wasn't really. I walked for a few miles down a lane until I came to a town and slept in someone's garden. Luckily for me, it was a rectory. The priest who lived there took a shine to me.'

'That was fortunate.'

'God bless that man. He found a job for me at a house nearby.'

'Working for Madame Petrovska.'

'That's right, cooking, cleaning, washing – a proper skivvy.'

Nuala looked up from her chores: 'Ah, good morning miss!'

Georgina Kingdom had arrived at the pool. It was clear that she had been doted on by her father from the moment she'd been born. She was well-spoken and I could tell that her calm self-possession, shining hair and coy smile would work like a charm – she obviously expected those around her to see to her every whim.

She acknowledged me and arranged herself, like Venus, on a patch of grass so that she could catch the sun.

'She will be wanting me to wash her clothes,' said Nuala.

'Well, don't.' I said. 'You are not her servant. She can do it herself.'

'Yes, sir.'

'Don't call me sir. You are not my servant either.'

'What shall I call you then?'

'William.'

'I shall then. William!'

Her laugh was like the tumbling of clear water.

Smoke rose lazily from the thatched Celtic huts. One could hear dogs barking and the bleating of sheep. Warriors were sharpening their weapons while their leaders were having important conversations. It had been reported by the Ordovices' scouts that the XXth legion had left the Wroxeter camp and was now only two days' march away along the Roman road, Watling Street. The XIVth was approaching from the south. The moon would be waxing again when the armies met.

The battle would not be fought in the Caer Caradoc encampment. Caractacus knew that the Roman battering rams and siege engines would make short work of the wooden fortifications and that the stockade would merely trap the Celts in a killing ground. His plan was that, after Beltane, the tribes would abandon the stockade. The women and children would be hidden deep in the forests that clad the hills to the west. The site of the battle had yet to be chosen; this was the subject of fierce debate.

•••

We did not take part in the Beltane celebrations that day, but we were certainly aware of them. From late afternoon, we heard the shriek of pigs as their throats were slit and we were conscious of people moving into the camp. Joseph returned triumphantly from his hunting trip with a small boar.

As evening fell, the delicious aromas of roasting meat drifted across the hillside accompanied by the sound of laughter and ribaldry.

That night, the full moon rode high and proud in a clear sky. Nuala and I were rarely apart. That evening, I placed my arm around her waist. The expectation of the coming battle meant that nothing needed to be said. She moved her body into mine.

In the middle of the night, the Beltane fires were lit. Acrid smoke billowed from the sinister wicker giants and we could hear the pitiful screams and cries for mercy of the sacrificial victims. We surmised that among them must be Kingdom's groom Snipe. The fellow was never seen again. We retired for the night when the awful sounds had stopped.

The screams and laughter from the Beltane celebration continued until long after it was light. Lying in the dark, I fancied that I could hear the crashing of giant timbers falling to the forest floor. Nuala was in my arms, her sweet breath on my face. She was a goddess and I longed for the morning to come, so that I would be able to drink in the beauty of her pale skin and blue eyes.

I felt perfectly safe.

25

Battle Plans

Caractacus resorted to the ultimate hazard, adopting a place for battle so that entry, exit, everything would be unfavourable to us and for the better of his own men, with steep mountains all around, and, wherever a gentle access was possible, he strewed rocks in front in the manner of a rampart. And in front too there flowed a stream with an unsure ford, and companies of armed men had taken up position along the defences.

Tacitus, The Annals

I shall never forget the war council. The largest circular hut in the stockade had been converted into a meeting chamber for the occasion. Boughs of rowan were placed around the entrances and the floor was scattered with oak leaves, so that the tree's strength would transfer to the warriors through their feet. A rowan fire burned in the centre of the hut to summon spirits to assist the tribes in the coming battle. The chamber was lit with fire brands held in iron staves.

From Wales were representatives of the Ordovices, Silures and a few Demetae. From England came the Brigantes, the Catuvellauni and the Iceni tribe, led by their flame-haired warrior queen, Boudica. The Brigantes' leader, Queen Cartimandua, was also a woman of striking physique and great beauty. Caractus leered at both these formidable women, despite his wife being present.

Druids had come from the sacred island of Anglesey. They stood in their black robes around the perimeter, some holding rattles in the shape of bull's testicles.

The meeting was presided over by Caractacus. He was the most ostentatious of the chieftains, his gold neck ornament and bracelets a blatant display of his wealth.

Caractacus declared that this was an important moment in the history of the Celtic nation. He reminded his audience that their ancestors had succeeded in driving Julius Caesar from the shores of Britain a hundred years before, so the Romans were not invincible.

'Do you want to live in servitude?!' he pronounced, staring fiercely into the hut.

'No!' came the resounding reply.

'Then take this opportunity,' he exclaimed. 'It is better to die a hero than to live as a slave!'

The Druids shook their rattles.

Now came the task of determining the tactics that would be needed in the coming battle. Caractacus and his principal leaders, including Boudica and Cartimandua, left the hut with cheers ringing in their ears.

•••

It was just after dawn. A straight-winged red kite hung motionless above us. It diminished to a dust-sized speck that dissolved in a blue haze.

Kingdom, Nuala, Georgina, Joseph and I were seated on a knoll beneath the peak of the mountain. The Icarus was hidden nearby. Should things go badly, we should be able to escape in the time machine – that was our plan.

Caractacus was a little way below us in his war chariot surrounded by his finest warriors. The sky was Wedgwood blue, the clouds sharply defined, like the finely etched figures carved on a cameo. We could hear, in a vast murmur, the whinnying of horses and shouts of men. The array of speckled dots that we could see in the distance was an army. It wound in a thick black crocodile back to the Roman camp.

The Celtic army had been divided into four, each occupying a hilltop. Each hillside had been carefully defended with walls and heaps of stones. The Celts would wait for the Romans to fall into their trap. The entire army and its equipment would be forced by the local topography to move down a track along the valley bottom, crossing the river at two fording points which had been strewn with boulders. Two miles away, clearly within our sight, Celts began firing arrows at Roman soldiers crossing the river. Caractacus issued instructions that were conveyed by riders to distant troops.

We watched the Roman army encroach for several hours – its endless cohorts of infantry and terrifying, horse-driven machines.

By noon, on the other side of the river in the valley, we could see the pennants and sacred eagles of the two legions. General Scapula must be among them. He was so close that a Celtic arrow could almost have reached him.

Caractacus raised an arm. On this signal, thousands of warriors blew their war trumpets. Each fashioned from bronze had a mouthpiece shaped like a boar's head with a gaping, open mouth. The vast, echoing sound was a call to war from the mountains themselves. Perhaps some Roman hearts froze at this sound, like an ancestral memory from the deepest, darkest forests of Gaul in which their comrades had fought savage painted enemies.

26

Beasts From The Sky

'This is not good,' Kingdom said, peering through a spyglass.

The two forces were now engaging. From our vantage point, we could hear the throaty bellows of men roused by the red mists of battle far below.

The XIXth, the Valeria Victrix, had been the first legion to cross the river. We watched its infantrymen link their shields into a testudo, or tortoise, formation – a moving wall and roof like a metal box. In this way, large numbers of soldiers could edge forwards, slowly but safely.

The legions moved steadily up the hillsides like an army of armadillos. Brave, sword-wielding Celts flung themselves at the massed shields but were easily despatched by Roman archers. The grass was soon littered with their bodies and slippery with blood. The frothy, scarlet river was dammed by fallen soldiers.

As evening fell, the sky was slashed with crimson streaks. The Romans were pouring more men from a seemingly inexhaustible source into battle and hauling their ballistae (or crossbows) and giant catapults into position.

The battle's outcome now seemed inevitable. Caractacus had lost a quarter of his army. Their bodies littered the hillsides like crushed ants. Brandon stepped from the shadows. Helped by another Druid, he carried the largest and most ornate carnyx that the Celts possessed. The mouth of the heavy instrument was shaped like the head of a fearsome python. The men rested the instrument on a stand. Brandon muttered a prayer and took a gulp of air into his lungs. He placed his lips to the mouthpiece.

•••

A spine-chilling, plangent sound rolled into the valley. We watched as clouds in the western sky assumed new forms – the shapes of giant bulls. The thundering of their hooves was deafening as the gold, crimson and orange beasts stampeded across the sky. Their horns were like razors and their great ironclad hooves crushed men and structures like paper. Within the next few minutes, every single Roman testudo and war machine had been trampled into oblivion. As quickly as the beasts had been summoned from the spectral realm, they vanished, melting back into the sky.

Celtic cheers filled the air. Warriors, with blue patterns inked on their faces, leapt over boulders. They chased and despatched the few Roman soldiers who remained. They would compete to lay their hands on the ultimate prizes – the eagle standards of the defeated legions. Later, clouds of ravens and kites pecked at the corpses on the battlefield.

News of the amazing victory would pass down through the centuries and travel to the ends of the known world.

Two Roman legions and their high official had been obliterated.

•••

Task: Publius Ostorius Scapula
Mission completed

Feel proud of yourself. You have whipped the Romans real good and they won't return to Britain for a long time – if ever. Well done. You are smarter and wiser now, so use your powers carefully. Here's a tip: sometimes, you must take a portion of darkness from your enemy in order to defeat them.

It feels weird not to wake up in a cave. Doubly weird because The White Lodge is extremely comfortable and designed to cater for every human need. I won't miss the aches and pains, but I will soon feel nostalgic for the 1st Century AD – listening to curlews, watching the sunrise, the scent of dew-misted grass. In particular, I will miss Nuala. Is it possible to fall in love with an avatar? I seem to've done.

The bedroom is fusty and unusually dark. I look out of the window. The sky is filled with swollen black clouds. Right on cue comes a flash of lightning and the ominous rumble of thunder. This reality is very theatrical. It is soon lashing down on the South Downs with fat drops of rain.

There are no e-mails for me. I wonder if Simon is still recording music for Strobe Kitson. What about the band? Do we have another gig? I always experience a sense of loss after completing a task in the game – like a performer who's just come offstage. I need to re-orientate myself to the normal world before re-entering the virtual one.

There is only one place to go – the bar. But first, as usual, I visit reception. Anita, the queen of the Cleveland Street brothel, is preoccupied. There's a tight frown on her face, and she barely notices me.

'Hi Chris,' she murmurs.
'Hi. How are you?'
'I'm fine, thank you.'
She looks tense.

Today's history talks seem intriguing. They are (from memory): The Ancient Wisdom of Helena Blavatsky; Pelagius and The Heresy of Goodness and Amy Levy: The Emancipated Muse. But that will be for later.

There is little point in asking for a copy of The Times from 50 CE to read about the triumph of the Celts. Cool beer is beckoning me. I walk across reception to a familiar door and push it open.

Pinch yourself Chris! Leaning over the pool table, beneath George Washington's benign smile, is a gangly man wearing a white suit and cowboy boots. He's peering down his cue, concentrating on his shot.

27

A Portion of Darkness

'Hey dude...'

A second after Kitson greets me, a red ball pops neatly into a corner pocket, leaving an inert white ball just behind it ready for the next shot.

I see that he's playing Simon. This should be an interesting contest. Unlike me, both are skilled at pool.

'Hail the conquering hero,' Kitson says, as he chalks his cue.

My night at the music hall in Camden springs to mind – the night Kitson was Jim Beam, Western Sharpshooter, with Little Plum, his companion in buckskin.

'I understand you gave Scapula a mauling,' he comments, bending over the table.

'Yes. We killed him and destroyed two of his legions,' I inform him.

'Nice work.'

His confident shot, an attempt to break up a small group of reds at the other end of the table and pot one of them, ends in failure. Simon stands up, ready to take his turn.

'How did you do it?' Kitson continues probing.

'I made friends with this Druid guy,' I explain.

'Brandon?'

'Yeh, that's him. Brandon knew Belenus, the Sun God, and, through him, Dagda. He's the Irish Zeus. We used Brandon's magic cauldron to call up Dagda and borrowed his fairy cattle to mash up the Romans.

'Belenus and Dagda are pals, they go way back,' Kitson informs me. 'You're certainly working your way through the ladies, by the way,' he adds with a wink.

'What do you mean?'

'Mary Jane, Phoebe, Nuala. You're potting those balls, son.'

I feel myself blushing. How does he know this?

'Don't worry. Everyone falls for Mary Jane. She was built by the best.'

'Don't you think it's wrong using people you know in your games?' I inquire, cautiously.

'You mean an infringement of their civil liberties? No-one's complained. In fact, most people like it.'

Simon, with ruthless efficiency, is working his way through the table.

'This guy is good,' the Texan comments. 'Good guitar player too.'

'I know.' I nod.

The game is soon over. The tropical fish in the George Washington bar look listless. Kitson greets the bar tender, who pours a generous measure of Bourbon and tops it up with ice and Coke.

'They say bad things come in threes,' Kitson confides.

'What do you mean?'

'Well, I might lose this place, the jewel in my crown. The rocket disaster screwed me and everyone is saying that I'm the Antichrist or the Beast of The Apocalypse. They are even saying on YouTube that I blew up my own spaceship just for the publicity. Reporters are sniffing round the hotel, trying to dig up dirt on me. And that's not the worst thing.'

'Oh?'

He takes a gulp from his tumbler.

'Some son of a bitch in Korea is selling games cloned from mine. That motherfucker has been stealing my code. I'm gonna sue him, obviously, but it's gonna cost me. Which is why some of my assets might have to be liquidated. Maybe this one. I love this place. I'd hate not to have my English retreat.'

He pauses, reaching into his jacket: 'Would you like a little helper?'

'I'm sorry?'

Kitson pulls out a familiar packet – Kingdom's Rocket Remedy.

'A rocket pill. They're made to my own recipe.'

I accept a single white tablet. Kitson gulps downs a handful, with a generous slurp of Bourbon.

'You know you're my best player, don't you? I get the daily reports.'

I say I'm glad about that.

'By the way, I'm having a party on Saturday at CloudCorp HQ in London to launch my new game. All my friends will be there. And my enemies. I hope you and Simon can play for me.'

'I'm sure we can.'

'Well, that's good.'

He slips off his bar stool. Unsurprisingly, his legs won't hold him up.

'What the fuck?'

Simon is watching from a nearby table, where he's sitting with Anya. The barman comes to the rescue, and it takes all of us to steer Kitson to the lift.

28

The Texas Vampire

It's hard to ignore the Daily Mail. The paper's like a nasty fungal infection that won't go away – you keep checking to see if it's still there. The following morning, the day before the gig at CloudCorp's London HQ, it is very hard to ignore. Copies are strewn around the hotel, lying on the reception desk and around the bar. I pick one up.

The Mail knows what its readers want and gives it to them unfailingly – old-fashioned morality, aspiration and sensation wrapped into neat human packages, like the lives of the saints.

Its editors are tyrants, mercilessly sarcastic to those who do not meet their standards; its reporters are skilful and resourceful; its sub-editors are imaginative and lack moral scruples. Once the Mail has settled on a victim, it goes for them like a thug in a dark alleyway. As far as I can see, most of today's issue, Friday 5th June 2020, is devoted to Strobe Kitson. There's a front-page story under a huge headline, 'Weird Cult of Evil', with the strapline 'special investigation'. There are more pages inside with interviews and pictures.

The paper must have been working on this for days. I sit down in the lobby and start from the beginning:

'Billionaire linked to missing teenagers

Police are searching for missing people who attended a games convention organised by Texas billionaire Strobe Kitson through his luxury hotel brand. Gamers attended the event at CloudCorps' central London HQ last year to help in the creation of the cult game Get The Bad Guys.

The Mail has learned that some gamers were put to sleep, allowing a device to be implanted in their brains. The police are searching for several participants who have disappeared.

A former employee of CloudCorp's flagship White Lodge Hotel, near Eastbourne in East Sussex, has confirmed to the Mail that drug-fuelled 'sex magic' takes place at the hotel.

Cult expert Professor Paul Pointing of Buckingham University told the Mail: 'We know that video games are extremely addictive. Here we have a game that's being used by a charismatic individual to promote his belief system to vulnerable young people. It is a toxic and dangerous combination which, in my view, should be stopped before more people are damaged – or worse.'

The Mail is calling on MPs this week to conduct a full inquiry into Kitson's business practices. Kitson (42) was unavailable for comment last night.

Business empire

Strobe Kitson began CloudCorp in 2010 in Brownsville Texas with his business partner Chuck Tyler. CloudCorp was floated on the stock market in 2018 with a value of $100bn. Kitson is known to own properties in the UK, US, France and Brazil. His UK assets include The White Lodge Hotel in Sussex and a house and recording studio in Holland Park. His main property is a 1,000-acre ranch in Texas. He is believed to have begun co-habiting with his wife, Tammy, when she was only 15 years old. They were legally married when she was 17.'

I read an op-ed article headed 'The Texas Vampire':

'It began as an American dream. Strobe Kitson was a high school dropout. His father deserted the family before he was five. He grew up with his mother in a trailer park in Brownsville, Texas. Kitson came from the wrong side of the tracks and was desperate not to stay there.

He tried to be a music promoter and set up a cleaning company. Both ventures failed. A spell in prison on minor drugs charges focused his mind. It was in Cameron County Jail that he met his future business partner, Chuck Tyler. Tyler was an app developer and video game enthusiast.

Get The Bad Guys became a cult without a cent being spent on advertising. The game took off because it used a new form of immersive reality based on cloud technology that made the user experience vivid and compelling. Best of all, this experience was available without the use of a VR helmet.

How could that be, experts asked? Some have speculated that Kitson must have been implanting tiny, almost invisible chips in gamers' brains.

Strobe Kitson has done well. He likes to boast that he is an ordinary, self-made billionaire. Like any mogul, he has accumulated multiple trappings of success – a succession of glamorous women and vanity projects, including his space company, which is seeking to build a hotel on the moon.

Weird cult

Kitson and Tyler are both billionaires. But the Mail has learned that Kitson's former business partner is now living as a recluse in a tumble-down shack, guarded by vicious dogs. His hair is unkempt, his clothes are dirty. He goes to sleep with a shotgun by his bed. We don't know the true story of how or why they fell out. Kitson's life is a weird mixture of fact and fantasy.

Kitson's hotels in London, Paris and New York are listed as offshoots of his AI company, CloudCorp. We know that they offer cheap rates to gamers, tempted with the prospect of being transferred to CloudCorp's luxury flagship hotel near Eastbourne, The White Lodge.

The Daily Mail has established that young people are lured to the private hotel, which is closed to normal residents, by limitless drugs and sex. It is the centre of a weird cult.

Some people have called Kitson 'The Texas Vampire'. Has he actually stolen the souls of his victims to construct his empire of evil? There are no limits to the ambitions of this metaverse mogul. But one thing is sure: the authorities are closing in.'

29

The Lone Stars

Kitson was happy that Simon, Anya, Ben and I had played the gig on Saturday to launch his new game, Temple of Solomon. CloudCorp HQ had turned into a circus. Alerted by the Mail, a scrummage of reporters and photographers were massed outside (it was like the Brotherhood Church all over again), as well as protestors carrying banners – 'Where are our kids?', 'Pay your taxes!', 'Go back to Texas JR!'.

By midday, there were more than a hundred people in front of the building. Some of the protesters had camped up in a local graveyard in multi-coloured tents.

More police arrived and soon there was a metal barrier positioned in front of CloudCorp HQ. Their main job was to keep the traffic flowing but that became impossible as the crowd swelled. Tweets were tweeted and videos livestreamed.

By the time Simon, Ben and I had arrived, the protest had acquired what the press would call a 'party atmosphere'. Music was playing from the church yard, people were blowing whistles and protesters handed out flyers. More people had piled in; a helicopter hovered overhead. The road had been closed off and the city was in gridlock.

By evening, the demo itself was a news story. The protestors had set up their own Facebook pages and websites. It was fodder for evening TV news bulletins and lengthy dissections in the Sunday broadsheets. The tabloids, with their deep pockets, were now pursuing everybody who had ever known Strobe Kitson, on both sides of the Atlantic.

•••

We'd entered the chapel at seven o'clock to a cacophony of boos and whistles, as the first evening news stories were airing on TV. We were being paid but that was not the main reason we were there. We liked Kitson and didn't think he'd done anything wrong.

He was nowhere to be seen but he'd issued a press statement, which made the following points:

1. No chips have ever been implanted in a gamer's brain. Those who have participated in game development have done so willingly and signed waivers permitting their avatars to be used as intellectual property.

2. No evidence has been produced that any game player is missing.

3. CloudCorp have paid all taxes required by law in the jurisdictions in which it operates.

4. Kitson will be taking legal proceedings against those responsible for spreading false and malicious stories, including on social media.

The launch was a listless affair. Many of the invitees did not turn up and those who did had been smuggled into the chapel via the back entrance. Champagne and warm red wine were duly drunk and canapés nibbled as the Temple of Solomon was demoed.

The idea of this game, a historical walkthrough, was to show how the world's Abrahamic religions are linked by common roots. Players can explore the ziggurats of Ancient Mesopotamia, get to know prophets and live with nomadic tribes in the desert.

Kitson made a speech, thanking his team of game developers. He said that if more people knew about how the major religions are connected, the world would be a better place.

He added that it was hard being a good guy when most people thought you were bad – like Jesus, or John Lennon. Things had ended badly for both of them. There was nervous laughter.

Most of those present were aware that rumours were spreading the improbable idea of a crypt beneath HQ in which the bodies of gamers have been cryonically frozen – a catacomb populated by the victims of The Texas Vampire.

•••

Few people were left by the time we went onstage. We'd settled on our name – The Lone Stars – earlier that day and had it printed up for my bass drum. Strobe's wife Tammy had flown over from Texas for the occasion.

Of course, she was the double of Mary Jane Kelly, Phoebe Brundle and Nuala. Did Kitson know that I'd slept with three versions of his wife? Obviously, he did but it didn't seem to bother him. At least it was only in the metaverse. The next time Tammy's avatar popped into a game, I would remember Strobe and Tammy locked together during one of our slow numbers.

There were no encores that night but as we were packing up, Anita the receptionist came over and complimented me on my drumming. She was wearing blue velvet trousers and a white top which she had beautifully embroidered. She seemed very pleased to see me, telling me she lived in Brighton and, in a roundabout way, that she was single. She mentioned she was working the next day at the hotel, and I said I'd see her there.

I watched Simon as he carefully coiled his guitar leads. He gave his Gibson SG a loving wipe with a yellow duster and put it in its velvet-lined case. Little was said as we were driven in a long white limo back to The White Lodge, gliding through half-glimpsed suburbs and the dark English countryside.

30

Machine Head

Perhaps I should have cut my losses at that point, walked away from the hotel and gone back to my normal life. But to be honest, my normal life wasn't that great. It was warm here and the food and drink were free. I didn't believe the Daily Mail's story. I couldn't see that Kitson had done much wrong – apart, possibly, from not paying his taxes. But, set against that, he had told me that he'd set up a charitable foundation with his wife.

Trying to catch up on a lost night's sleep never works. Napping fitfully in my room, I had a weird dream. It began in the Camden Hippodrome. Jim Beam The Western Sharp Shooter was spinning Little Plum on his wheel of death. The audience were gasping with anticipation. He fired his silver Winchester. A hole appeared in her head; her buckskin tunic was splattered with blood.

Stalin stood up in his box. He was clapping and cheering. Lenin frowned.

Then I was sitting on a hard upright chair, dressed in a dinner jacket with a high white collar. Queen Victoria's dissolute grandson, Prince Albert Victor, stood in front of me. His glassy-eyed stare was gone; now there was a lascivious look on his face. He licked his lips as he stared at me. Suddenly, the room was thrust into darkness. There was a bar of yellow light under the door. I crossed the room. Outside was a landing illuminated by a sickly pink light.

There was a door. I opened it and entered a dimly-lit, sinister room. Culadar was sitting in a chair. Not only had the poor man's throat been slashed but he'd been gutted like a fish.

Small white candles were arranged around the chair. They formed the shape of a five-pointed star. I saw Culadar's moist red lips twitch. There was a hole in his forehead, exposing his brain. No brain tissue was exposed but, rather, the silver cogs of a watch's interior...

His eyes opened. He was alive.

•••

In reception, Anita had a welcoming smile on her face. She looked great in her crisp uniform and white shirt.

'Good night,' she said.

What did she mean? My night had been terrible. Then I realised it was a statement, not a question. She'd been referring to the gig.

'We've played better,' I said.

'Well, I thought you were fantastic.'

She had been at the front dancing, for nearly all of the set. I had tried not to look at her, but, a few times, our eyes had met.

'Thank you. Most people don't notice drummers.'

'Well I do, Chris.'

It was the first time she'd used my name.

'Any sign of Kitson?' I asked.

'No. They say he's flown back to America.'

'Any messages for me?'

'No. I'm sorry.'

I turned away. Then I thought better of it.

'Anita?'

'Yes?'

'Anita...would you like to go for a drink, sometime...or a meal?'

She grinned.

'Of course, I'd love to.'

I went upstairs to my room breathing pure oxygen. She was beautiful and sexy. But our date would have to wait. I'd decided I would definitely finish Get The Bad Guys, whatever it took. What prompted this decision? I think it was the dream. Some elusive reality was hidden in the game – which may be terrifying, but I must confront it to achieve resolution in both my real and virtual lives.

I entered my room and turned on the TV. Strobe Kitson's Texan drawl welcomed me back into the game.

31

The Chateau d'Auteuil

Task: Adolf Hitler

You've got this far so you must have a knack for it. It's my guess that you can read people's minds, you're quick on your feet and you can speak any language. Impressive skills dude. Try this one: the big H! Now, here's the thing...

The Allies are aware that lots of people on his own side want him dead. You'll be working undercover. Deep undercover. Attention to detail is key in this task. If you want to stay alive, you'll need good table manners combined with the cold heart of a killer. Remember, there are no rules in this game. It's not cricket, old boy. It's war.

Time: 1943
Lives remaining: 4
Special powers: Level 2

Hitler knows that he will have to break us in this island or lose the war. If we can stand up to him, all Europe may be freed and the life of the world may move forward into broad, sunlit uplands. But if we fail, then the whole world, including the United States, including all that we have known and cared for, will sink into the abyss of a new dark age made more sinister, and perhaps more protracted, by the lights of perverted science.

Winston Churchill, Speech to the House of Commons, 18th June 1940

I was drifting down through space. Fortunately, there was a parachute above me; I was secured from the shoulders by stout webbing straps. Flakes of snow floated upwards through a leaden sky. To my right, a corolla of golden sun was breaking free from the earth. Was it dawn or sunset? I sensed the former, with an impending dread.

The landscape below me was dusted with snow – flat fields and patches of woodland. It was rushing up to meet me, rather quickly. Below was a dark red building with a steeply pitched roof and tall chimneys. It was substantial – a manor house or chateau. The property's estate of whitened grass extended around it.

An issue was causing me anxiety: I had never learned how to land in a parachute. But this was not to be a problem, as it was the outer branches of a tall poplar tree that my boots touched first. As I fell through these, I was brought to a wrenching, brutal stop that jarred every bone in my body.

I looked down. A man in a tweed suit with a deerstalker type hat was peering upwards at the strange object dangling from the tree. He was holding a double-barrelled shotgun.

•••

This is the life, I told myself. The Chateau d'Auteuil – the building I'd seen from the parachute – was very different to an English country house. Take the room I was in, for example: a drawing room or lounge, yet nothing about it was meant to be comfortable or relaxing. There was no squishy sofa covered in Labrador hairs, no tennis rackets or board games or copies of the French equivalent of Country Life lying around. The furniture invited one to sit upright rather than lounge. There was no carpet but a polished wooden floor. Around the room were cabinets containing highly polished glassware and porcelain. On the walls were prints of horses.

My host, the man who'd assisted me down from the tree and helped me to burn my parachute, was doing his best to put me at ease. Because of my newly-acquired language skills, we were able to converse easily in his native tongue, French, of an aristocratic variety.

My ribcage was battered and bruised. The pain was excruciating and caused me to wince, but I said nothing. Stiff upper lip and all that.

My charming host was a nobleman, a count, he explained, from an ancient family of Picardy, the de Kergorlays. He loved horse racing and, before the war, he'd bred Arab stallions at this chateau, entering them in many competitions. There was even a race named after his family, the Prix Kergorlay, in Deauville.

His ancestors had been soldiers for generations. At the beginning of the war, he'd commanded a battalion in the Ardennes Forest. He'd seen half his men cut down by the relentlessly advancing Germans.

The Count, a slight, fastidious man with grey eyes, noticed that my glass was empty and, with a bottle in hand, moved to where I was seated.

'I apologise for this poor vintage, sir,' he said. 'Since the occupation, my cellars have been running down. I have lost my best bottles and have not been able to replace them. You will understand that many things have changed under the Germans.'

'I quite understand,' I nodded.

'Would you prefer a whisky – a Johnnie perhaps?'

'I'm sorry?'

'A Johnnie Walker. I have a bottle from my last trip to London.'

'No thank you.'

The Burgundy seemed excellent to me – as rich and smooth as anything I'd ever tasted.

'Are you from London?' he asked.

'Not originally,' I replied, 'but I live there now.'

'I visited in 1934 with my Edith,' he recalled wistfully. 'We saw the Tower of London and Buckingham Palace and we went to your Derby Day. What a fine occasion that was.'

'Edith?'

'My wife. She is living in Perpignan, to be safe. After she lost our baby...well, it seemed best that she live in the south with her grandmother.'

'That is sad. It must be hard for you.'

He shrugged.

'Not really. What is my story compared to those of the poor souls that the Germans have slaughtered? Charlotte and I rattle around this house like dried peas. She is my cook and housekeeper. I am able to shoot pheasants on the estate and the occasional boar – the few that the Germans have not killed with their machine guns. But it is hard for us to keep a good table. Do you like pheasant,

Major Wilkins? I hope that one of my birds will be acceptable for lunch.'

So I'm a major, am I?

I murmured that pheasant would be entirely acceptable.

'I know that game is too rich for some,' the Count commented solicitously. 'I would offer you roast beef, if I could, but alas…'

He refreshed my glass, almost filling it to the brim.

'Anyway, to business,' he announced.

He glanced at the windows to check that no-one was trying to look in. We were at the front of the house. Outside, the snow-frosted estate was lit by winter sun. The first few acres were grassland; then there was dense woodland, the ancestral hunting ground of the de Kergorlays.

'You will know that I am a member of the local resistance.'

'Of course.' I nodded.

'I am not their leader, for I am far too well known for that role. I merely help them when I can. It is my misfortune that a unit of the SS is based in our local village, Berneuil-en-Bray. The Germans visit me from time to time and I am forced to break bread with them. They love to snoop around this house.'

'I imagine they do,' I said. 'It is a very nice house.'

'Thank you, sir.' He leant forwards, solicitously. 'In the normal course of events, Major Wilkins, you would have received your orders directly from the Special Operations Executive in London. However, in this case, the operation was initiated by me. I requested, through our local cell, that a suitable operative be sent; they chose you, I understand, because of your excellent knowledge of Paris.'

My excellent knowledge of Paris? I'd never been there…had I?

'And because you know Winston Churchill.'

'I…'

'I understand that Mr Churchill is taking a close personal interest in this operation. He regards it as crucial to the outcome of the war. I am sure that he has told you that.'

'Um…yes.'

'I have heard that the SOE training is very thorough – hand-to-hand combat, cryptography, how to behave under interrogation and so forth...'

'That's right,' I tried not to stutter.

Interrogation? I was starting to feel sick.

'Only the toughest and bravest get through so you have done well, Major Wilkins. Very well.'

'Have I? I mean, well, yes! Thank you.'

'You are far too modest,' he commented, with a steely look. 'However, happily, this mission is simple. It should be over quickly, a week at the most. It will be, what do you British say, a cake walk?'

He chuckled at his witticism.

'I hope so.' I was beginning to wonder what I'd let myself in for.

He glanced again at the window.

'As I explained, it was my idea. You see, I know your countryman PG Wodehouse. We met at his house in Le Touquet, Normandy, in 1938, through a mutual acquaintance. We played baccarat together at the casino.'

'PG Wodehouse?' *(PG Wodehouse?!)*

'He is a charming man, isn't he – the perfect English gentleman. I am fortunate to have several signed first editions of his books on my shelves.'

I was sinking in deep water. My head was swimming from two very large glasses of red wine. He turned away and crossed the room. Reaching behind a chintz-covered sofa he pulled something out – a package wrapped in oilskin.

'Major Wilkins,' he declared, holding the package, 'to cut to the chase, your mission briefing, your identity details and your documents are all contained in this package. I am going to leave the room and see how Charlotte is getting on. When I have left, you will read through the instructions carefully and memorise them. Then you must eat them – they are printed on rice paper. Don't eat your identity card. You will find it rather indigestible.'

His smile put creases around his brown eyes.

'Do you understand?'

'I do.'

He handed me the package.

'I shall return in 30 minutes.'

'Thank you, Count de Kergorlay,' I acknowledged, with a lump rising in my throat.

'Please, call me Pierre.'

He smiled again. Then he was gone.

Oh Jesus, I thought to myself again, *what on earth have I got myself into?*

I read the words that I would be required to eat...

32

One O'Clock Jump

SOE: F section
TOP SECRET

Mission: PG Wodehouse

The comic novelist PG Wodehouse was detained by the Germans at his residence in Le Touquet in June 1940. He was transported to Upper Silesia in Poland and placed in an internment camp. Wodehouse was released in June 1941 just before his sixtieth birthday and moved to Berlin by the Germans. He agreed to make some broadcasts for them on short-wave radio. His talks on life in an internment camp were badly received in Britain, with some people accusing Wodehouse of being a traitor and calling for his execution.

In September 1943, he was allowed by the Germans to move to the Bristol Hotel in Paris, at number 112, Rue du Faubourg Saint-Honoré. Here he still lives with his American wife, Ethel, and their Pekingese dog.

Wodehouse is a man of precise habits. Each morning, he takes his dog for a walk. He returns to the hotel and writes for the rest of the day.

Your task is to make contact with Wodehouse, who is known by his friends as 'Plum', and to engage him casually in conversation. You have two main objectives:

The first is to tell Wodehouse that a joint Commonwealth and American invasion force is to attack the coast of France imminently. Give Wodehouse the impression that the attack will take place at the Straits of Calais.

We believe that Wodehouse has made the acquaintance of Willhelm Canaris, the head of the Abwehr, German military intelligence. Canaris is a double agent who, on several occasions, has offered to help us.

Your second objective is to tell Wodehouse to make Canaris aware that Heinrich Himmler is about to take him into detention and to assure him that he has the full support of the Allies in his secret plan to assassinate Hitler. Ask Woodhouse to invite Canaris to communicate with Winston Churchill through secret channels and to make him aware that Allied assistance will be available, both to kill Hitler and to organise a succession government.

Cover identity: Arthur du Coquetot

Du Coquetot is your cover in France. You were born in Perrone, Picardy, in 1903. You have a heart condition which exempts you from military service. You are a wine merchant based in Beauvais, dealing in wines from the Aise, Oise and Somme regions. Your work frequently takes you to Paris. You are sympathetic to the Germans and have previously met with the Gestapo and the SD to inform them of local resistance members and of people you believe to be of Jewish origin. As du Coquetot, you will be able to move freely in the occupied area. However, in the presence of Wodehouse, you may drop your cover and explain that you are English, working on secondment for the British government.

All this information was typed onto a single sheet of paper but, even so, it was hard to swallow. After memorising Wodehouse's address in the Rue du Faubourg Saint-Honoré and certain other details, I managed to force it down my gullet with the help of a glass of water.

Also in the packet was an identity card for Arthur du Coquetot. It specified his place and date of birth, occupation, height, hair, eye colour and build. There was a fingerprint on the card and a black and white photograph. Coquetot had dark hair and a black moustache. We bore a striking similarity.

I glanced at the carriage clock on the mantelpiece. It was twelve o'clock. Just as the clock began to chime, Pierre walked into the room. There was a smile on his face.

He looked me up and down.

'My word,' he said. 'It is remarkable how much you look like du Coquetot. You are his image. Your hair and moustache are a little light, but we can easily dye them.'

'You know him?' I asked.

'Knew him,' he replied. 'He is dead. He was my nextdoor neighbour. I killed him with my bare hands, actually at the very spot where you are standing.'

I looked down at the immaculately polished floor.

'The man was a pig, a traitor and collaborator. He bullied his poor wife to death and he was about to betray me. I had no choice.'

'I see. When did you kill him?'

'It was a month ago. Nobody has noticed that he has disappeared yet. He was a sour man who lived on his own. We buried him in the forest. The pigs will have dug him up by now and eaten him. There won't be much left, I imagine – a few chewed bones.'

'I see.'

'It was imperative that the SOE found someone who looked like him for my plan to work. I must say, they have succeeded perfectly.'

'Thank you.'

'Of course, I will have to teach you his table manners and mannerisms; his way of talking, and so on. He has a strong Picardy accent – the accent of a shopkeeper. He is a coarse man, he does not speak as we do. We can begin the lesson over lunch. He has a mistress, by the way, who lives in Paris. You will be able to stay in the apartment that he uses for his liaisons with her.'

'Who is she?'

'Some floozy. It is shameful how French women will drop their pants for the Germans. By the way, I retained du Coquetot's clothes so that you can wear them.'

'The clothes that you killed him in?'

'Don't worry, I throttled him. There was no blood.'

'That's fortunate.'

'Not much blood, anyway.'

He saw that I'd noticed a piano at the side of the room.

'Do you like jazz?' he asked, suddenly.

I said that I did; in fact, I had been known to play the drums in jazz bands. At this he brightened. It was clearly a subject of great interest.

'My Edith loved to play Chopin,' he explained. 'She hated jazz. Would you like to hear a gramophone record?'

'Very much,' I acknowledged.

He was evidently proud of his carefully assembled record collection and gramophone, which was the latest kind.

He carefully slid a 78 rpm disc from its cover.

'It is my fellow aristocrat, Count Basie,' he said, grinning.

The record was One O'Clock Jump. Its happy, syncopated rhythm, led by piano, saxophone, trumpet and trombone, filled the room. Edith's lips would have pursed with distaste.

My fingers were twitching for a drumkit, but I was content to tap out a rhythm on my thigh. We listened to the disc numerous times, as if we had been transported to New Orleans.

The door opened and Charlotte entered the room with a trolley bearing our lunch. In this avatar, she was extremely shy, but her face gave her away. Charlotte was Mary Jane (and Tammy, et al). Her hair, which was tied back, was the shade of red that comes from henna, a colouring favoured by French women. She seemed diffident and tentative, as if a loud noise would make her jump out of her skin. She wore the same uniform as at Colebrooke Row and in Sevenoaks – black skirt, white apron, black stockings, only with no cap. She studiously ignored me, only once making brief, nervous eye contact before leaving us to our meal.

•••

'So, how does du Coquetot hold his knife and fork?' I asked at the table.

'Like this: like a peasant digging potatoes.'

He held his knife and fork in an awkward way.

'What does he like to eat and drink?'

'He's not bothered. Quantity is more important to him than quality. As for wine, he deals in it, but he would drink literally anything – even vinegar. He would not recognise one bottle from another.'

'Do I sound like him?'

'You must put more of a sneer into your voice, as if there is a piece of gristle between your teeth.'

'Like this you mean?' said I, attempting to adopt Pierre's suggested dialect, with a sneer and imaginary gristle.

'Yes, exactly.' Pierre laughed.

'Du Coquetot is a man who is uncomfortable in his own skin. He will always follow the lead of the richest or most important person in the room and hang onto their every word, like a lap dog. He holds people with no power or money in contempt. He speaks with no passion until he gets onto his favourite topics.'

'Which are?'

'Jews, bankers and communists. The people whom he believes have ruined France.'

'And gypsies?'

'He would be very happy for all of them to be exterminated.'

'Would have been,' I corrected him.

'Yes, that's right.'

'Well, let's drink to Monsieur Arthur du Coquetot,' I announced, lifting my glass.

'To the bastard's bones. May they be ground to dust!'

Pierre finished his wine. He refilled our drinks from the dusty bottle on the table. The pheasant was delicious – succulent and with a satisfying gaminess. The wine my host had chosen complemented it to perfection.

He told me that he himself had shot the birds that we were eating. I said he was lucky to have such an excellent resource at hand, as food must be scarce.

'Yes, but for how much longer?' he said. 'The Germans have their eyes on this house. I don't know why they haven't requisitioned it yet. Perhaps it would be better for me to burn it down before they take it. Would it be such a loss?'

'Of *course* it would!' I emphasised. 'It is part of your patrimony. Besides, the Germans might not win the war, you know.'

'Ah, you are an optimist.'

He looked wistfully around the elegant room with its pale grey walls and polished wood and crystal. It was he, Pierre told me, who had painted the delicate watercolours of horses. He was an artistic soul.

'But you have a point, William. Some people think that the war is turning in our favour, thanks to your Montgomery at El Alamein. He is a fine general.'

'He certainly is.'

Fortunately, I'd seen a film about him once, fighting against Rommel in the western desert.

We weren't just ignoring the spirit of the blackout imposed by the Germans at curfew; the room was literally blazing with light that must have been visible for miles. We were listening to jazz played by negroes – a form of music despised by the Nazis and therefore banned by them. The delicious meat that we had consumed had been killed using a privately-owned weapon that should have been handed in to the authorities.

Did we think that nothing was going to happen?

We were sipping Calvados and listening to something mellow from Pierre's record collection when there was a thunderous knocking on the door.

Pierre's face turned white.

'*Merde!*' he hissed. 'Get the hell out of here!'

33

The Forest

I ran hastily up the stairs into the shadowy regions of the house normally occupied by servants. Catching my breath on the first-floor landing, I heard bolts drawn back as Pierre opened the door. The sound of heavy boots clumping into the house reached my ears, followed by muffled voices.

I made my way as quickly and quietly as possible to the servants' corridor at the roofline to find a hiding place. Most of the rooms were empty, others filled with boxes and bags of clothes. The rooms smelt of damp and dust. The one at the end was Charlotte's. I tapped on the door.

The poor girl looked petrified when she opened the door, as if I was about to kill her. Her wardrobe was the best hiding place we could find and Charlotte closed me into the dark space. I breathed in the aroma of dresses, fur and mothballs. I was in there for a long time. She kept checking through her tiny window until, finally, the German car left, and she let me out.

I saw that she was dressed for bed in a white, cambric nightgown. She was as beautiful as ever and utterly French. This Mary Jane (more 'Marie Jeanette') had the pale, freckled skin of Nuala and an abundance of coppery hair that tumbled across her shoulders. Her eyes were deep brown, almost black.

She looked at me, and my sixth sense divined her tragedy. Her young sweetheart had been killed in the first weeks of the war, before they could marry – before he had even come home on his first leave. She had never slept with a man.

For two years, his serious face had stared out from a photograph by her bed. He looked handsome in his uniform, his beret shadowing a solemn face. She kept his letters tied with a ribbon in a secret box, with the photograph of her first communion and some secret tokens of their love.

She was sitting on the bed. Her nightdress had ridden up, showing her thighs. She had dancer's legs, taut and supple, but I looked away. Her face crumpled as she began to sob. I drew her to me and held her close.

∙∙∙

The following day, Pierre told me what had happened. It was a detachment of the SD who had dropped in – the military police used by the Nazis to enforce their rules on local populations. They were jobsworths but not psychopaths like the SS, whom they worked alongside, or the Nazis' merciless and sadistic inner circle, the Gestapo. The SD men had seen lights from the lane and swung their Mercedes into the poplar-flanked drive of the chateau. There were four of them.

The Count had been deferential and apologetic. He said he was extremely sorry about the violation of the blackout – it had been an oversight. The SD captain observed that the dining table was set for two. Yes, Pierre explained, he'd been eating with his housekeeper. His servant? A woman? Yes, a woman. He was screwing her, was he? Well, yes, Pierre had replied, conspiratorially, his wife was away. The nights were cold and lonely. What was a man supposed to do?

What about his records? Beethoven and Brahms mainly, Pierre told them, and indeed he was an admirer of the great Berlin conductor, Willhelm Furtwangler. Apologising for not doing so himself, he'd watched as the brutish captain examined and smashed his jazz discs one by one. Fortunately, most of his jazz collection was stored in the attic.

They didn't ask about his gun, but they did say that shots had been heard in the woods. Did he know anything about that? Alas, no.

To his great relief, the men did not demand to search the house. However, they said that they would return soon. He thanked them. They'd left as abruptly as they had arrived.

∙∙∙

The morning brought no reprise of the previous day's sun – only a leaden November sky. Patches of snow lingered on the grass. Pierre took me hunting deep in the woods with his little dog – a Picardy Spaniel. The sharp leaves crunched beneath our feet. The air smelled vaguely of smoke. The woods seemed dead. It was unsurprising that there were no birds fluttering into view nor shy rabbits lingering before darting for cover, offering themselves to Pierre's gun.

Neither of us spoke much. His mood was subdued. The previous night's visit from the SD had been a close call and he must have felt that he was now on borrowed time. It surely wouldn't be too long before du Coquetot's absence was noted by the German officials to whom he'd ingratiated himself. I did not tell Pierre what had happened with Charlotte. She was giving some shy downward glances and blushing as she served our breakfast, embarrassed no doubt at her forwardness and my subsequent rejection.

I was dressed as du Coquetot today. His sober black suit and shiny cuffs and black hat made me feel like a minister. He liked to slick down his hair with sticky green oil that smelt of parma violets. Pierre insisted that I do the same, adding a little black shoe polish; that I shave carefully and use the same alcohol-based preparation on my cheeks. Du Coquetot's black shoes were too tight for my feet, so we darkened my well-worn brown brogues. A tiny detail but such things, Pierre insisted, could mean the difference between life and death.

I tried to talk like him on our walk. Pierre said that du Coquetot had always been jealous of his neighbours, the aristocratic de Kergorlay family. Part of him must have rejoiced when the Germans had arrived and disrupted the old order.

We passed close to where his body was buried, in a clearing in the ancient forest of oak, beech and hornbeam. The grave, Pierre noted with relief, seemed undisturbed. Coquetot's car, a Delage coupé with a long bonnet and extravagant, sweeping wings, had been driven down a narrow track and hidden. Pierre said I would be able to use it to drive to Paris. It was here, deep in the forest, that I would begin my 60-mile journey.

First, we ate lunch, this time in the kitchen. It was a practical arrangement. Since the range was permanently lit, the kitchen was by far the warmest room in the house. Pierre gave me a gift for the journey – a flask of brandy.

We were just finishing our meal when we heard a heart-wrenching sound. Charlotte, who was working in the scullery, was crying again.

'Excuse me,' I said.

'Of course.'

I scraped back my chair and left the room. I took Charlotte's freckled face in my hands. I told her that it was very sad but Jean, her love, was not coming back and she must move on. She was a beautiful woman; she had her whole life ahead of her. One day, perhaps, she would have children.

'Are you coming back?'

'I don't know,' I replied. 'I might not.'

I kissed her brow.

'Will you write to me?'

'Of course I will,' I said. Sometimes it is best to lie. 'I am glad I came here.'

'So am I.'

I held her for just a moment, not wishing to give her the wrong impression and then break her heart again.

'Goodbye.'

'Goodbye, William.'

•••

To our relief, the low-slung Delage sputtered into life after only a few cranks of the starting handle. The sun had barely appeared today, the day in eternal dusk. I was wearing du Coquetot's trademark black leather coat – the one that, Pierre said, made him look like a Gestapo officer. In the coat's lapel was an enamel SD badge – something he wore brazenly and with pride.

Deep in the coat's right-hand pocket was a gun – a Webley Mark IV army issue top-breaking revolver that had been provided by the SOE armourer. Strapped to my leg was another lethal weapon – a double-edged Fairbairn-Sykes knife of the kind used by commandos.

The SOE had provided me with a handy gadget – a fountain pen that fired tear gas from a tiny cartridge. They had added a pair of gold cuff-links (useful currency for a penniless agent). My leather wallet, as well as a plentiful supply of francs, contained something that might be used as a last resort should I face torture from the SS or the Gestapo – a cyanide capsule.

The engine was running. I wound down the window and took Pierre's hand.

'Good luck, my friend,' he said, with a smile.

'Thank you, Pierre. And thank you for all that you have done. I'll see you in London.'

'Of course.'

After giving him the thumbs-up, I released the handbrake. The Delage began its slow, lurching progress down the woodland track. It was only when I was on a proper road and heading south for Paris that I realised one element had been curiously omitted from the SOE's mission plan – how to get back to England.

34

Avenue Victor Hugo

Well, this is pleasant...

I was lying in a warm, soapy bath. The hot water soothed my bruised ribs. I lay back, enjoying a Gitanes cigarette and a delicious glass of red wine.

Whatever services du Coquetot was providing to the Germans, he was being well paid for them. His second-floor apartment was located at one of Paris' best addresses. It was well-furnished with the most up-to-date appliances. The main attraction in the principal bedroom was a canopied love throne – a huge bed bedecked with drapes and tassels that must have been carefully chosen by du Coquetot, a man of no taste. The spotless bathroom gleamed in black and gold.

The following day, I would be making my way to the Hotel de Bristol in the Rue du Faubourg Saint-Honoré to make my acquaintance with PG Wodehouse.

Getting into Paris early that morning had been surprisingly easy. I'd been waved through checkpoints with only a brief look at my papers – some of the SD men had even seemed to know me.

The Parisians' faces betrayed little emotion. It was dangerous to show one's feelings in public, but I'd sensed an underlying hostility towards this swaggering creature in the black leather coat, this French gauleiter I was impersonating. That was all to the good. It would help me pass through the occupied city unhindered by the Germans. Perhaps this mission would be, as Pierre had said, a 'cake walk'.

I took another drag on my cigarette. The French tobacco was rich and sweet, almost like a cigar. I was looking forward to a deep sleep in clean sheets, the loaded Webley close to hand. My big toe nestled in a tap like it used to when I was child. More hot water was needed.

I heard a knock on the door.

Oh Lord. I ignored it.

The knock came again. It was insistent but also tentative.

I stood up and climbed out of the bath, putting on the silk-collared dressing gown I'd borrowed. Barefoot and dripping, I opened the door, holding my revolver beneath my gown.

The woman in the hallway smiled. She was tall and slim and had bright red lips and chestnut hair. I sensed that she had been here before.

'Hello, my darling, your Odile is here.'

Her beauty, like the colour of her hair, was peculiarly French. Her unblemished face and perfectly arched eyebrows could have come from any canvas in the Louvre.

She waited. I was expected to kiss her. I stepped forwards.

'My sweetheart,' I improvised.

'Are you going to shoot me, my love?' she said, as my gun-wielding hand came into view.

'No, of course not! But one must be careful.'

'Of course.'

I put the gun down. Her lips brushed my cheek. I removed her fawn coat, beneath which a thin black dress of a sophisticated cut clung to her supple figure. She was no street girl.

As the coat slid from her shoulders, she looked startled. Perhaps I was being too familiar.

'Arthur?'

'Yes, my love?'

'Nothing.'

She smiled again. Her eyes were pale grey, almost green, and seemed almost translucent. She was waiting for me to do something, but what? Carefully, I hung up her coat.

'Would you wait for me please while I get dressed.'

I was being too polite, I realised. Du Coquetot would not speak like this.

'Drink?' I asked, more brusquely. I must try to be less polished.

'Yes, please.'

Du Coquetot would be ill-at-ease in the company of a beautiful woman. What the hell should I give her? I had already explored the cocktail cabinet and knew there were several options.

She made her way into the sitting room and sat on an elegant sofa covered in pale cream silk. She regarded me with interest. I selected the bottle that I had already opened and poured her a glass. She seemed surprised.

'Not my Chartreuse this evening?'

The sickly green stuff. That must be how Comte Arthur got his mistresses tipsy.

'No, my love. I thought it was time for a change.' I paused. 'I'm sorry, if you would like your favourite…'

She laughed and said she hated Chartreuse.

'Good, then. Please excuse me. I must get dressed now.'

I looked down at her. Her breasts were thrust upwards by her low-cut dress. A pearl pendant on a thin, silver chain nestled in her cleavage.

Odile looked puzzled. Evidently, what would normally happen within seconds of her entering du Coquetot's apartment is that he would grab her, his sour, coarse breath in her face.

'Arthur…'

It was the delicacy of her neck and curve of her breasts that drew me; her clear eyes, the delicious scent that enveloped her. I could not help myself. I leaned forwards. Her glass tipped, emptying its crimson contents onto the sofa. Our lips met. Soon, my tongue was probing the softness of her mouth. One hand touched her shoulder, another reached down her back.

•••

She leaned against me on the ridiculous bed. The blue smoke from our cigarettes mingled. Our clothes were heaped on the floor. I studied her pearl pendant.

'Look, I am not really…' I began.

'Yes, I know.'

She drew back to study my face.

'I knew that you were not du Coquetot when you took off my coat and when you did not force me to drink Chartreuse. He is a pig. And now I see clearly that you are not him.'

She placed a fingertip on my torso.

'Your chest is smooth. He is hairy, like a monkey.'

'What was your relationship with him?'

'I think you know.'

'Why did you become his mistress?'

She did not speak, merely blowing twin streams of smoke from her nose.

'You are English, aren't you?'

'How did you know?'

'I don't know. I can just tell.'

'And you are in the resistance.'

A non-committal look crossed her face.

'I'll take that as a yes.'

•••

There was a crash. A few moments later a large man in a brown leather jacket was glaring at us from the end of the bed. He was carrying something long and dark. A shotgun.

'Please, no!' she exclaimed.

She placed herself between me and him. The intruder's eyes were hard and narrow.

'He is English!' she said desperately.

There was no expression on the man's face.

Odile was attempting to cover the top half of her body.

'He is English, I am telling you!'

The man did not respond.

'I am you know.' I spoke in my own language.

The man blinked. He looked coolly at Odile as she reached for her underwear. His grip on the shotgun did not relax. He stared directly into my eyes.

There was a sound at the door, and another man came into the room.

'What the fuck is going on? You were supposed to kill him not tickle him.'

Odile began to remonstrate with the second man.

'Look, I am *telling you*...!'

It became apparent that, in her role within the resistance, she had come here tonight to lure the collaborator du Coquetot into a trap. He was to be killed and his body dumped in the street as a warning to other collaborators.

The contretemps continued. At least I hadn't been blasted to oblivion. A compromise was reached. It was agreed I would be taken away to be interrogated. They allowed me to get dressed but took custody of my gun. Odile remained in the apartment.

'Goodbye. I am so sorry,' she said.

'I am sorry too,' I responded. 'You are lovely.'

The door closed on her anxious face.

The two men bundled me roughly downstairs. It was still dark, just before dawn. They pulled a hood over my head and thrust me into the back of a grey Citroën van. Soon we were driving, in a series of lurches, through cobbled streets.

35

The Interrogation

I would've been angrier had I not been so weak. My interrogator was well-dressed and well-spoken. Look, I am English, I insisted. How many times do I have to tell you? I'm an agent in France on a mission. I cannot, of course, divulge the details.

'I see.'

He was a tall man with an air of calm authority. Black was his predominant colour – it was the hue of his polished shoes and well-pressed trousers, the neat jacket hanging on the back of his chair. His deep brown eyes were set in an intelligent face. At his neck, he wore a grey foulard. It gave him an aristocratic look.

The curtains were drawn. The dimly-lit room had the stale air of a space that is seldom used. My inquisitor spoke a precise and accurate English.

'Would you like a smoke?'

I shrugged. Why not? I was getting used to Gitanes.

'Thank God for tobacco,' said the Frenchman. His fingers were stained orange, he was obviously a chain-smoker; a man who twitched with nerves.

'It was certainly one of his better inventions.'

The man laughed.

I was thinking of the rich, gamey venison that I'd eaten at the Chateau d'Auteuil. I could still taste it. I longed for the sublime oblivion of a bed – even a typical French one, with its hard bolster, clammy sheets and uncomfortable mattress.

The man crossed to the window and peered briefly between the dirty beige curtains. I guessed from the stained carpet and magnolia walls that this was a hotel room of the cheaper sort, a 'chambre de passage' from which the bed had been removed.

My wrists were red and sore where they had been bound. The interrogator turned back from the curtains. He must spend his life in rooms like this.

'So, you are English but you will not tell me why you are here, or why you have taken the identity of a Frenchman...'

'I can't,' I said.

'You know that we were about to kill the man you were impersonating, don't you?'

'A man can't be killed twice,' I said.

'What do you mean?'

'He's already dead, buried in the middle of a forest.'

'Who killed him?'

'I can't tell you.'

'I see.'

He breathed out smoke, thoughtfully. He was a patient man. He slowly reached into his pocket – and pulled out a pistol. It was a French kind I did not recognise.

'I am sorry, but I will have to kill you.'

He raised the gun to my head.

'Have you heard of PG Wodehouse?' I asked desperately.

'Yes, of course.' He looked at me quizzically.

'He is the reason that I am here.'

He lowered the gun.

'I'm here to make contact with him. We, the Allies, believe he can be useful to our cause, especially when a second front is opened with the Americans.'

'Go on.'

'A joint invasion is imminent which will drive the Germans back to Berlin. We wish to plant false stories through certain contacts in France as to where the invasion force will land, to increase the element of surprise. We are promoting the idea that the attack will be in the Pas de Calais area. But it won't be there. Also, we believe that Wodehouse has made contact with a certain senior German official who could be of use to us.'

'Which German?'

'I can't tell you. That would jeopardise my mission.'

He nodded.

'So, you are with the SOE?'

'I am. F Section.'

He seemed reassured. I had been lucky to find one of the few Frenchman to have heard of Wodehouse.

'You speak French very well,' he said.

'I studied it at Oxford University.'

'At what college?'

'Christ Church.'

I did not blink. He said that, regrettably, although my story appeared credible, I would have to remain locked up until certain inquiries had been made.

As he spoke, his grey foulard shifted. I saw that beneath it was a deep red welt where the carotid artery is. Either the man had attempted to take his own life, or someone had slashed his throat.

I spent another night locked up by the resistance in a secure, guarded room. The following morning, they returned my gun and dagger, my wallet with the money and cyanide pellet in it, my trick fountain pen and my papers. They didn't, however, give me back the flask of brandy, but it didn't take me long to work out what had happened to it. I couldn't blame them.

They released me at dawn into a narrow, cobbled street. It was a grey, drizzly morning and I was yearning for coffee. I could tell that this was not the XVIth arrondissement in which I had spent my first night in the city but a far poorer quarter – one where tourists rarely ventured.

•••

After a shot of bitter coffee and a tot of whisky in a workmen's café, I began walking in a westerly direction. Under the brooding, thundery sky, the city of light seemed to have turned dark. German soldiers and checkpoints were everywhere. I saw the grey invaders in the backs of lorries, standing at checkpoints with rifles and sub-machine guns and walking along the pavements.

At night, grey Gestapo vans sped through the streets searching for the radio signals of the resistance; German officers had claimed the city's swankiest cafés and restaurants as their own. Close up, one could distinguish the SD units from normal soldiers and the SS with the death's-head insignia on their caps. It wasn't a good idea to get too close.

Petrol was scarce. There weren't many vehicles on the roads, other than those of the Germans. Paris had become a city of bicycles. They were stacked everywhere in squares and in front of buildings. It would have been a simple matter to steal one but, for the moment, I was happy on foot.

I came to a large vegetable market. This must be the Paris version of Covent Garden. The porters looked elderly. Yellow stars were painted on walls and doors here. It must be a Jewish quarter. Already, in the dark, narrow streets a few prostitutes in tight skirts and beehive hairdos were plying their trade.

As soon as the shops opened, queues of women formed with shopping bags, waiting to redeem their ration tickets. Only a few people would wake up to fresh bread and newly-ground coffee. This was a city merely enduring from day to day, virtually asleep and living through a nightmare.

My papers were checked first in the Rue de Rivoli, close to the Louvre. An expensive, prestigious street – a Paris Mayfair, with its pavement running beneath a classical colonnade. Between the columns, the invaders had draped giant swastikas, asserting their presence in crisp red, white and black. A banner arrogantly proclaimed 'Germany victorious on all fronts'.

Paris is a theatrical city, a stage set; the Germans, alert to how they were viewed by the French, had imposed upon it their own scenery and stage equipment.

At this checkpoint, the soldiers were suspicious. I tried to ingratiate myself with them by speaking scraps of schoolboy German, as du Coquetot would have done.

They asked me questions as to my business. Puffing myself up, I adopted an attitude that walked a thin line between obsequiousness and truculence. Reluctantly, they let me through, and I now entered the city of grand statements – huge squares, formal gardens and famous buildings. I saw from here, for the first time in my life, not merely as a photograph, the famous Eiffel Tower. No doubt it was bedecked with swastikas but they were too far away to be visible. It was just before eight o'clock when I wandered into the famous Tuileries Gardens.

I asked a miserable flower seller for directions and was given a grudging reply. By sheer chance, the Rue du Faubourg Saint Honoré was only two blocks away.

I was looking forward, later, to collapsing in du Coquetot's vast bed.

36

The Café des Ministères

The broadcasts, in point of fact, are neither anti- nor pro-German, but just Wodehousian. He is a man singularly ill-fitted to live in a time of ideological conflict, having no feelings of hatred about anyone, and no very strong views about anything... I never heard him speak bitterly about anyone – not even about old friends who turned against him in distress. Such temperament does not make for good citizenship in the second half of the 20th Century.

Malcolm Muggeridge, quoted in PG Wodehouse by Joseph Connolly

It was a matter of lurking outside the hotel like a shadowy private detective, waiting for the Englishman to leave the building for his daily constitutional. I hoped I wasn't too late. Would the heavy grey sky and the threat of rain lead him to stay in his warm bed? Not if he was a typical Englishman of his age and class.

There was a checkpoint further down this street, in front of an important-looking building. This was not a good place to linger. The Hotel Le Bristol looked like the other pale, stone-fronted buildings that ran down both sides of the street. It stood out only because of its gilded porch and wrought iron balconies. I lit another Gitanes.

At eight-thirty, my waiting was rewarded. I identified him at once – a man of medium height and light build in a brown tweed overcoat. He was wearing thick, horn-rimmed spectacles and a scarf. A little dog was snapping at his heels. This must be his Pekingese, Wonder. The dog was a golden brown colour that stood out in this world of grey.

Man and dog set off at a fast clip. I followed them, sometimes ducking into doorways, at what I thought was a safe distance. Wodehouse looked purposeful, as if this was a familiar routine. He did not stop to study window displays. He turned briskly into the Avenue de Marigny and entered the Jardins des Champs-Elysees.

How unlike London parks these Parisian public places were. The grass and flowerbeds were as neat and formal as the verbal interactions that the French favoured; one could not simply lounge about in them, as one would in England, without inviting disapproval.

He stopped in the gardens to exchange a few words with a man at a stamp stall. This must be part of his routine. There would be a few Parisians who knew this Englishman who walked through the parks each morning with his little dog.

Had Wodehouse brushed up his schoolboy French? Parisians spoke the language with a lazy drawl and their own slang that would be almost unrecognisable to someone who had learnt formal French in a schoolroom.

He glanced at the Theatre Marigny. The circular, lead-roofed building looked like a mausoleum. Was he wondering whether, in happier times, one of the comic musicals for which he had written songs would be performed here?

He surprised me then by heading south at the end of the Avenue des Champs Elysees. This man was a serious walker. I supposed you had to be if you spent hours every day sitting in front of a typewriter and wanted to avoid becoming flabby.

Why would a sane man stroll through the centre of the Place de la Concorde? This stone prairie, one of Paris' major public places, had become, by default, one of the centres of the Wehrmacht. The square bristled with barbed wire, sentry boxes and grey-coated soldiers. Wodehouse was unabashed. I saw him go through a paper check. I cursed him as I would have to do that too.

On the other side of the Concorde Bridge, one could see the Palais Bourbon, home of the French National Assembly. True to form, the Germans had draped an enormous banner across the width of the building, proclaiming their eternal victory.

Damn you, Wodehouse. I watched his figure recede onto the bridge as an SD man checked my papers. 'Arthur' oozed from me with his ingratiating and cowardly arrogance. My business here was tourism, I explained. I was from the countryside and merely wished to investigate Paris' Left Bank, particularly – and I spoke the name with a Picardian twang – the famous Boulevard Saint-Germain.

Plum and Wonder had almost reached the other side of the bridge by the time I was allowed through. I walked as fast as I feasibly could, keeping my eye on the old man and the dog. I nearly lost them – it was only because Plum lingered in front of the Palais Bourbon to light his pipe that I was able to catch up.

He made his way purposefully down the Rue Aristide Briand – another street lined with classical buildings in beige stone. Was he in a hurry so as not miss an appointment? If so, with whom?

•••

So, this was the old man's destination. The Café des Ministères in the Rue de l'Université was overshadowed by far grander establishments nearby. Most of its narrow frontage was hidden beneath a large awning that announced, improbably, 'brasserie de la mer'. It was more of a place for workmen than for the politicians and civil servants who worked in this quarter.

The sky thundered. The first fat drops of rain plopped onto the awning as Plum walked in. I stood on the opposite pavement, watching. Was this the place to introduce myself? Why not? I felt nervous. I checked the cold metal of my Webley revolver's stock.

The café had the look of a place that was not cared for. There were no customers in the front room. A solemn barman in a maroon gilet nodded at me indifferently as I entered. Naturally, he was polishing a glass, with the smouldering stub of a cigarette resting on his lower lip. *Très Français*.

Plum had selected a table in the back room, which was as gloomy as a cellar. I was surprised to see that he was sitting with another man. This fellow wore a plain black reefer jacket and had a shock of white hair. His skin was wrinkled and sallow. Wonder the dog had positioned himself compliantly beneath the table.

The barman arrived at their table with a tray and deposited two cups of coffee and small glasses of spirits in front of the two men. Who was this other man? Was he German? I fingered my gun. It was now or never.

I approached their table.

'Mr Wodehouse, I would like to talk to you, sir,' I said in my best English.

Plum did a double take. I must have looked like a travelling salesman.

'I...'

'It's quite all right.'

The older man had spoken. His English was good but accented with German.

'If this gentleman wishes to talk to you, I quite understand. Perhaps he is one of your many admirers, Mr Wodehouse.'

Plum smiled.

'I shall leave you for a minute,' the man in the reefer jacket said.

•••

I explained to Plum that, despite my appearance, I was actually English. I knew who he was and of his literary celebrity. I had come to Paris bearing a message from Britain. He did not seem pleased or flattered by this. On the contrary, it was clear that he did not wish his life, with its rigid habit and routines, to be disturbed. Our meeting was not going well.

'Mr Wodehouse,' I said. 'Do you know a gentleman called Wilhelm Canaris?'

'Why do you want to know?' he asked suspiciously.

'It is very important that you answer my question.'

He noticed that his pipe had gone out.

'I have done nothing wrong you know.'

'I am not saying you have.'

'Well, I do know a gentleman of that name, as it happens. As a matter of fact, he is my companion today.'

The man in the black reefer jacket was smoking contemplatively in the corner.

'That's Canaris?'

'Well he told me that is his name. I have no reason to doubt him.'

'Do you know who he is?'

'He is a businessman, that is all I know. He is a cultured and well-travelled man and knows an awful lot about the theatre, books and opera. I like to talk to him.'

'I see.'

I believed Wodehouse. It was apparent to me that he would always be locked in the 1920s world of silly asses and cocktail parties that he had created for the world's pleasure. He barely lived in this one. He was an innocent. It was feasible that he had no idea that the white-haired fellow with whom he was sharing a coffee was one of the most powerful men in Germany.

Still, the poor old duffer had been through a hell of a lot – whisked out of his luxury house in Normandy, transported across Europe in a lorry, banged up in a prison camp. And he had endured his fate stoically, saying that his place of internment was no worse than an English public school. He may have done absolutely nothing to help the Allied cause in the war, but he had done nothing to impede it either. Perhaps it was best to leave him in his state of denial.

I abandoned the first objective of telling him about D-Day. What was the point since he had no interest in the war? At least, through him, I'd gained access to the prize – Canaris. I stood up and was about to shake hands and leave him to the whimsical, nostalgic world of his imagination when I heard a noise. Turning round, I saw that three men had entered the back room. They wore field grey great coats and peaked caps with silver braid and winged swastikas. Christ. It was the SS.

37

Fire with Fire

The ID check was going badly. Very badly. The lead SS man, a lieutenant, was glaring at me with a look of hatred. I think that Arthur's eau de cologne had aroused in him a fierce loathing.

'Disgusting pervert,' he said in German.

'Excuse me?'

'Don't you know that sodomy is a capital offence?'

'I'm sorry?!'

'You were seen trawling for trade in the Luxembourg Gardens. You then followed this old man here, which is a known haunt of sodomites.'

He gestured towards Wodehouse. The writer had shrunk with fear. Canaris was smoking another cigarette. He looked calm.

I could hardly deny that I'd been trailing Wodehouse. I began to stammer a reply, but the officer asked bluntly:

'What is your business with him?'

Was it okay to say that Wodehouse was a famous writer? Surely this could not harm the situation.

'I am an admirer.'

'An admirer!'

He spat out the words with disgust.

'There is a place for filth like you!'

The two other SS men were standing by. One was holding a submachine gun. The lieutenant grunted at them.

'Take him into custody.'

That could not be allowed to happen! I'd be banged up in a police cell, summarily tried and end up in prison or, more likely, a death camp – one where homosexuals were gassed.

I reached into my pocket for the Webley. The lieutenant moved back. His pistol was in his lanyard. There was no way he could remove it quickly.

I had never fired a revolver in real life or, indeed, any kind of gun, apart from the ones in fairgrounds. I hadn't reckoned on it being so hard to pull the trigger. I began to squeeze. I was shakily pointing the wavering weapon at the officer's forehead.

I felt a sharp concussion as a bullet entered my temple. One of the other soldiers must have whipped out his pistol.

The impact knocked my head back like whiplash, and I saw stars. Whoops. Back to base, Chris.

•••

I did not want to be here, in a fusty hotel bedroom. I went straight back to the game.

Task: Adolf Hitler
Time: 1943
Lives remaining: 3
Special powers: Level 2

This time, I was not floating over Picardy attached to a parachute harness. I was standing outside the gloomy Café des Ministères on a dismal winter day.

I went in and made my acquaintance with Wodehouse in the backroom. Canaris, his sallow-faced companion in the reefer jacket, excused himself. Wodehouse and I started chatting.

This time, I quizzed him about his time at Dulwich College. It was a famous and expensive boarding school for the sons of the rich. Wodehouse, who had disappointed his father by abandoning a career in banking, brightened. He asked me how I knew about Dulwich. I said I lived in South London, not too far away.

He asked me about the school's cricket and rugger teams. He said he liked to follow their progress but since his incarceration and forced exile, it had been hard.

I said I understood.

At any moment, the SS patrol would enter the brasserie. This time, I would intercept them in the front part of the café. That would give me more time.

My hearing was sensitised. I heard the front door open.

'Please excuse me for a minute, Mr Wodehouse.'

I stood up.

•••

The three men were standing menacingly just inside the door. The barman – probably a veteran of the First World War – was pretending, as hard as he could, that everything was normal.

'Hello blondie,' I said, mincing my way over to the lieutenant. 'Are you looking for company?'

He looked nonplussed.

'That's a *fabulous* uniform,' I said. 'It fits you like a glove. I bet your mother is very proud of you.'

I needed to be fairly close to him – three or four feet away.

He was trying to get some words out as I pulled the disguised fountain pen from the breast pocket of my jacket. I had practised using it at the Chateau d'Auteuil.

First, I removed the cap.

'Could I have your autograph please?' I said. 'You know, I am a huge fan of the SS.'

I pressed a clip.

A cloud of teargas hissed from the end of the pen. It enveloped the officer's face, blinding him. I was already reaching into my pocket. This time, I knew how hard the trigger was to pull.

One of the other soldiers was bringing his MP40 submachine gun up to his shoulder. The other was fumbling for his pistol.

I dealt with the pistol man first. A shot to his body did the trick. There was a flash. The recoil was a lot stronger than I had expected.

Happily, the MP40 was still being raised to a level position when I got off my next shot. I slugged its owner between the eyes and he went down like a skittle. The first soldier was sliding on his stomach across the floor, moaning, blood oozing in a crimson trail from his wound.

I copied something that I'd seen in countless films. I simply walked across the room and shot him calmly in the head. His body convulsed. He lay still.

There was still the blinded officer to deal with. That took two shots. Five bullets, three dead Germans. Well done, Chris!

I could swear the barman had barely moved and that he was still polishing the same glass.

The bar was full of blue smoke. Wodehouse was sitting still, his face like a mask. Perhaps he could write a short story about this – 'Bertie Wooster and The SS Patrol'.

Canaris walked calmly into the scene of carnage.

'That was excellent,' he said in English. 'You are a good marksman, sir.'

I thanked him.

'Calmness in battle is the first requirement of a warrior,' he replied. 'And *that* you have demonstrated.'

Fortunately for us, the street outside was deserted. It seemed that no-one had seen or heard the fire fight. I suggested that Wodehouse skedaddle as quickly as possible. The writer's face was grey. He walked out of the brasserie without a word and disappeared into the Parisian morning, as if nothing had happened. What would he tell his wife? Most likely, he would simply erase this regrettable incident from his memory.

Canaris knew exactly what to do. We dragged the three bodies to the back of the brasserie and piled them into a cupboard. I felt sorry for the barman. Mopping up that blood was not going to be easy. And the Germans would be back.

38

The Fox

It was now that my life and the fate of Europe changed. A chance encounter in the streets of Paris, in November 1943, led me to be confident that Britain would assist in the removal of the Führer from office, by any means necessary. History should thank the brave secret agent who conveyed this news to me in Paris, liberating my country from the spell that had led it to barbarism and lifting the veil of evil that had darkened the world.

Memoirs of Wilhelm Canaris, Berlin, 1953

Who would believe it? I was walking down the Boulevard St Germain with Admiral Wilhelm Canaris, head of German military intelligence, the Abwehr. This man was one of the most senior officials in Hitler's Wehrmacht. And he hated Hitler's guts.

Our destination was the Abwehr's Paris HQ at 45 Boulevard Raspail. He liked to take a stroll in the mornings and that was how he had met Wodehouse, purely by chance. Finding that they had many interests in common, their chats had become a weekly occurrence.

I had heard of the Boulevard St Germain and the Left Bank. It was supposed to be a haunt of writers and philosophers and their glittering 'café society', but they weren't much in evidence today. Cafés were open but they weren't doing much business. In some, German officers in grey uniforms were taking coffee.

There was an aura of power around Canaris, despite his casual and anonymous form of dress. The soldiers that we encountered seemed to know him; some even saluted.

'What do you make of the City of Light, Major Wilkins?' he asked.

'I'd rather see it without the swastikas,' I commented.

'So would I. I am no admirer of Corporal Hitler, I assure you. Your Neville Chamberlain should never have made terms with him. It was a black day for Europe when he came back from Munich clutching his little piece of paper.'

'Do many German people wish to see Hitler deposed?'

'I would suppose so,' he replied.

'Do you?'

'As you saw, I was happy to help you just now. The SS are disgusting. They have no morals or scruples. They are not soldiers but street fighters. Their leader Himmler, the Reichsführer, is a monster.'

'Indeed.'

'Let me tell you about this man,' Canaris began. 'Himmler was a chicken farmer before the war; you may have noticed his narrow Slavic eyes. Do you know he almost fainted when he saw Jews being executed on the Eastern front?'

'No, I did not know,' I said.

'He is a disgrace to Germany's military traditions. That is why I no longer wear my uniform. It has been dishonoured. But, as you have noticed, people still know who I am. They have a nickname for me. Have you heard it?'

'I haven't, no.'

'They call me The Fox.'

He stopped to offer me a cigarette and lit one for himself.

'You know of my record, I suppose?' he continued.

'Not in detail.'

'I was a U-boat commander in the first war and was awarded the Iron Cross. I was promoted to admiral in 1940. At first, I was happy to go along with Herr Hitler in his rise to power, although I did have my doubts. And when I saw Jews being slaughtered in a synagogue in Poland…'

He paused.

We had reached the Rue de Bac metro. It was a broad thoroughfare with a central tree-shaded strip, perfect for a game of pétanque on a summer evening.

As we strolled along, Canaris expressed the view that the war was effectively over. As soon as a second front was opened, the Germans would be helplessly trapped between the Allies and the Russians. Hitler's card was marked.

'You know that time for a second allied front is coming soon, don't you?' I said.

'It would seem likely,' he replied.

'It will be next summer. Preparations for the landings are well in hand. We are trying to spread rumours that the landing will be near Calais but, actually, they will be in a different location.'

'I had suspected as much,' he said.

'You are well-informed.'

'It is my job to be so.'

Further down the boulevard, the Abwehr's HQ loomed over the Square of Sèvres-Babylone like an ocean liner. Bedecked with swastikas, it radiated from a central, curving tower – a marvel of balconies with iron grilles and decorative stonework. This was a famous building – a monument to Art Nouveau. Until the fall of Paris, it had been the well-known Hotel Lutetia.

'My office,' Canaris gestured. 'Would you like to see it?'

'Yes, but perhaps it is better that we talk outside,' I suggested. 'I have some information of a sensitive nature for you. It comes from Mr Churchill himself. It will be of great interest to you.'

'I understand.'

As it happened, there was a café in the square and Canaris invited me to sit at one of the tables outside, as his guest.

•••

'We know that you are involved in a plot to assassinate Hitler,' I revealed. 'Mr Churchill would like you to know that you have our complete support. Britain will deploy its special forces to ensure the plot is a success. Once Hitler is dead, we will assist you in forming a provisional government. But we must advise you to go to a place of safety immediately. Himmler knows of your plans.'

Canaris leaned forwards.

'Thank you for confirming what I already suspected. I will go to Portugal. Your man Menzies is there at the moment, I believe.'

'Menzies?'

'The head of MI6...'

'You know more than I do. At least the weather will be better in Portugal.'

'Indeed. Do you like to sail, Major Wilkins?'

'I have never tried.'

'I'm sure that you would like it. Would you like to see a picture of my yacht?'

How could I refuse?

'It is in my office.'

He sensed my reticence.

'You are perfectly safe, you know. I am a fox, not a wolf.'

He smiled, showing the ravages of tobacco on his teeth. One sensed that this man lived by his wits and nervous energy, ever alert to danger. So far, remarkably, he had survived.

•••

The vestibule of the Abwehr building was a glistening concoction of marble, mirrors and chandeliers. Little had been done to disguise its former function as a luxury hotel.

Typewriters tapped busily and faces looked up at Canaris as he passed, with smiles and greetings. No-one shrank in fear, they all seemed to like him.

We took a lift to the fifth floor, passing through an anteroom to his office, where more secretaries sat.

On the walls of his office were pictures of the admiral on his yacht, of his family and his favourite Dachshund.

He positioned himself behind a huge desk and then spoke to me in French.

'Please, take a seat. Thank you for offering to help the Abwehr, Monsieur…?'

'…du Coquetot,' I finished, playing along.

He nodded.

'We are extremely grateful for the assistance that you, as a loyal citizen, have provided to the Reich. Please would you give me your papers?'

He spoke slowly. This office would surely be fitted with hidden microphones. I felt a pang of fear. Was I about to be cuffed and taken to the cells to be interrogated (again)? I reached into my jacket.

He did not flinch.

'Have no fear, I am going to provide you with a letter carrying my signature to ensure that you can travel freely anywhere in France as an honorary member of the Abwehr.'

'Thank you, sir. It is an honour.'

Du Coquetot would have been immensely proud. There was only one thing to do – I rose to my feet, snapped my heels and gave the familiar salute.

'Heil Hitler!'

The phrase was returned.

The eyes of the Fox wandered around the room. Perhaps he was bidding it farewell.

39

Business as Usual

Hitler is dead. The war is over. Germany has surrendered unconditionally to Great Britain, the United States and Russia and resistance has ceased in all areas. The announcement follows a secret operation at the German Eagle's Nest headquarters in Rasenburg, Poland, involving the RAF, local partisans and British special forces.

British Prime Minister, Winston Churchill, has been in contact with Colonel Count von Stauffenberg, head of the German provisional government, to discuss the terms of the surrender. Later today...

The Times, 10th December 1943

Task: Hitler
Mission completed

Fancy footwork amigo! You have just killed the Big H. Not on your own, of course, but you skilfully brought together the ingredients of the poison brew that finished him off. That shows a special kind of talent. You're going to need it when you pit your wits against the next badasss. Good luck!

'Hi Anita.'

'Oh hi, Chris,' she said. 'You're in a good mood.'

She must have seen the spring in my step. I didn't tell her the reason for it.

The smile vanished from my face as I looked at the front page of the Daily Mail on the reception desk:

'Texas Vampire: suspicious death investigated.'

The story reported that a police raid had recovered a dead body stored in a chest freezer in the CloudCorp building in City Road. The victim was a young male.

'Oh dear,' I said. 'Has Strobe been arrested?'

'Yeh, this morning. It was on the TV news.'

'Has he been charged with anything?'

'I don't know. They didn't say. There's an e-mail from him. Have you seen it?'

'No, not yet.'

'Well come and have a look.'

She stood next to me. The perfume that permeated from her starched uniform was distracting.

'To: All Staff
From: Strobe

I am sure that you have all heard the news about City Road. I'm co-operating fully with the police in their inquiries and I have offered my condolences to the young man's family. I would like to make it clear that he died of natural causes.

Some of you will have been reading the ridiculous stories about me in the Daily Mail. You have my full assurance that none of the allegations are true. That is why I will be suing them and anyone else who repeats this nonsense.

Believe me folks – I am not a vampire! Well, only in the bedroom!

We'll get through this. I would like to reassure you that I'll be returning bigger and better than ever. So have faith. And, yes, I know you've all been asking, there will be a summer ball for all staff. You put the loud in CloudCorp! I'll be busy with lawyers for the next few days, but I'll be more than happy to answer any of your questions.

Peace to all.'

'It doesn't read like he wrote it,' I commented, suspiciously. 'Even the jokes.'

'He didn't. His PA will've written it.'

'His PA?'

'Samantha.'

'I've never met her.'

'She's mainly based at Holland Park.'
'Let me guess, she's tall and blonde?'
'Yep.'
'Well, there's a surprise. Oxford graduate?'
'Cambridge.'
'But of course. Hey Anita,' I said in a sudden flash of inspiration. 'You must be finishing your shift soon. Would you like a coffee?'

She looked delighted.
'Thanks Chris. I would love one.'

•••

We chose a table that looked over the lawns at the back of the hotel.

Chiffchaffs and willow warblers were singing; swifts and swallows wheeled in the azure sky. The white cross of the helicopter pad stood out sharply from the grass. I remembered the day that we'd flown to Brazil.

'Imagine owning all this,' I said.

'It reminds me of my grandparents' place in Jamaica. It's up in the hills near Montego Bay. It's beautiful there.'

'Do you go there?'

'When I can. I try to go every year. Mr Kitson was going to buy some land there. But it fell through.'

'Did you help him?'

'A little.' She looked uncomfortable.

'Do you like Kitson?'

'I used to. He was very generous and kind to me when I first came to work here.'

'What happened?'

'He made a pass at me.'

'You surprise me.'

'I didn't mind that,' Anita continued. 'I'm a grown woman. It was the language he used that I didn't like, it revealed a less pleasant side to him.'

'Was he embarrassed?'

'Embarrassed? Of course not! He's not embarrassed by anything. He asked me to go to one of his parties.'

'What parties?' I asked.

'The sex parties. There used to be lots of them. I never went myself.'

'Do you know that you're in Get The Bad Guys? A Victorian brothel madam?'

She smiled.

'I believe that Strobe uses me when he needs a black female character – like a jazz singer.'

'Bit of a racial stereotype, isn't it?'

'I don't mind. I used to be in a gospel choir.'

'So, you have hidden talents then...'

'Some people say so.' She paused. 'You'll have to find out what they are, won't you?'

'I'd love to,' I replied with a smile.

40

The Wheatsheaf

Task: Aleister Crowley

This opponent is going to test you. He's a well-connected sociopath who has acquired, through occult practices, a full gamut of psychic powers. He doesn't follow the rules that most humans do and he's worked hard to earn his nickname in the British press – The Great Beast. You'll need to pull something really special out of your bag of tricks to beat this son of a bitch. Even then, it may not be enough. Dig deep my friend. Good luck.

Time: 1941
Lives remaining: 3
Special powers: Level 2

There must have been an air raid here. Broken glass and other detritus crunched underfoot. I looked around at the houses with their taped-up windows and realised I was in wartime London. It was evening. No doubt, many of these Georgian houses had sandbags inside. *Could this be the work of Zeppelins?* No – World War Two.

The West End, Fitzrovia probably. Yes, I was walking down Charlotte Street. Oddly, I was only one block from Cleveland Street, famed for its brothel scandal of 1899, of which I now had intimate knowledge.

I was wearing a dark grey suit, double-breasted with wide lapels, a smart pair of shoes, a black trilby. I had a moustache again. My right leg felt stiff, as if it was attached to a splint.

Evening was falling. Between Tottenham Street and Goodge Street, a row of shops had received a direct hit from German bombs. Burnt timbers jutted from blackened brickwork like the skeleton of an old ship. Policemen and air raid patrol wardens in steel helmets were guarding the smoking ruins.

My watch told me it was ten to eight. Why was I here? A young man in a khaki uniform bumped into me. He asked for a light. I reached into my pocket – but, instead of matches, my fingers curled around a thick cream envelope. The letter had already been opened:

> 'Lower Barracks
> Southgate Street
> Winchester
>
> 15th April, 1941
>
> Dear Bill,
>
> I was sorry to hear that you were banged up in your Hurricane. I hope that you are not in too much pain, old chap, and that your wounds are healing. You must be in a hurry to get back to your squadron.
>
> It's good news about your divorce. Quite honestly, you are better off without Ileana. She didn't suit your easy-going ways and I could see how unhappy she was making you. You deserve better old man.
>
> This is mainly to say that I shall be on leave next week and it will be a good opportunity to meet up, if you want to. The Hampshires are resting between ops but the word is that pretty soon we'll be off to the desert in North Africa. They've made me a captain, by the way. Remember those lead soldiers that we used to have at school? Hours of fun.
>
> I have lots of other news, but I'll save it for when we meet. I suggest The Wheatsheaf in Rathbone Place at eight o'clock on the evening of 3rd May. It's full of pretentious types but at least it's central and the booze rarely seems to run out.
>
> My pal on the Express, Tom Crabtree, will be joining us. He's an odd character and a pacifist but, take my word, he is utterly sincere and entirely harmless. I have also invited your old flame, Katie. I hope you don't mind.

Please drop me a line or send a telegram to confirm, but I hope to see you there my old friend.

Best regards,

Captain Harry Walden, First Battalion, Hampshire Regiment.'

I guessed that the invitation was for tonight. Fortunately, The Wheatsheaf was only a few minutes away, at the southern edge of Fitzrovia where it touched Soho.

Soho had always had a seedy, glamorous edge to it. But the war would have quickened its pulses, adding more opportunities for crime and jeopardy. As the night wore on, its streets would fill with servicemen, theatre goers, tarts, spivs, boozers and hustlers.

•••

'Bill, you old devil!'

The man who rose to greet me in the crowded pub was wearing a suit in the latest style, similar to mine – double-breasted with a generous lapel. His was pin-striped. His colourful silk tie and matching breast pocket handkerchief added a dash of *joie de vivre*. So, this was Captain Walden.

The saloon bar was jammed. There were men in uniform, women in their Saturday night finery and some distinctly odd types who looked very Fitzrovian. Seated at the bar was a chap in a cream-coloured suit with a canary yellow waistcoat. He wore dark glasses and was smoking a cigarette with a long holder.

A woman wearing a beret and cashmere sweater was moving from table to table. I saw with horror that she was raising her sweater, giving The Wheatsheaf's patrons the opportunity to glimpse her breasts.

The room was deafeningly loud and filled with smoke. Blackout boards had already been fitted neatly to the windows, sealing in all light.

As I struggled to the table, Harry placed an arm around my shoulders.

'Welcome my friend. Look, we've saved you a place.'

There were two other people at our table. One was a stick thin character in a pale green moth-eaten cardigan. His thinning hair had a reddish tinge and he had a half-hearted beard and shining eyes sunk into hollow sockets. It looked like he needed a glass of milk and a decent meal.

Sitting next to him was a beautiful black woman. She wore a simple dress of blue silk, cut low at the front. Her hair was long and straight; her eyelids were an iridescent green.

'Everybody!' Harry announced importantly, 'this is Bill. We were at Winchester together. Bill is a fighter pilot, he's serving in Number One Squadron, protecting us from the Hun. Or at least he was, before his injury. That's right isn't it, old boy?'

'It is,' I confirmed.

'He'll be far too modest to tell you himself, but he shot down a German bomber earlier this year. Only the silly bugger got shot down himself, didn't you Bill? He bailed out and managed to fall through a roof, damaging his legs. Am I right?'

'Yes,' I said, sheepishly.

'Bill, this fellow is Tom Crabtree. Tom is a writer and columnist on my newspaper, the Express; he is also a dowser and collector of folk tales.'

'And an author,' the man interjected.

'Yes, that's right. What are some of your books?' He paused briefly. 'Oh yes, there's Badger's Bottom, My Life with Owls and – what was the other one? – Living with Bees.'

'Living with Trees,' the author corrected him.

'Trees. I'm so sorry, Tom. He lives in a cottage in the woods in deepest Sussex.'

We shook hands. Crabtree had pale artistic fingers. His grip was as weak as a baby's.

'This lady should need no introduction, Bill – Katie, the jazz singer, or, as she is known professionally, Kitty Star. You met her in the Café de Paris last year, remember?'

'Did I? I mean, yes, of course, the Café de Paris...'

'I can vouch for that. It was the famous night that we saw Ken "Snakehips" Johnson. Katie sat in with his band. She sang a couple of numbers. Didn't you take her back home to Balham, Bill, in your little Austin, after the show?'

I shrugged.

'Lost your memory?' Harry asked with a wink.

'Ah yes, that's it,' I improvised. 'When I fell through that roof, I banged my head really hard on a chimney breast. There are lots of things I can't remember.'

'Sounds a bit worrying.'

'Oh, you know.' I shrugged.

Katie (aka Anita) stood up to greet me. She was glowing with fulfilment. Her perfume wafted around her like a flock of tropical birds. She planted her moist red lips on my cheek.

'You poor darling,' she cooed. 'It's lovely to see you again.'

'Right, let me get some drinks,' Harry announced.

He meant mainly for himself and me. Crabtree's small glass of pale liquid was barely touched and Katie was only halfway through a large red wine.

'What would you like, Bill?'

'I er…'

'The usual?' he asked.

'Yes, the usual. That would be excellent.'

Was it possible for more people to be jammed into one not-very-large room? In central London, yes. The conversation in here was becoming more frantic; the air growing thicker by the minute with eye-watering tobacco fumes. And the evening was only just beginning.

41

The Great Beast

The role of jazz singer would suit Anita perfectly. That is, if she could sing. (I was hoping she could.)

Crabtree, the author, seemed self-absorbed and somewhat detached. He was resigned to being here but I could tell that he'd be a lot more at home in a cosy country pub with beams and pewter tankards, sitting next to his dog.

Katie, by contrast, was delighted to be among the clientele of The Wheatsheaf – the beau-monde of Fitzrovia.

'I'm so sorry I can't remember meeting you,' I said.

She smiled.

'It happens a lot. Don't worry, Bill, you were the perfect gentleman, I can assure you. You drove us through the blackout and got me home. Don't you remember? Then the sirens went off. So you had to come into my flat.'

'I came in?'

'You spent the night with me.'

'I did?'

'On my sofa. It must have been horribly uncomfortable.'

'They usually are.'

She laughed.

'It was very kind of you to put me up,' I commented. 'I'm so sorry I can't remember. You see, since that awful bang on my head …'

'We understand, don't we Tom?'

Crabtree's mind seemed to be elsewhere. We made small talk for a few minutes until Harry, the glue that held us together, finally made it back to our table, precariously clutching our drinks.

'Christ,' he puffed. 'That was hard going.' He placed the drinks on the table. 'I bought you another drink Tom. You can't just sit there all night with half a pint. For you, Katie, another rather nasty Algerian red.'

After we'd grabbed our respective drinks, Harry gave us a thumb-nail impression of the room. 'The woman behind the bar looks like a man. She has a moustache! And you see that fellow in the yellow waistcoat, Bill?' He pointed to the bar. 'That's Julian MacLaren Ross, the writer. He's such a crashing bore. Do not, under any circumstances, try to talk to him. He has only one subject – himself. And his breath smells like a cat's arse.'

'Harry, you can't say that!' objected a shocked Katie.

'Sorry, like a cat's paws then.'

I knew that there were many dubious and deluded characters in the environs of Soho – self-aggrandisers, repetitious from drink. For every genuine genius, there were a hundred pretenders. Most deceived no-one but themselves. Some were con artists. Harry was still scanning the room:

'See that woman?' He pointed. 'That's Nina Hamnett. She was a famous artist's model in the '30s – Picasso's muse, so it's said. It's hard to believe that now her looks have faded. She's reduced to showing people her tits in return for half a crown.'

He finally sat down, took a gulp of his drink and sighed in satisfaction.

'Well, this is agreeable. My favourite place with my favourite people,' he said, his eyes shining. 'A toast?'

'Yes,' Katie said. 'But to whom or what?'

'To Flight Lieutenant Bill Wilkinson,' Harry announced, 'of His Majesty's Number One Squadron, "first among equals"! May he continue to protect our skies from the Luftwaffe.'

We raised our glasses.

'Some ground rules for tonight,' Harry announced. 'I am a warrior, obviously, a brave infantry captain who is on leave, serving my country in battle, as well as being a well-known foreign correspondent on Britain's best-selling newspaper, the Daily Express. Bill here is a flyer, with a confirmed kill under his belt.'

'It was nothing, really,' I said. 'I…'

'Katie is an up-and coming jazz singer. She has already performed for the Prince of Wales and is the toast of Soho. The world is truly her oyster. Tom here is a conscientious objector…'

Harry was already clearly drunk, knocking back Irish whiskeys as if there were no tomorrow.

'We can forgive him this – because the spirit realm, of which Tom writes, has yet to mobilise against Hitler, at least as far as we know. Perhaps they are fairy fascists!'

'I object to that Harry.' It was the first time Crabtree had spoken. 'I've explained to you many times, or tried to: this war is not just being fought in our everyday physical world, but also in the spiritual realm. The forces are finely balanced. It won't take much for one side to gain dominance.'

'I take your point Tom,' Harry responded. 'But I was going to suggest, as the first of my ground rules for this evening, that we must not talk about the war.'

'Wasn't Tom speaking on a metaphysical or even metaphorical basis?' I suggested.

'No, not at all.' Crabtree seemed glad that someone was taking him seriously. 'The conflict of which I speak is just as real as that which is taking place between men in uniforms.'

'Good versus evil,' Katie said.

'No, I don't mean that. Good and evil are Judaeo-Christian concepts. It is not so clear-cut. You see…'

'Fighting the Nazis seems pretty clear-cut to me,' Harry cut in. 'It must be to Bill here, with his peg leg.'

Peg leg! Oh my God. I touched my right calf. I felt something hard and unyielding beneath the fabric of my trousers. So, I had lost one of my limbs. *Oh, great.*

'Come on, Harry,' Katie interjected. 'Stop being beastly to Tom. I thought he was your friend. He's a sweetie! He is entitled to his beliefs, just as you are to yours. Isn't that why we're fighting this war?'

'I withdraw my comments,' Harry said. 'They were not meant to be unkind, I do assure you. I hope you know that I respect you, Tom, both as a writer and as my respected colleague on the Express. There is no question as to your bravery. Good God, you like to swim in the pond on Hampstead Heath in the buff. It takes a brave man to do that, in winter.'

'Thank you for bringing that up Harry,' said Crabtree. 'I do like to take a swim on the Heath when I am up in London, as many do.' He took a sip from his beer.

'Naked?' Katie asked.

'Of course,' the writer replied.

'I agree with you, by the way,' Katie said.

'What do you mean?'

'There are spirits all around us.'

'Can you see any now – apart from this one?' Harry pointed at his glass.

'Can't you take anything seriously?!' said the singer.

Harry must have realised that he'd over-stepped the mark.

'Oh dear, I must now apologise to you too, my dear. If you say that we are walking amongst the spirits of the departed, who am I to disagree…Bill, are you all right?!'

He must have noticed that my face had turned pale. I was searching with my fingertips for my missing limb.

'Yes, I'm fine,' I murmured.

'This is all far too solemn. You see, I was right. Let us talk no more of the w–'

Just as he was uttering that final syllable, a shrill wailing of banshees filled the pub – air raid sirens (not supernatural beings). After the loud, soul-tugging sound had stopped, there was a moment of silence. The hum and clatter resumed almost immediately. Most people, including us, had elected to stay indoors, concluding that we might as well die with a drink in our hands. A few purposefully left, heading for the nearest shelter.

A sign that filled one with dread had appeared in front of the bar pumps – 'No more beer'. The establishment had run out of its most vital commodity. The remaining drinkers would have to make do with other sources of inebriation.

•••

We all noticed him at the same time – a bulky man in black clothes seated at a neighbouring table. He had a pale, fleshy face and deep-set, staring eyes. He was sitting alone. It was easy to see why: there was an aura around this man – a force field that discouraged casual conversation. To me, with my Level 1 and 2 special powers, it was clearly visible – a yellow light glowing from the top of his head.

'It's Aleister Crowley, isn't it?' commented Crabtree. 'Don't you know him, Harry?'

'Yes, I've met him a few times…'

'Don't they call him The Great Beast?'

'Some people do.'

'Is he a black magician?' asked Katie.

'Some people say so,' Harry said thoughtfully. 'He likes to practise what he calls "sex magic".'

'What's that?' asked the singer.

'Basically, he's a randy old goat who is capable of hypnotising vulnerable people, male and female, into doing his bidding, which normally means one thing. He used to be a member of the Hermetic Order of the Golden Dawn, a kind of Masonic order for poets, but that didn't satisfy his need to be in charge. Also, it's a rather stuffy organisation. They objected to his sexual proclivities. So he set up his own religion. It's called the Cult of Thelema.'

'In reality,' Harry continued after quaffing his whiskey. 'He is merely rebelling against his wealthy upbringing by the Plymouth Brethren. At first, he did it by mountaineering – oddly – and then, when he was up at Cambridge, by writing poetry. Terrible poetry. It took him a long time to get to his ceremonial magic. It's a perverted form of Christianity – the Eucharist is performed with blood and er…semen. Crowley intones mumbo jumbo which he's stolen from many places, including Indian religions and the ancient Egyptians. It's all complete balderdash.'

'You seem to know an awful lot about him,' Katie pointed out.

'Well, I've written many stories about him. He makes great copy. Crowley depends upon people like me to build up his reputation as "the most evil man in Britain" and I'm more than happy to oblige. Our readers love it.'

He raised his glass, hoping that the man he was talking about would notice. The gesture was not seen, or perhaps it was just ignored.

'Is he evil?' Katie asked.

'Is he evil?' Harry repeated the question. 'Well, a few people in his inner circle have ended up mad, or dead. But, happily, he doesn't have the capacity to do too much damage. He's essentially an attention seeker. He is rather peeved at the moment that no-one is writing about him – and his health is not good. That's another thing I didn't tell you – he's a drug addict. He likes to inject himself with heroin.'

'Lovely,' said Katie.

'He has a catchphrase, doesn't he?' I remembered. "Do what thou wilt shall be the whole of the law?" I felt pleased with myself. I had read a book about Crowley once, at university.

'That's right,' said Harry, impressed.

The folklorist, Crabtree, seemed drawn to the bulky stranger. He couldn't take his eyes off the man.

'I'm going to talk to him,' he suddenly announced.

Katie tried to dissuade him, and even Harry tried to pull him back.

'Tom, I really wouldn't…'

It was to no avail.

Crabtree stood before The Great Beast. He extended a hand for the man to shake.

Crowley ignored the hand and said, somewhat arrogantly: 'Who are you?'

'My name is Tom Crabtree. I am an author. I have a column in the Daily Express. It's called…'

'Piffle,' Crowley commented.

'I'm sorry?'

'Do you think I am interested in the trivial chatter of newspapers?'

'I, too, believe in the fairy realm…'

'You poor fool! We have nothing in common. You are a non-entity, a fairy yourself. A man fairy.'

Crabtree stammered in protest.

'Go away.'

The Great Beast raised his hand in a dismissive gesture. He cast a peculiar look at our table and nodded at Harry, confirming that he knew him. The light emanating from his head was flaring like a gas jet. *Uh-oh.* For a moment, our eyes met. That was to cost me dearly later. Crowley had sensed that I, too, had psychic powers, although they were less than his.

Crabtree sheepishly returned to his seat.

'That went well, Tom,' said Harry.

The folklorist looked down at his untouched glass of beer.

'Look, they're running out of drink here. Let's go somewhere else,' my friend continued. 'What was that place you were telling me about the other day Katie, the one down in Dean Street?'

'You mean the Gargoyle Club?'

'Yes, that's it, the Gargoyle Club. It sounds fun. Let's go there.'

It seemed like a good idea.

Two companions had joined Crowley. The man, with a thin moustache, had the appearance of a sadistic scoutmaster. His female companion sported a cold expression, black bobbed hair and crimson lips. They formed a peculiar trio.

Harry scraped back his chair.

'Come on, let's get out of here.'

42

The Gargoyle Club

We had lost Crabtree at some point. His encounter with Aleister Crowley had been bruising. I don't think the idea of going on to a louche night club in Soho filled him with much excitement.

We'd left The Wheatsheaf just as last orders were called. Some of the patrons would now cross the road. It was well known that certain public houses in the neighbouring London borough were licensed to stay open for longer.

Harry, Katie and I crossed Oxford Street, traversing the invisible boundary that separates Fitzrovia and Soho. One sensed an area that was barely in control. Part-time prostitutes, the so-called Piccadilly Commandos, were out in force. They seemed to be present in almost every dark passageway. Some of the women used torches to light up their faces. The patches of light stippled on the darkness gave this street scene the feeling of a weird masque performed in an experimental theatre.

The bomb damage was extensive. For the whole journey, we were crunching through broken glass. In Dean Street, we saw people fighting and vomiting. The proximity of lonely men on leave, alcohol and the Piccadilly Commandos had created a bacchanalia. A few times, we heard the shrill blast of whistles and sound of running feet. Harry led the way, like a general at the head of his troops. His face was shining. In his extravagant suit and colourful tie, he looked oddly at home.

It was a relief for Katie and I when we reached the club, a white-fronted Georgian building on the corner of Dean and Meard Streets. It was only now that we noticed Crabtree had disappeared. With luck, he would get back to his cottage in Surrey on the milk train, to lick his wounds in peace.

•••

Harry told me that this establishment had been the creation of a bohemian aristocrat. He had wanted to put a little bit of Montparnasse in London, creating a congenial environment for artistic and literary types in which to let their hair down. He said that it was very popular with people from the BBC and civil service.

A tiny, underpowered lift transported clientele into the club. It was only big enough for two people, so I went up first with Katie. Being pressed tightly against her, breathing in her perfume, was not unpleasant. She didn't seem to mind either.

We emerged into a wood-panelled room hung with brightly coloured prints. They were lithographs by Matisse, Harry explained, when he came out of the lift. The club's interior had been designed by the famous artist.

'Come on peg leg,' he said. 'You haven't seen the best yet.'

In the dining room was one of Matisse's most striking paintings. The Red Studio was a slab of scarlet within which floated luminous objects, as if in a dream. One sensed in this marvellous canvas the optimism and luminous colours of the Mediterranean. It offered a vista of light that had not been obliterated by darkness – the kind of visual stimulation that the underfed and light-deprived people of London would need to get them through the war.

Harry, who knew the famous creator of the club (he seemed to know everyone), led us up an art deco staircase fashioned from steel and brass. I was keenly aware of my artificial leg as I swung it from step to step. Katie graciously offered to help me. Harry merely stood at the top with an idiotic grin on his face.

'Come on,' he said. 'Is that the best you can do?'

The Moorish ballroom was a world of crimson and maroon, the signature colours of the club. The walls were covered by shards of mirror; a sea of gilt and velvet chairs and tables with small red lamps were spread out before us.

At the end of the room, a band was setting up. The music stands were decorated with double interlocking letter As.

In the centre of the stage was a tall, thin man in a dinner jacket with slicked-down hair and a black moustache.

'That's Alec Alexander,' Katie explained, 'it's his orchestra.'

Recognising our companion, he abandoned what he was doing and crossed the room. Close up, one could see that his face was thickly coated with foundation cream and that beads of sweat were breaking through. His pupils were swollen like tadpoles. He clasped Katie's hand:

'Darling, I am so glad you're here! I hope you'll honour my little orchestra by singing some numbers with us.'

Katie murmured that she might.

'That's wonderful!'

He became aware of Harry and I, and introductions were made.

'You know how marvellous she is, don't you?' gushed the band leader.

'Oh yes,' Harry said, 'she's a star in the making.'

'She certainly is. Do you mind if I borrow her, gentlemen?'

We graciously bade Katie goodbye. Alexander led her across the room as if he was trailing an expensive racehorse across a paddock. Soon, she was amongst the band talking shop.

'Well Katie's popular isn't she?' Harry commented. 'I understand that the Prince of Wales is smitten with her. Did you notice that man's eyes, Bill?'

'What do you mean?'

'He's high as a kite on something. I have yet to meet a musician in Soho who doesn't take drugs.'

•••

Whatever substance the man had taken, it was very effective. He was a blur of nervous movement, a hyperactive stick insect. This energy transferred itself to his musicians, then to the audience, where it was amplified and thrown back until lift-off was achieved – the ecstatic moment when the Holy Spirit enters the room. Its presence was welcomed tonight. The audience – men in dinner jackets, women in long evening dresses – were desperate, just for a few hours, to leave the war outside.

The crooner who came on first was competent enough but he was soon to be eclipsed. When Katie stepped up to the mic, it was as if a switch had been turned on.

Her voice was subtle and immensely powerful. Its timbres were shades of magnolia, coffee and ebony. Leading the brass instruments or twining around the lead line of a clarinet, her voice could move in an instant from a soft whisper to a powerful, operatic contralto.

Harry and I moved to the front. Singing a slow ballad, Katie looked down at where we were standing. There was a curious expression on her face. Harry nudged me in the ribs, implying that she was performing for me. Was she? All I knew was that it would be painful not to look into her face or to hear her smooth, caressing voice. I didn't just want to sleep with her. I was truly in love with Anita...I mean Katie. Well, both.

She finished her set and the band switched back to dance numbers. As she descended to the world of mortals in her tight, silk dress, she seemed to be filled with light. All eyes in the room were watching her but it was me who reached up to help her down from the stage. Her hot, scented body pressed against mine.

43

The Dream of Baphomet

Katie's place was in South London, just off Balham High Street. The location was convenient for her work as a ward nurse at Lambeth Hospital.

We'd hailed a cab on Shaftesbury Avenue. It was dawn when we arrived at her flat, and streaks of yellow sun trailed across the pink and grey sky. I recall the smell of bread wafting from a nearby bakery.

She took off her shoes and we climbed a steep set of stairs. Inside, she collapsed in a tiny hallway, rubbing her feet. She was crying with mirth. We'd been laughing the whole journey. Her make-up was smudged. It was hard to believe this was the same woman who'd held an entire room under her spell.

'Oh, Bill.'

'Come on, you have to get up,' I said.

'Do I?'

'I'll help you.'

I reached down.

It was a hard job, dragging her to her bedroom. Soon, the bed loomed ahead of us like a boat in a stormy sea. As she pulled me on top of her, she began to moan.

•••

Later, we sat up in bed smoking. The room was very small. Through the net curtains was a landscape of yellow London brick and grey rooftops. Here, at the back of the house, the sun rarely seemed to penetrate.

I noted a large suitcase on top of her wardrobe. Next to the bed were an alarm clock (essential for nurses) and a photograph of a small black girl in a white chiffon dress with, presumably, her parents, dressed in formal clothes. No-one was smiling.

Katie pulled the bedclothes back and we looked down. Where my lower right leg should be was a smooth wooden attachment.

'Who dressed your wounds?' she asked.

'I don't know. They must have done it in the hospital.'

'Which hospital?

'Er…Westminster.'

'You mean St Thomas'.'

'Yes, that's right.'

'Perhaps they were in a hurry. They made a terrible job of it.'

She placed a finger on the jagged stitches of a scar.

'You poor darling. I wish I'd done it.'

'It's a shame you didn't. Do you like being a nurse?'

'Sometimes.'

She looked serious.

'It can be very hard, especially after an air raid, when they bring in the wounded. You can't be sad when you are doing your job – but later, when you think about what you've seen...'

'Of course, that must be terribly difficult. Why don't you become a singer?'

'I am a singer.'

'I mean a full-time, professional singer.'

'That's not going to happen, is it? Perhaps I could but I don't want some slimy business manager running my life. Besides, I like my job.'

'Are you working today?'

'Yes, but I'm on the late shift. I don't have to leave until this afternoon. You are very thin, poor Bill. I'll need to feed you up.'

'I would like that.'

I reached for another cigarette and lit it.

'Who are the people in the picture?'

I pointed to the photograph on the bedside table.

'Oh they were my parents in Jamaica. My father was a minister. He was called William, like you. He was a strict, God-fearing man. I ran away and went to live with my grandmother in the mountains. I was there for a few months but he came and brought me back. He said she was a witch and that she was corrupting me.'

'Was she?'

'Well, she knew about healing with herbs and the spirits of nature. And she could speak to people who had passed to the other side. Is that a witch?'

'Did she teach you some of her skills?'

She turned.

'What makes you think that?'

'Well, you have an aura.'

'What do mean?'

'It's a faint light that shines from your head and shoulders. Aleister Crowley has one too, the most powerful that I have seen. Didn't you notice it?'

She looked away.

'Why did you come to England?'

'I told you, I was a bad girl. I was sick of my father beating me, so I ran away. I met a sailor in Kingston and he took me away on his boat.'

I sensed that the memory caused her unease.

'It must have been fun escaping on a boat,' I said, attempting to change the mood.

'It was until the captain caught me.'

'What happened then?'

'He beat me and then…' Her voice trailed away. I reached over to hold her, but she tensed so I withdrew. She continued.

'When we arrived at the West India Docks, I ran away again. I had an uncle in London, so I stayed with him while I was training, in Cricklewood.'

'Training?'

'To be a nurse.'

'Are there many black nurses?'

'No. And yes, some patients are horrible to me.'

She glanced at her little clock.

'Any more questions?'

'I'm sorry,' I said. 'I'll stop asking you things, I promise.'

'You'd better, mister.'

It was midday. Should we get up?

'Are you hungry?

'I don't know. What are you offering?'

'Well, I have some bacon and an egg.'

'You mean one egg?'

'We can share it.'

Time seemed to be suspended over the next few days and nights. It felt like we were in a British black and white film of the 'kitchen sink' variety, our temporary domesticity punctuated by the rattling of trains from the nearby railway line. We became accustomed to the mournful sound of their horns and the vibrations every time they passed.

Mostly we stayed in bed. Katie did her shifts at the hospital and, in between, we listened to jazz records. I didn't know much about jazz (well, apart from what Pierre had played me in another life). She started me off with Fats Waller, Sidney Bechet and Billie Holiday.

She was sharing her rations, so there wasn't much food. But it didn't matter. She told me about the delicious dishes that she would cook one day, if plantain and bananas ever returned to London.

One night, the sirens sounded. The sky over London was criss-crossed with beams from the searchlights in Hyde Park. We decided to stay in. We would die under the covers, in her creaky bed. Luckily, this time it was a false alarm.

•••

On the third night in her flat, I woke up in the middle of the night. I had no idea what time it was. I felt the side of the bed where Katie should be. It was empty.

She was sitting in the living room cross-legged facing the window, wearing a loose blue robe. There was a full moon, its silver light filling the room.

She must have sensed that I was behind her.

'Come here. Sit before me.'

I did as I was told, with difficulty.

She placed her hands on the sides of my head.

'I, Katitia, daughter of Selene, sister of Hecate, pray that the blind one sees. May the moon rise in him. May my eyes be his eyes.'

Energy, like a current, passed through her fingers into my temples.

I shut my eyes. Although I was facing away from the window, I saw what she saw. London was burning. This was not a series of unconnected fires that the Blitz had brought; the entire city was a cauldron of boiling lava. Relentlessly, war machines crossed the sky like a sinister shoal of fish. They were discharging bombs and parachute mines. The aeroplanes met no resistance, there were too many of them. Nothing could control the terrible inferno that they carried. The city was doomed.

Now the scene changed. We looked down, as if from the rafters of a chapel. The building had a chequered floor and mullioned windows. In the transept was an altar covered with a black cloth. On it, I could see two black candles, a chalice and a knife.

A man knelt in front of the altar, facing the eastern window. Red and yellow panels in the rose window glowed faintly. I knew him. It was Aleister Crowley.

44

Hot Club

I had got used to the bitter taste of chicory in coffee and eating only one slice of toast for breakfast. On the radio in the background, the Home Service was playing a dance band tune in an attempt to cheer up the waking masses.

Katie was on her early shift today. We were sharing a seven o'clock breakfast before she left for the hospital.

'What did our dream mean?' I asked.

'It wasn't exactly a dream,' she said.

Her nurse's uniform was not dissimilar to the one she wore as Anita in The White Lodge Hotel – crisp, starched blue. It suited her.

'Through me, you entered the astral plane. Time does not constrain those who are on it. When one is there, it is possible to travel through time and place at will. My power entered your body.'

'Your power?'

'The power of Katitia.'

'That's your witch name, is it?'

She frowned.

'It is my astral name.'

'So, what did it mean, our vision?'

'Isn't it obvious?'

'Not to me.'

'Oh, Bill. You know that tomorrow is a full moon, don't you?'

'Is it?'

'Yes. On those nights, there is often an air raid. What we saw in our vision is the raid that may happen tomorrow night.'

'Are you saying that this will definitely happen?'

'No. It is a possibility – one of many possibilities. Did you notice the floor of the chapel? It was chequered. Crowley was in a room which is normally allocated to masonic rituals.'

'What does that mean?'

'It means that, using his blasphemous magic, he has re-assigned a Masonic lodge to something far worse.'

'To what?'

'To a temple of Baphomet, the hornéd god. Crowley was preparing to summon Baphomet to the earthly plane.'

'Why?'

'Isn't it obvious? The energy discharged by such a summoning would destroy our radar defences and illuminate every light bulb in England. London would be powerless to repel a large air raid. Crowley's allies, the fascists in their black and brown shirts, would crawl out of the woodwork, like woodlice. By the way, Crowley is an Ipsissimus. That means he can imitate any person with perfect accuracy.'

'So?'

'It means that he will have Churchill killed and take his place. He will then tell the King and the British people that they were wrong about Hitler. Britain will become a vassal state to Germany.'

'It's a little far-fetched isn't it?'

'Is it? We have seen the first part of the plan with our own eyes.'

'*You* have seen it.'

'Yes, but you saw it through me.'

'So, what are we supposed to do?'

'Do I have to tell you?'

'Yes!'

'You must contact your friend Harry and tell him. He's a spy, isn't he?'

'How do you know?'

'Well, he doesn't exactly hide it. He is one of the least discrete men I have ever met. He will inform the authorities.'

'What will they do?'

'I don't know. But it's worth a try, don't you think?'

'Won't he think I'm mad?!'

'He might do.'

The look on her face made it clear that there was no alternative.

'Do you know Harry's telephone number?' she asked.

'No.'

'I do, he gave it to me.' Of course he did. She scribbled down the number.

'There will certainly be a raid tonight – we don't know how severe it will be – so the hospital will be busy. I'll see you when I can.'

She gave me a lingering kiss and left.

•••

Just my luck. It was the only time I'd been out of the flat for days, and it was raining. It wasn't easy to find a telephone box and when I did, two people were already waiting to use it. One of them must have been collecting pennies for weeks, in order to telephone an elderly relative who was clearly deaf.

I finally got through. Fortunately, Harry was in. He didn't seem surprised that I wanted to see him. He pronounced himself delighted that I was staying with Katie and asked me when the big day was – our wedding day!

I felt myself blushing and told him not be ridiculous. I said I had some important information for him, which I did not wish to share on the telephone. Unfazed, he asked me to come over to his house. How about joining him for lunch, he suggested?

From Balham to Sydenham was a complicated journey. It required me to take a train, the tube, then another train. By midday, I was standing in front of a large Victorian house set on a rise well back from the road. A sloping path fringed by a flowerbed led up to the front door.

•••

He must have been polishing something – his sleeves were rolled up and he was wearing gloves.

'Come through to the kitchen, Bill.'

He led me through a broad hallway with Victorian floor tiles to a large room at the back of the house. Katie's entire flat would've fitted in here.

'I've been cleaning some silver,' he said. 'It was my father's. I'm going back to the barracks on Monday, so I'm trying to get the house ship-shape before I leave.'

He was smoking a cigarette as he worked, restoring the shine to a silver candelabra. He, too, was listening to the Home Service. Some light classical music was playing.

'It's amazing the stuff that my father collected. Do you like this music, Bill?'

I shrugged. 'Not really.'

'Have a look through my discs.'

Harry was also a jazz fan. I picked one at random.

'Ah, the Hot Club de France. Excellent choice.'

As Django Reinhardt's jaunty gypsy guitar filled the kitchen, accompanied by Stefan Grappelli on violin, I told Harry of Aleister Crowley's diabolical plan to take over Britain by assisting the Luftwaffe.

'I see,' he said, finally. 'Well, it doesn't really surprise me. In fact, we know all about Crowley's interest in the war. But our take on it is rather different. By *we*, I mean certain people who work for the government. Crowley has been feeding us stuff for ages. But you've got it wrong, Bill. He is offering to help the Allies to beat Hitler, not selling us to Satan.'

'Couldn't he be working for both sides, playing one off against the other?'

'He could be. That would certainly be in character.'

In this suburban kitchen, the combination of the cheerful jazz and aroma of Harry's tobacco conjured up the carefree atmosphere of pavement cafés in Paris.

'Funnily enough, I was chatting about Crowley with my friend, the spymaster, Maxwell Knight yesterday. By a strange coincidence, it seems that The Great Beast has invited the great and the good down to a country house in Sussex. He is going to demonstrate to them a supernatural plan designed to reduce Hitler's power.'

'Really?' I said. 'When is this taking place?'

'Tonight.'

Harry had finished his polishing. He placed the gleaming candelabra on the table.

'Another record?'

'Yes, please.'

'Maxwell will be there and a load of stuffy officials with peculiar titles – sheriffs and lord-lieutenants and the like. I can't abide all of that. I tell you what, I'll go, just for you. Actually, you can come with me. How's that? We'll drive down this afternoon. The meeting is in the Ashdown Forest. We won't announce ourselves. We'll sneak around the back and peak through the windows. When you see that Crowley is not calling up the Devil, you'll be relieved, won't you?'

'I suppose so, yes.'

'We can drive down there in my new Bentley. But first, lunch…'

Harry rustled up a very respectable meal. For some reason, the strictures of food rationing were not affecting him too badly. We ate it drinking a delicious Chateau Margaux, listening to Bix Beiderbecke playing his jazz clarinet. Perhaps the war was not so bad. Afterwards, we enjoyed port and Cuban cigars.

We left by the back door at five o'clock. Harry kept his Bentley in the old stables at the rear of the house. He loved fast, expensive cars (he'd done some racing at Brooklands before the war).

The Bentley was the two-door, 4.25 litre model known as the 'silent sports car'. He was very proud of this vehicle with its synchromesh gearbox and electric starter. He told me that it was capable of reaching the amazing speed of 95 miles per hour. I hoped he wouldn't test this claim on our 30-mile journey to the Sussex countryside...

45

Ashdown Manor

We drove through South London suburbs that I'd vaguely heard of but never visited. They all looked the same. A couple of times when the road was clear, Harry opened up the Bentley to her full potential. It was terrifying.

We took the Eastbourne Road. Once we'd passed through the village of Godstone, the real countryside began. The narrow lanes that ran through the beech woods cloaking the North Downs were like green tunnels leading us into another world. After East Grinstead, we started to climb into the High Weald.

The Ashdown Forest is not actually a forest but an upland heathland. The predominant trees are silver birch and pines and there are pockets of ancient woodland. There are also open areas clothed in heather and gorse. The views from this plateau midway between London and the English Channel are spectacular.

On a sketchy track, Harry came to a halt for a magnificent roe deer with spreading antlers. The creature studied us for a while. We could have been hundreds of miles from London. The heath felt like a creation of fiction. One could imagine smugglers meeting here on moonlit nights, highwaymen galloping across tracks.

Ashdown Manor was observing the blackout. Even so it, it commanded the plateau like a pale, ghostly ship. It was part mediaeval abbey, part castle, part railway station. The architect had added an authentic-looking Gothic church with pointed arches and tall narrow windows to the side of the main house.

The car park was half-filled with important looking black cars. So, the meeting was on. We crept across the moonlit courtyard that lay between the house and the church and made our way to the rear of the building.

•••

Peering through one of the windows on tiptoes, we could see a discreetly luxurious interior. With its soft lighting, embossed wallpaper and leather chairs, this room could have been found in a gentlemen's club or the Houses of Parliament.

The left-hand side was dominated by a long table. A row of men was seated along one side of it, the majority wearing dinner jackets and decorated with some kind of chain of office or one or more medals. One, who was standing, wore a blue and red apron decorated with peculiar insignia, indicating that he was a Freemason.

It was easy enough to spot Crowley. He wore a plain black garment that looked like a priest's robe. He was standing in the middle of the room, explaining something to the assembled men. Crouching beneath the windowsill we could catch indistinct snatches of what was being said. Whenever Crowley said something, his audience would murmur in response.

We decided to move to the front of the house. Why not? It was dark now and it should be easy to stay hidden. Harry was ahead of me. We could easily have been guests of the meeting, strolling around in the grounds. He stopped at the corner of the building. Stepping into the courtyard, he was soon out of my sight. I heard a loud crack and a cry of pain. God, what was happening? I walked as quickly and stealthily as possible, given my missing leg, to the corner of the building and peered round.

Four men were standing in line on the opposite side of the courtyard. They wore black jumpers and balaclavas. One had a still-smoking pistol in his outstretched arm. I looked at Harry – his face was contorted and blood was streaming onto the flagstones from a wound in his thigh.

'Bill!' he cried.

It was too late. One of the four attackers was holding something far more potent than a pistol – a Thompson submachine gun with a circular magazine, the kind that gangsters used. A noise that sounded like a cross between a bark and a cough resounded through the air. I watched as clouds of chipped stone bounced across the courtyard in slow motion. Bullets crossed Harry's chest and jerked him backwards in a haze of blood.

I felt a sharp pain, like a bee sting, in my upper arm. The next impact, in my neck, severed an artery. Life spurted from my body in a scarlet fountain. As the killer lowered his weapon, I fell forwards onto the unyielding stones.

46

Deus Ex Machina

Task: Aleister Crowley
Time: 1941
Lives remaining: 2
Special powers: Level 2

Oh Christ, I only have two lives left. I'd better make them last!
We were driving along the track close to the manor house. The roe deer blocked our path. *What a magnificent beast.* It skittered away.

As we pulled into the car park next to a black Lagonda, I asked my friend a question:

'Harry, do you have a gun?'

'Yes, I have my service revolver, in the glove compartment. Do you think we'll need it?'

'We may do. Is it loaded?'

'It is.'

'Good.'

He pulled out the gun. It was a Webley Mark IV, the same weapon I'd used in Paris on the Hitler mission.

'Have you ever fired one of these?' he asked.

'I have.'

I didn't tell him I'd recently killed three men with one.

'Right then, let's go.'

In stealth mode, we made our way to the courtyard. A full moon floated over the roof of the house.

'Good night for German bombers,' Harry said.

'Indeed,' I said. 'The RAF will be on full alert.'

We peered through the casemented windows at the dull meeting of civic dignitaries. Crowley was mouthing his nonsense. I knew that, after his lecture, he would lead the dignitaries outside and they'd be mown down by his goons. It was part of his plan to deliver Britain to the Nazis.

I made a suggestion to Harry.

'We need to check the front of the house. Crowley may have called in reinforcements.'

We hid behind some bushes close to the front of the building. A large four-door saloon drove slowly into the car park and stopped. It was a fast model, a Railton. Four men climbed out. One of them was holding a Tommy gun.

'Give me your revolver, Harry,' I said.

'Why?'

'I can fire at them and draw their return fire, acting as a diversion. You can make your way to the Bentley and leave at high speed. They'll have to follow you.'

He handed me his weapon.

'Good luck.'

I knew I would have to act quickly. Holding the heavy revolver with a double-handed grip, I moved into plain sight. The man with the Tommy gun was my target. I fired a round into his chest and he went down.

Harry was already sprinting to his Bentley. To keep Crowley's goons occupied, I fired more shots at the other men. More by luck than judgement, I clipped one of them in his shoulder. I heard him scream.

I saw Harry leave the car park at high speed. The two uninjured men conferred and one of them ran to the Railton to give chase. That left one functioning thug. I fired at the thickest part of his body but missed. Damn! Only one bullet left...

•••

That bullet was for Aleister Crowley. I made my way down a stuffy, maroon-carpeted corridor. It was wood-panelled, with scenes of hunting and country houses decorating the walls.

There must have been forty or fifty people in the dining room. They were astonished when I burst in and levelled my weapon at The Great Beast's head.

His lips formed into a sneer. I thought of what his men had done to Harry in my previous life; they'd shown no mercy. My sensitized ears – my sixth sense – detected a noise behind me.

It was the fourth man cowering outside the door. He didn't even have time to raise his gun before I plugged him in the middle of the forehead. My last bullet!

Watched by the assembled dignitaries in their chains of office and aprons, Crowley stared at me:

'What are you going to do now?' he scoffed.

'Shoot you down like a dog.'

I levelled my right arm.

'But you have fired your last shot.'

'How do you know?'

A smile crossed his face.

I was about to lunge at him when he drew something from beneath his robe. It was a small-calibre pistol.

'Gentlemen,' he said, 'please excuse us.'

Crowley directed me down the corridor with his gun. We passed the sprawling corpse of his hired man, his head resting in a pool of blood. It matched, perfectly, the colour of the carpet.

•••

The interior of the chapel was exactly as I had seen it through Katie's eyes in her flat – the altar covered with the black cloth, the ceremonial objects and flickering candles.

'How fitting that you will end your life here,' Crowley smirked. 'What a superb offering for the hornéd god. Move forwards to the altar, would you? That is where I am going to kill you. I will then cut your throat and fill my chalice with your blood.'

I spat a ripe word at him. I'd resigned myself to losing another life and nudged forwards.

'Hurry up!' he barked.

There was a loud creak as the double doors swung open. I looked round. Katitia the priestess was standing in the entrance, framed by the iron-clasped oak doors.

47

The Crossroads

But the cowardly, the unbelieving, the vile, the murderers, the sexually immoral, those who practise magic arts, the idolators and all liars – their place will be in the fiery lake of burning sulphur. This is the second death.

Revelations, 21:8

'I am Katitia and I am your doom, evil one.'
'Is that the best you can do?' said Crowley, sarcastically.
'Oh, and did I say how fat you have become?' *Ouch.*
I was hiding in the shadows. He fired a shot at the priestess. It missed.
'Leave Bill. Now!' she hissed.
As I passed her, she pressed something hard and warm into my hand – a gold sovereign, the gateway to the next power. It would take my special powers to Level 3. This, I knew, included the ability to enter the astral realm and to assume the form of an animal.
She was wearing a tight, figure-hugging dress. Her long hair flowed from a blue silk turban.
I lingered in the doorway. The priestess deployed a psychic weapon against The Great Beast. A huge black jaguar emerged stealthily from the shadows at the eastern end of the chapel. The creature prowled towards Crowley.
He clicked his fingers. From the vaulted roof and the shadowy corners of the room came a writhing black cloud formed of thousands of bats. The creatures clamped themselves to the back of the jaguar. It writhed and snarled in pain.
'Go!' Katitia exclaimed.
Leaving the chapel, I was delighted to see Harry striding towards me. He was carrying a jerry can.
'What happened to the Railton?' I asked.
He smiled.

'Crashed into a tree at the first bend,' he replied. 'Couldn't keep up with the Bentley.'

'And the driver?'

'He survived the crash. I tied him up with my tow rope. Didn't kill him. Should have.'

'What's that for?'

'This you mean?' He lifted the jerry can. 'I keep it for emergencies and that's exactly what this is.'

Harry said that he intended to burn the chapel down, so that it could never again be used for diabolical purposes. It seemed like a good idea. I gripped the sovereign between my thumb and fingers. Its mysterious powers surged up my arm and into my body.

•••

I was flying. I was a graceful, long-winged bird with a curved beak and long, sharp talons – a buzzard.

Beneath me was the Ashdown Forest. It was a clear summer morning, a little after sunrise. I could see from this aerial perspective how the pine-tipped sandstone bluff was the natural extension of a landscape formed over millennia. It squatted on the glacier-smooth Weald between the North and South Downs.

I must have left the 21st Century, for there was no great house below. To the north, there was no sign of the metropolis of London either – merely an expanse of dark green woodland touching the silver ribbon of the River Thames as it broadened into a huge estuary.

I rode on currents of air experiencing the sheer pleasure of travelling weightlessly in this new element, dipping and swooping on invisible currents. My powerful eyes could discern meaning in the slightest movements and patterns below. Life, in many forms, was apparent on the heath – and so was death. The carcass of any creature would be fair game to my talons, as would other birds and smaller animals.

Even a buzzard eventually exhausts the pleasures of flight. I decided to seek a landing place. Where two tracks crossed at the highest point of the heath was a gibbet. It was a good place to settle.

Close by was a timber-framed building with a thatched roof. A sign proclaimed that it was a tavern – The Hatch Inn. It was a lonely spot for such an establishment but it was well-chosen, next to a crossroads where many travellers would pass. Adjacent to the tavern was a large, ramshackle barn.

•••

The door of the inn opened and three men emerged. The first was smartly dressed in a black jacket and breeches. He wore a wig and tricorn hat. He was carrying a document. His two companions were dressed in rough, homespun clothes. One of them was a giant of a man. He opened the door of the barn and his partner went inside. He emerged with three men attached at the ankles with leg irons. They were sad, ragged specimens – bloodied and bruised from ill-treatment. Their hair was matted, faces streaked with dung.

The man in the tricorn looked at the gibbet. He would not have been surprised to see a buzzard perched there. A white shape fluttered down to join me, a bird with a flat heart-shaped face and huge dark eyes – a barn owl.

'Good morning, Bill.'

It was strange to hear Katie's voice coming from a bird's beak.

'Here for the hanging?'

'It would appear so,' I replied.

'Let us watch. The crossroads is where the Devil likes to claim his own.'

The six mismatched men were making their way to the crossroads, the prisoners clanking along in their chains. It was a good place to signal a warning to others. Their bodies would be left dangling as they slowly decomposed.

Katitia and I moved to a branch on a nearby tree. We watched as three ropes were slung over the gibbet's crossbar. Stools were placed beneath each noose.

The man in the tricorn hat rang a hand bell, then spoke in a rich, deep voice:

'Oh yay, oh yay. As the Lord Lieutenant of the County of Sussex, I act by the powers vested in me by King George to enforce the laws of his realm. For those subjects who steal game, who are house thieves, cutpurses and highway robbers, no mercy will be shown. They will be taken to a common place and left to hang, in punishment for their malfeasance.

'As their bodies return to the natural elements, may their souls rise to a better place for the judgement that awaits us all. As we see today, all men must suffer the inevitable consequences of their wrongdoing. Let the common men be first, then the necromancer.'

The first prisoner was dragged to the gibbet. The giant lifted his head into the noose. With no ceremony, he kicked away the stool. The man's end would not be swift. This was a short drop, so that he neck would not break. He would suffer a slow death by strangulation as his face turned purple. He was still writhing as the second criminal was lifted into position.

Crowley was the third to be hanged. There was an odd expression on his face – indifference blended with contempt. The giant winced as he lifted the heavy body onto the stool.

My sensitive eyes had detected a ragged army approaching from the far distance, creeping through the trees. Thousands of ghosts had converged from all directions – the spirits of those who had been despatched at this lonely spot – poachers, cutpurses and house thieves – and other lost souls who were merely curious.

Crowley's weight meant that he died relatively quickly. His face turned almost black, his eyes bulging grotesquely. His yellow aura faded to grey, then flickered out, as his soul floated free from his human form.

•••

We heard a spine-tingling sound. Hooded men waving scimitars were running through the trees, shrieking blood lust. Each man was a blur of movement – they were masters of some deadly martial art.

They chopped up the phantasmal criminals in a matter of moments. Soon their severed heads were rolling on the forest floor.

I heard a crash. Katitia and I looked in the same direction. A huge Tyrannosaurus was smashing through the trees, snapping them like matchsticks. It gave a roar. A stream of liquid fire issued from its open mouth; the trees in its path burned like candles. We fluttered upwards, far out of reach of the black-cloaked warriors and the strange fire-breathing creature.

The Lord Lieutenant and his two henchmen were running for their lives across the heath. Half the wood was on fire now, issuing dense black smoke from an orange core. The dinosaur was destroying everything in its path.

48

Last Chance Saloon

Task: Aleister Crowley
Mission completed

That wasn't so hard, was it? You dealt with The Great Beast like a cat playing with a mouse. This means that you are a skilled, A-class predator, close to the top of the food chain. Well done my friend! An even more cunning adversary now awaits you and he can match you, power for power. I hope you're ready for him. Eat your greens and get to bed early! Good luck, amigo.

The White Lodge was exceptionally quiet. Most of the guests had left. I realised, standing in reception, that I now had no reason to stay. Strobe Kitson was clearly an unsavoury character – using people to achieve his goals in life: sex and money. Also, I didn't need to play a game to hang out with Anita; I knew her in real life. I could see her whenever I wanted to.
'Hi!'
As ever, she was in a cheerful mood. 'How are you?'
'I'm fine, thanks,' I replied pensively.
'How was the game?'
Did she know that we'd spent a week together sharing a bed in a cosy flat, and that we knew every inch of each other's bodies?
'It was challenging,' I replied.
'Did you see me sing?'
'I did. In a club in Soho.'
'And?'
'You were amazing. You have a fine set of pipes. Why don't you sing in real life?'
'Don't be silly, Chris, that's ridiculous. Have you seen the Mail?'
She handed me a copy across the desk. At the top of the front page was a teaser:

'Texas Vampire linked to teen's death. See page 6.'

'What does it say?'
'See for yourself.'
I took the paper and walked across the lobby.

•••

The story was dominated by a photo of a solemn mother and father. The mother was holding a photo of her son.

'Mystery of missing teen solved

Mick Mahoney loved video games. He wasn't the outdoors type and since he lived off the beaten track in Tasmania with his mum and dad, there wasn't much else to do.

Mick's parents, Ron and Robin, emigrated to Australia when he was nine. When he was fifteen, they moved to their current home in the small, remote town of New Norfolk on the island of Tasmania. Ron is a warden in the Southwest National Park and Robin works as a part-time carer.

Seventeen-year-old Mick left the family home in March with a ticket to London in his pocket. His dream was to turn his hobby into a job.

His parents drove him to the airport and said goodbye. They said they were sad but happy that he was doing what he'd always wanted.

At first, they received Tweets and e-mails. Mick had begun a blog describing his experiences in London. They followed his daily entries, until they abruptly stopped.

The last time Mick was seen alive was on 2nd April 2018 on the morning of his interview with CloudCorp at the company's City Road HQ.

It was the week of his eighteenth birthday. Mick confided in his blog that he was excited. He was applying for an opportunity to develop a new game that he'd seen advertised on a flyer, with a really cool company.

When the police raided CloudCorp's offices this week following a Daily Mail tip off, they made a grim discovery. A body had been dumped in a catering freezer. After an autopsy, it was confirmed that it had been there for more than a year. The body was identified as Mick's from photographs and dental records, with the Mail's help.

Ron and Robin are desperate to find out what happened to their son. They believe that CloudCorp has a case to answer – particularly Texan billionaire Strobe Kitson. He is out on bail, but that could soon change.'

•••

This was the final straw. I packed my bag.

I'd almost reached the front door of the hotel later when a familiar figure appeared, someone I really didn't want to see: Kitson.

'Hey, where are you going?' he asked.

'I'm leaving.'

'Leaving?' He seemed surprised. 'Why?'

I saw no reason to explain myself. I merely stood still, waiting for him to let me pass.

'The backpacker?'

'Yeh, the backpacker,' I replied stonily. 'And other stuff.'

'Other stuff?'

'Do I have to tell you?'

'Yes.' He paused and sighed, perhaps realising he'd been rather abrupt and continued more affably. After all, I was his success story.

'Well, listen, have a drink with me, or a coffee, or whatever. If, after that, you still want to leave, I won't stop you.'

Reluctantly, I went back to the bar with him. His face looked tired and drawn. He asked the barman to put a shot of Bourbon in his coffee.

He offered me a cigarette, which I declined, reminding him that smoking was not allowed in the hotel. He merely shrugged.

'Right, the backpacker. Let me explain...' He drew on his cigarette. 'This was when we were busy demoing Get The Bad Guys. One day last year, this young guy turns up on our doorstep. He's called Michael, or Mick. He's come all the way from Tasmania, for Christ's sake, and he's obsessed with video games. Naturally, we welcome him.

'The thing is, the early versions of the game sent some people into a deep sleep, almost a coma. They always woke up but one day Mick didn't. It was nothing to do with us. He had a congenital heart condition...'

'Why did you put him in a freezer?!'

'It wasn't me. I was furious when I found out. At that point, we didn't know what to do. He had no ID on him when he died, so there was no-one to get in touch with. Yes, we should have contacted the police. But we didn't. We ended up doing nothing, which was wrong. Very wrong. Hands up. I have to live with that. Have you read about the coroner's report?'

'How could I?'

'It confirmed that Mick had a heart defect – a defective aortic valve. The report said he literally could've died at any time.'

'That's no consolation to his parents!'

'I know that, and I know they hate me. They have every reason to hate me. I would. I'm going to meet them. I want to tell them my side of the story.'

'What about the orgy thing?' I asked suspiciously.

'What?'

'The sex parties at the hotel that they wrote about in the Daily Mail.'

'Do you believe what you read in that rag?'

'Not everything, no.'

'Yes, we had some parties and they may have got a bit wild, but I never forced anyone to take part. If they didn't want to, that was cool.'

'What about Anita?'

'What about her?' He stubbed out his cigarette. 'Look, I had a thing for her but she wasn't into me or the orgies – and that's okay. She's still working here, isn't she? I'm perfectly civil to her, like I always have been. I have enormous respect for her. Hands up, I like sex. I do. But I'm not a monster. And all this has cost me my marriage.'

'What do you mean?'

'Tammy is leaving me.'

I didn't say anything. He looked around the empty bar.

'What about your partner Chuck Tyler? The Mail said he's in hiding, in fear of his life.'

'Let me explain about Chuck. He's a genius but he's paranoid, always has been. As soon as the dollars rolled in, his drug use got out of control – coke, crack, MDMA, you name it. He became a recluse and bought a bunch of guns. He believes that everyone wants to kill him, especially the CIA – and, of course, me. I can't convince him otherwise. It's tragic.'

He lit another cigarette.

'I would love your band to play for me again.'

'Maybe.'

'And I need you to finish the game.'

'Why?' I asked.

'You know that Korean hacker I told you about? He's messed about with my code. Did you see anything strange last time you played?'

I thought for a moment.

'Yeh, I did actually. Little dudes in black cloaks with swords. A fire-breathing dinosaur.'

'Ninjas. That's the hacker – Moho's his name. That dinosaur has burned up most of southern England. There's one more piece of code. The hacker needs it, but it's hidden in the game and he can't find it. Since you are such a hotshot, Chris, I'm thinking you might be able to get to it before he does.'

'Where is it?'

'The code is hidden in the centre of an iconic monument, that's all I can tell you.'

'An iconic monument?'

'When you see it, you'll know...' Kitson finished his cigarette.

He stubbed it out and looked around the comfortable little world he'd created.

An awkward silence followed. I really wanted to just leave and to hell with it all. I was about to do so when Simon walked into the bar.

'Ah, here's your pool buddy,' said Kitson. 'Look, I'm gonna leave you. Stuff to do. Hope you don't mind... You don't think I'm a bad guy do you?' he added, giving me his toothy, crooked smile.

'Probably not.'

'Probably?'

Simon's entrance had changed things. Seeing him reminded me of the band and how much fun it was playing with The Lone Stars. Plus I hated unfinished business – I had to finish the game, whatever I thought of Kitson. So I told him I would stay.

Simon looked at us from across the room.

'I hope you guys will play another gig for me at the hotel with your hot little band.'

I said I'd have to ask Simon.

I guess I did really want to stay, I just didn't approve of some of Kitson's behaviour. But the hotel had become a second home. In the ballroom was a Ludwig drumkit, the best that I'd ever played and there was Anita too. Was I a bad guy?

Simon slouched across the room as Kitson left. He'd be itching to thrash me at pool.

49

Ten Pound Poms

Task: Abdullah Ismael Omar

> *Now, this is interesting – a full-blown international crisis. An evil dude is holding the world to ransom. This twisted playboy has a black belt in evil. He makes Aleister Crowley look like an amateur. You'll require a spy's tradecraft, street fighting skills, all your charm at the dinner table and your best magic just to get near him. Even then, they may not be enough. My advice? Look for a chink in his armour. Strike swiftly, grasshopper!*

Time: 1953
Lives remaining: 2
Special powers: Level 3

Her prow cut smoothly through the water, her lines smooth and clean. The SS Oronsay was the pride of the Orient Line, capable of carrying 1,500 passengers and travelling at 22 knots. She was painted in the line's colours with a buff hull, a white superstructure and yellow funnel.

The Oronsay left Tilbury Docks in London bedecked with Union Jacks on the day of Queen Elizabeth II's Coronation, 2nd June 1953. She was headed for Australia. The ship had already rounded the Bay of Biscay, steamed into the Mediterranean and crawled down the Suez Canal into the Red Sea. Next, she would cross the Indian Ocean before reaching her destination, Darwin.

I knew all these facts because I had gleaned them from my fellow travellers. The majority of them were 'Ten Pound Poms' – British people who had purchased a subsidised ticket in order to embark upon a new life in the Antipodes.

They would have begun the voyage with high hopes, waving goodbye to their misty-eyed relatives at Tilbury. Now the Egyptian sun was playing havoc with their pale skins. Most of them were red and blistered. Too enervated to play quoits on deck, they sought shadows or lay in deckchairs, dads in white shirts open at the neck, mums in cotton print dresses. Their children roamed the ships in gangs. They weren't all Cockneys – their accents were a gazetteer of Britain.

My cabin was in an obscure part of the ship, well beneath the water line. A drive shaft in a steel tube passed through it, gently quaking the hull. It was unnaturally hot; an electric blower merely pushed warm air around ineffectually. I slept well, considering. There was something reassuring about being encased inside a vast, humming machine.

•••

Why was I here? As usual in Get The Bad Guys, that was yet to be made clear. To the economy passengers, the Ten Pound Poms, I was a curiosity – an unattached male lacking a wife and a brood of children. The first-class passengers were equally puzzled but they were less inclined to talk to me, suspecting that I was member of the 'Ten Pound' contingent.

The first-class facilities were located in the forward section of the ship. This was a world of bridge games, cocktail parties, dressing for dinner and stilted conversation. The pride of first class was the Veranda Lounge, whose wood-panelled walls, attentive staff and starched tablecloths imitated a luxury hotel. Here, all tableware was monogrammed and everything had been polished to within an inch of its life. The most favoured guests, on the formal occasions that punctuated the voyage, would be allowed to sit in this well-favoured saloon at the Captain's Table – something to tell their grandchildren about.

Whoever had packed my large leather suitcase had given me multiple options. I had shorts, tennis pumps and light, short-sleeved shirts for outdoor purposes, a sports jacket and slacks for informal socialising but also a dinner jacket for more formal occasions. They had even provided me with a sun hat and some pink calamine lotion to protect my skin. Calamine was ubiquitous amongst the Ten Pound Poms. The mothers dabbed themselves and their children with it constantly, so that their skins were blotched with pink patches; its sweet marzipan smell filled the sun deck.

•••

For a few days, I simply relaxed, accustoming myself to the rituals and routines of the ship. After her week of crawling through the Suez Canal, the Oronsay was making up time, breasting the turquoise water of the Red Sea. The flat bluff lands to either side were a mystery. There were often electric storms, when bolts of white lightning crackled across the sky. But rain rarely fell. At night, the sky was encrusted with stars. They seemed so low that one could almost reach up and touch them. It was getting hotter and hotter. Those who knew said the temperature would cool once we had crossed the equator. For now, however, both days and nights were almost unbearably hot. Some passengers took to sleeping on the deck – or trying to.

If anyone asked me where I was travelling to, I told them that I was emigrating – I was a draftsman and had obtained a position in Darwin. If they asked me about my wife, I said that she and my two dear children were to follow, once I had established myself in the new land.

Out of sheer boredom, I began to take part in the ship's social activities. The economy lounge was frequently enlivened by games of bingo, beetle drives and children's parties, with sausage rolls and balloons. The first-class passengers put on dinner jackets and diaphanous dresses and danced to a small orchestra.

The huge advantage of these occasions was that the Veranda Lounge was somewhat cooled by languorous fans that attempted to push back the oppressive heat that rolled across the ship – a luxury unavailable in economy. I toyed with the idea of a shipboard romance, but then rejected it. There were few unattached females on the Oronsay, other than the pubescent girls who played hula-hoop on the sun deck and the wealthy maiden aunts who were using their private incomes to cruise in the tropics. It was like something out of an Agatha Christie novel.

•••

One night, an intriguing poster outside the Veranda Lounge caught my eye: 'Kitty Star and The Kittens – eight o'clock tonight!'. Beneath this announcement on the poster was a blurry photograph of a black female singer in a cocktail dress: Anita. It declared in tiny print at the bottom, 'Courtesy of Ember Records'. So, she had a recording contract. A light went on in my head; I sensed this concert would be key to my mission.

The Kittens were interesting, a scratch band assembled by the Orient Line. They looked like the kind of men one sees hanging around Soho – beatnik types with bright eyes and wispy goatee beards, only these guys were dressed for a wedding. The pianist was not really a jazz musician; he peered at his scores through thick-lensed spectacles. The drummer was so ancient and frail, he looked like he could've dropped dead at any moment – although, strangely enough, he seemed the most enthusiastic band member. His rhythm was as tight as a metronome. In the fast numbers, he spread the power of an express train through the rest of the band; in the slow ones, he swept his brushes over his skins like a pastry chef whisking a meringue.

The guitarist was Simon. In this incarnation, he too looked like a habitué of Soho coffee bars – a 1950s existentialist who would slope around in a duffel coat with the latest philosophy book in his pocket. He seemed ill at ease in the formal clothes he was required to wear as a Kitten. He had an arch-topped jazz guitar plugged into a vintage valve amplifier. In all the time that the band played, I never saw him even glance at his music. He was one of those players whose understanding is instinctive and intuitive. His left hand seemed to form complex chords naturally. The music simply flowed through his body into his fingers.

I was sitting on my own at a small round table close to the stage. At the beginning of the night, the Veranda Lounge was pretty sparse but as news of the beguiling, sexy singer spread through the ship, it soon filled up.

She wore a tightly clinging dress of shimmering red sequins. Her eyes were bright. Kitty filled the room with her presence, inspiring the band, who had seen better days, to play out of their skins.

She seemed to notice me once, although there was no recognition in her face. I was a stranger to her, but I'd been expecting that. She worked her way through a series of ballads, all featuring Simon's dextrous guitar. The band started out at a fast clip, then slowed down for songs that suited the melancholy yearning in her voice. One of the numbers was Lover Man, the song she'd directed at me in the Gargoyle Club and that we'd listened to endlessly in her flat in Balham, sung by Billie Holiday. After it ended, I applauded politely like everyone else in the room.

I noted that there was something strange about her demeanour – her eyes were glazed, as if she was not in the room.

•••

I realised that someone had joined me at my table. An Oriental gentleman dressed in a white linen jacket, he had a thin black moustache and large, sad eyes. He wore a silk tie embellished with red and yellow diagonal stripes.

I recognised my new companion from a dark, shabby boarding house in the East End, when I had been on the trail of Joseph Stalin. It was Culadar!

'Please don't get up, William,' he said. 'It is good to see you again, after all this time.'

'For me also,' I replied.

'She's good isn't she?'

He lit the Balkan Sobranie cigarette in his long holder.

'Too good for the Oransay. I think everybody here knows that. She is exceptionally talented. Did you think that she would recognise you?'

'Not really,' I said.

'Ah, you have become wise,' he commented. 'Almost as wise as me.' He gave his trademark laugh, like a harsh croak.

'All is not as it seems here, Mr Wilkins. I am sure that you are aware of that. You must have some questions.'

'I do, yes,' I said.

'Then would you like to join me for a night cap in my cabin?'

'I would.'

'Excellent.'

He rose to his feet.

People were surprised that we were leaving before the end of the performance that had made the hot, balmy night so special. Kitty did not register our departure.

Without a whisper of any kind of breeze, the stifling, humid air made it hard to breathe. The ship seemed to be following the direction of the Milky Way – the thick creamy band wrapped around the earth.

50

The Spell

It was cool in Culadar's cabin. He did not have to suffer, as I did, in the bowels of the ship, or like the poor creatures who flopped onto the promenade deck at night, gasping for air like stranded fish.

The cabin was luxuriously appointed in a modern, unfussy style – beech furniture, oatmeal fabrics and a few tasteful, well-chosen decorations.

'Take a seat Mr Wilkins,' said Culadar. 'Would you like a drink? A Singapore sling perhaps – that is what one drinks in the tropics, isn't it?'

Miraculously, a tall glass appeared, loaded with crushed ice and decorated with a slice of lemon.

'Chin chin,' he said, lifting his glass. 'By the way, you may be curious about my tie.'

I wasn't, but I let him continue. Not that I had much choice.

'It is that of the Marylebone Cricket Club, of which I am a member. I have two passions in life. One is jazz and the other is cricket.'

I wondered why he was telling me all this – some kind of preamble before he told me why he'd invited me to his cabin?

After he had returned his glass to the table, he filled his opium pipe.

'This does not count as a passion,' he said. 'It is an addiction.'

He lit the pipe. With his first inhalation, contentment seemed to flow into his small frame. Wouldn't the drug's sickly aroma insinuate itself into the corridor outside and attract suspicion? Quite possibly, but it wasn't my problem.

'I must cut to the chase,' Culadar finally said, blowing out a lungful of smoke. 'Kitty, as you observed tonight, has been placed under a powerful spell. She has been bewitched. By whom, you ask? Who would do such a thing to a poor, defenceless creature?'

He paused.

'The answer is Abdullah Ismael Omar. You may be wondering who he is?'

He didn't wait for my reply.

'Omar, as we may call him, is an Egyptian-born businessman. He is immensely wealthy, mainly from his interests in shipping and oil. Omar is utterly ruthless. He will remove any obstacle that gets in his path, by any means necessary. Blackmail, torture, extortion, murder, they are all grist to his mill – he has used all of them. It is said that he killed his own father. He also has formidable supernatural powers, acquired from certain nomadic tribes when he was living in the desert.

'Omar is on the radar of the security services because he is planning to bring down Colonel Nasser's government in Egypt, which will not only destabilise the Middle East but, potentially, the entire world. Not least, this will give him control of the Suez Canal. It is believed that he may have built a crude atomic fission device – an atom bomb – and that he intends to blow up something prominent, perhaps one of the pyramids, in order to impose his will. Needless to say, this cannot be allowed to happen.'

'I understand,' I said, 'but what does this have to do with Kitty?'

'An obvious question,' Culadar commented. His eyes widened as he drew on his pipe again. 'Kitty is his mistress – one of many. They met in Paris when she was singing in a club on the Left Bank. He can be very charming, as you can imagine. He showered her with vintage champagne and mink coats. She is totally under his spell. Literally, because, as I say, he has bewitched her.'

'What do you mean exactly?'

'Omar has used an ancient Arab curse to make her his golem. It means that she will do his bidding at all times and that she is immune to the charms of other men. Also, he controls her memory.'

'Can this charm be lifted?'

'Oh yes.'

'How?'

'Quite easily. Any man who makes love to her will restore her, instantly, to her normal senses.'

'You mean...'

'Yes, William, that is the role that has been assigned to you by the forces of light in this corrupted world. And I am here to help you.'

I began to speak.

He raised his palm.

'The Oronsay is to dock in Aden next week. By that time, you will have released Kitty from Omar's spell. The British authorities will be waiting there to fly both of you back to London. Kitty will be interviewed by MI6. They will quiz her on Omar's intentions, the names of his associates, his plans and so forth. You will then be sent to Cairo. Armed with the intelligence obtained from Kitty, you will check into the Shepheard's Hotel. That is where most British people stay in Cairo. You will make contact with Omar's Egyptian contacts or they will find you. You will infiltrate his gang and you will then...'

'What?'

'You will kill him.'

Culadar's laugh filled the cabin.

'Well, that's easy for you to say,' I commented, once the wheezing had subsided. 'How am I going to win Kitty's affections? She won't even look me in the eye.'

'Mr Wilkins,' Culadar said. 'I have thought of that and have come up with a solution. There is an infallible way to get to Kitty's heart and it will certainly work for you.'

'What is it?'

'Music. Or, in your case, the drums. By the way, would you like another drink?'

'It's rather late,' I said.

The opium fumes had made me light-headed.

'I understand. Time for bed. Oh, Mr Wilkins?'

'Yes?'

'Why don't you have a look in your pocket?'

I did. It contained a gold sovereign.

'Press on the coin, would you, in the privacy of your cabin. It will raise your powers to the fourth level. You will need them in order to defeat Omar. Believe me, he is a formidable opponent. Congratulations, by the way.'

'What for?' I asked.

'In pressing the coin, you will have acquired the fourth degree of The Ancient Order of The Sons of The Dragon. That is the highest degree. You will now be classed as a Master of The Order and an Ipsissimus – that is the state of spiritual acuity that Aleister Crowley reached, God rest his soul.'

'My life is now complete,' I said, with irony.

He smiled serenely.

'That is truer than you know, Mr Wilkins. I must counsel you to use your powers wisely in the trials that lie ahead. And, believe me, you will need all of them.'

I said that I would try, and left for my cabin.

51

The Stand-In

The follow morning, I followed my usual routine. I put on my white flannel trousers and deck shoes and went for breakfast, preferring to take the first meal of the day in the economy part of the ship, where the food was greasy but plentiful. Some of the families here had already befriended me and knew my name; the people in first class were merely curious about my position in the social hierarchy – whether I was above, equal to or beneath them. This would determine how they would talk to me.

Kitty would be a hard nut to crack in order to get to the next stage of the game. Culadar had said that music was the way to her heart. But how was that to be achieved?

As usual after breakfast, I wandered around the ship. Passing the Veranda Lounge, I was surprised to see the word 'Cancelled' daubed in black ink on a poster advertising tonight's repeat performance by The Kittens. This was worrying, especially as alarming rumours were flying round the ship that someone had been found dead in their cabin and taken to the ship's mortuary. Could the two things be connected? (Was I actually *in* an Agatha Christie novel?)

Through a purser, I located the ship's entertainment officer in his staff quarters. Fishing for information, I said how tragic it was about the death. Yes, he replied, poor old Sid, he had a dicky heart. What a shame about the band having to cancel tonight's gig, I commented. Yeh, Sid was a good drummer, an old-school jazz man, he responded. I'm a jazz drummer, I hinted, a professional (I lied). *How hard could it be?* I told him that I had lots of experience and that I possessed a dinner jacket. He was delighted and told me he'd arrange for me to rehearse with the band that afternoon, as a stand-in.

It was obvious that no-one had any expectation that I could play, especially Simon. The expression on his face made it clear that he thought my auditioning was a waste of time. However, as I played on one of the faster numbers, which had some tricky stops and fills, his expression softened. So, I could play. And I wasn't going to pop my clogs any time soon. That was a bonus.

When I turned up for the gig that evening in my penguin suit, Simon actually smiled. We were soon conversing like old friends, comparing musical experiences, discovering we were both from South London and around the same age, the youngest members of the band.

•••

As we began our first set that night, Kitty did a double take when she noticed it wasn't Sid sitting behind the drumkit. I'd studied the old boy carefully and, although our techniques and grips were different, I was able to copy some of his tricks. She liked that.

After the second set, we chatted as the band was packing up and, later, we shared drinks on the promenade deck. Kitty's expression was still glazed and there was no sign of her normal aura – which had been suppressed by Omar's spell.

But I had powers too – the considerable ones of an Ipsissimus. By talking to her and studying her face, I was able to sense the hypnotic power of Omar. Using the full force of my psychic influence, I could feel some of her free will returning.

Our gin cocktails helped, as did the abundant shooting stars and romantic glow of moonlight over the Red Sea. Kitty told me about her small flat in Balham and her old job; about how she had been spotted singing in the Flamingo Club in Wardour Street by a music impresario; and the agent who'd obtained a record contract for her and booked her to play on this cruise. She loved singing. She said she'd like to go to New York one day to see her musical heroes. I assured her that she would.

The following morning, she was a little stiff and cold with me. Omar's spell had re-asserted itself but I managed to wear down his influence again, mainly through making her laugh – something that he could never do.

The first-class passengers enjoyed the use of a small, private swimming pool, a suntrap at the ship's bow. We spent the afternoon there with Simon, swimming and drinking cocktails. Kitty looked adorable in her white swimsuit and film star sunglasses. Several passengers asked for her autograph and she graciously obliged. Simon read his book by the pool and smoked cigarettes, far too cool to show emotion.

That evening brought a tropical storm, with thunder and flickering tongues of lightning. To everyone's amazement, it began to rain in buckets. The economy passengers were cock-a-hoop, raising their sunburnt faces to the fat warm drops and laughing. It was just like being at home. The temperature had dropped from unbearable to merely uncomfortable.

We were soaking. Kitty asked if I would like to dry off – in her cabin. Her quarters were in first class, in the same corridor as Culadar's. We had no sooner pushed through the door than she pulled my body towards hers. The door snapped shut. We crashed back against the wall. My mouth found hers and my hand began to fumble in her clothes.

As we were about to fulfil our desires, my sixth sense detected a movement in the cabin. I ignored it – fatal mistake. I felt something hard impact the back of my head. Lights out, Chris.

•••

There had been someone hiding in the wardrobe. A bad guy, one of Omar's men. He must've been insinuated on the ship as a spy. And he had been waiting for us. Well, he wasn't going to kill me a second time.

I went straight back into the game for round two with the gorilla.

Task: Abdullah Ismael Omar
Time: 1953
Lives remaining: 1
Special powers: Level 4

'Would you like to come back to my cabin and dry off?'
Our clothes were very wet.
'I would. Thank you.'
Aware that I now had only one paltry life left, I followed Kitty down from the sun deck to the first-class cabins.

She fumbled with her key and went into her quarters. I hung back. I knew someone was hiding in the wardrobe.

'Kitty,' I said. 'Do you have a tie or a piece of rope, or something like that?'

'Oh, William...' she said, her tongue moistening her lips.

'No, it's not for that,' I said.

With a silk dressing gown cord, I firmly tied the wardrobe door handles together so they couldn't be opened from the inside.

We made love.

Afterwards, we slept.

When she woke in the morning, her manner was different. She was alert. Awake. Her shining aura had returned. She knew something had changed.

'What happened to me?'

'I'll explain later.'

We heard a muffled sound from the wardrobe.

'What was that?' she said.

'Someone is hiding in there. They're trying to kill me.'

'What?! Who?'

'Just somebody.'

I now had the ability to summon spirit animals to help me, as Katie had done in the chapel in the Ashdown Forest. What animals should I conjure up? Snakes? How about the nastiest, most venomous snakes known to man?

I thought hard and made it happen. In my mind, I could see the wardrobe filled with slithering, writhing creatures with sharp fangs.

We heard a scream. The man must've died from heart failure. When I opened the doors, his body toppled to the floor with a heavy thud. His eyes were wide with terror. Blood trickled from his nostrils and the side of his mouth. Lying next to him was a wooden cosh.

'Bill!

Kitty clasped my hand.

We had a serious problem – how to dispose of a corpse on a ship without attracting attention.

We were reflecting on this dilemma when a tremor rippled through the ship, like the aftershock of an earthquake.

52

Cairo

We could see fire licking around the funnel, where the Oronsay had already been hit in an aerial attack. To the east, an ominous shape was silhouetted against the luminous sky. It was an aircraft carrier.

Three more warplanes were on their way. They were white planes with red roundels – Japanese Zero fighters, familiar from my model making phase. The ship's klaxons sounded and people began running around in panic. Crew members were unfurling a fire hose on the foredeck where a column of dirty smoke was billowing from a jagged hole.

Nothing was going to save the ship. The lead Zero made its approach from the bow, so low that we could almost see the pilot. The first bomb destroyed the bridge, the second hit the section where economy passengers were sleeping – their bodies were flung over the side like chaff.

A terrified family ran past us to a lifeboat. A woman screamed. The second and third aircraft dropped their bombs. The crew members with the fire hose were blown to smithereens.

Passengers emerged from their cabins to the stench of burning and blood and body parts scattered across gangways and decks. A few desperate souls jumped into the sea.

'We're helpless,' Kitty cried desperately.

'Look!'

I directed her attention away from the stricken ship. Tracks of broken water were streaming towards us where the sea was being unzipped: torpedoes.

This was clearly the work of Moho – the man who had unleashed Godzilla and the Ninja warriors in the last level of Get The Bad Guys. He'd added a submarine to the Japanese aircraft carrier.

There were two explosions as the first, then second torpedo tore through the hull. The pride of the Orient Line was broken in two.

'Kitty?'

She had disappeared.

On the ship's rail in front of me was a large white eagle.

'I suggest that you shape-shift too,' said the bird. 'We can't do anything here. We'll have to escape.'

Using my special powers, I, too, transformed myself into an eagle.

●●●

We were above the listing ship. Its wailing sirens were like the cries of a dying animal. A thick black stain was spreading from its side. Ahead of us was a dense white cloud.

The bird whose astral body I'd assumed was far larger than the buzzard form I'd adopted in the Ashdown Forest. My outstretched wings were as long as a man.

We were at a high altitude. Ice burned our skin. The cloud was like a dense, freezing fog and Kitty was obscured. When I finally emerged into bright white light, she had disappeared.

Below, the Red Sea was a silver carpet laid across a world of shifting sands. I remembered my ink-stained school atlas – I knew that I had merely to follow it, with the rising sun to our right, to reach my goal.

Saudi Arabia, to the right, was a barren world but Egypt, on my left, was watered by the sacred Nile. It writhed through the khaki and buff landscape, widening into a sparkling delta of paddy fields to the north.

It was early morning when I descended. The ancient city grew closer and I noted the cliffs and escarpments solidified from sand and the plains scattered with hamlets of mud-baked cubes. Where the Nile touched the desert, it had sprung magically to life in a patchwork of green and brown strips, like twists of yarn.

Cairo is the mother of the world. The city was a jumble of brown and beige – a dead land breathed into life by water and sun. Here, the Nile was a stream of molten gold. I saw the City of The Dead, a sprawling cemetery in which families lived in stone mausoleums amidst the bones of their ancestors. Its citadel dominated the skyline – a great brown stump topped by the graceful silhouette of a mosque. Ancient spirits jostled with the living in a smoky confusion of donkey carts and car horns.

Culadar had told me that the Shepheard's Hotel was located in the Ezbekieh district – a part of the city dominated by colonial buildings, oases of emerald grass and banyan trees. A perfume market was hidden somewhere below in a covered bazaar. Its enticing scent would guide me to the right place.

The stone-fronted hotel was almost as vast and ornate as Versailles. Its name was picked out in metal letters that floated above a tower topped by a Greek pediment. Initially, I perched on the letter 'S' as I studied the waking city, breathing in perfume, traffic fumes and the sweet, rotting smell of decay.

A huge red sun was refracted through the shimmering mists that rose from the Nile as the morning call to prayer summoned the inhabitants of this dusty bowl. An echo of an ancient time that lived on, congealed in the mud and stone.

•••

Now I was in human form. I had chosen the persona of someone who'd be able to cope with heat, exhaustion and the attention of bad guys armed to the teeth – a 1950s secret agent.

My lightweight suit was pale grey, with a touch of mohair that made it shine. I wore a plain red knitted tie. My dark hair was cropped close to my skull. My lower face was darkened by bristle, half shading the faint white zigzag of a scar that, one would assume, was the result of a knife fight.

I was carrying a pistol – a Beretta that nestled in a leather holster beneath my left shoulder. I was no thug, however. I would fit easily into the society of the Shepheard's Hotel.

It was now evening. Residents and their visitors were gathering in the palm-fringed lobby like a flock of exotic birds at a waterhole. They were the city's elite en route to dinner or the opera. I mingled with businessmen in fezzes with their fur-wrapped Levantine mistresses, Egyptian officers in elaborate uniforms and European types in sweat-patched linen suits, listening to their conversations. I had no particular sense of purpose. I was simply waiting to see what the game would offer me.

The most fragrant and well-dressed of the hotel's patrons were clustered around the padded doors of the hotel casino.

Perhaps I should join them; there was enough money in my wallet to place a few bets. Why not?

A figure strode towards me. He was tall, in a spotless cream suit. Gold accessories, expensive cologne. He smiled.

'Name's Dillmore. Gordon Dillmore. Mind if I join you?' I felt like I was in a James Bond movie!

'Please be my guest,' I gestured.

He was in his fifties. His pale face was darkened, presumably from years in the tropical sun, and blotched from drinking spirits no doubt – I could detect stale whisky on his breath. I saw through him at once. Beneath the leathery skin and flashy smile, he was a chancer, an opportunist, the kind whose role in life is to hang around the wealthy, looking for a good bet. A man like him would rob a wealthy widow of her savings or leave a companion bleeding in an alley, in a heartbeat.

'Are you on business here?' he asked.

'Er…yes.'

'What kind of business?'

I tried to think of something so boring that it would deter further questions.

'Marine turbines,' I said. 'What about you?'

'Oil.' He was clearly lying.

He produced a grubby card from his wallet.

'My company is exploring drilling options in Yemen. But this Suez Canal business…'

'Yes, it's terrible isn't it?' I said.

'Lot of wogs in here tonight.'

I merely nodded. It was the disgusting term used by some colonials for Egyptians. He was the kind of narrow-minded bigot you would encounter in the bar of any English golf club, who would boast about his latest sports car and extra-marital affairs.

'Do you like the wheel?'

'I'm sorry?'

'Roulette? You're a baccarat man, are you?'

I mumbled something. Gambling was a complete mystery to me.

'They have a good table here.'

'Do they?' I replied vaguely.

His watery blue eyes swivelled to left and right. Like a crocodile, he was sensing his prey – some wealthy old lady to whom he could attach himself. I realised he was not alone. The hotel was a meeting place for every corrupt official, double agent, arms dealer and gigolo west of the Levant.

•••

We entered the gaming room behind a western woman wrapped in a sheath of red silk. She seemed too high rent for Dillmore; anyway, she was with an Arab gentleman, the kind who never spoke but exuded immense wealth and importance.

This was a place of hushed conversation and carefully observed rituals, of tight concentration and of cigarettes smoked to the nub. The click of balls and chips and the clipped calls of the croupiers were a reassuring backdrop.

Dillmore played roulette cautiously. There seemed to be no skill involved; it was merely a game of chance dressed up in the flummery of chips, tobacco smoke, French expressions and green baize.

I watched him until I'd grasped the rudiments of the game. My first bet was unsuccessful, as was my second. After my third, a single chip on red 7, I began to win steadily. By the time an hour had passed, a small crowd had gathered at the table to witness my spectacular good fortune. The audience included the blonde lady whom we'd admired on the way in.

Dillmore had lapsed into silence as my bets became more audacious. A final turn of the wheel quadrupled my winnings. I had no intention of losing them.

'Time to call a halt,' I said.

'Yes, indeed. Well done.'

I was soon holding an unfeasible quantity of grubby Egyptian currency, stained with the sweat of many palms.

'Look, I know a club near here,' Dillmore murmured. 'It's an after-hours establishment, if you know what I mean?' I nodded. 'Why don't we go there and celebrate your success? Perhaps this charming lady would like to accompany us?'

It was the blonde. He said her name was Geraldine. I saw in the tired, dim light of the casino that there were crow's feet at the corners of her eyes and that her hair was bleached. I could faintly detect the Home Counties in her accent.

I realised that they were working together. The Arab to whom she had previously been attached had merely been a stooge.

What they wanted was bulging in my jacket – a fortune in creased, dirty notes. I said I'd be delighted to accept Dillmore's invitation.

53

The Blue Lotus

Geraldine was hanging on my arm. Dillmore was in front of us – a tall white figure gleaming in the dark. Above the Ezbekieh Gardens a full moon hung in the star-clustered sky.

It was hard to breathe. There were so many smells here: exotic scents from the Orient, rare spices, piles of rotting vegetables and suppurating offal. Geraldine tottered on her high heels as we crossed the romantic square, giggling and pulling down on my arm.

Wagh el Birket, our destination, had been the pride of Cairo in the days of the Belle Epoque. Now the street was a seedy red-light district. Its imposing buildings, with their colonnades and wrought iron balconies, had succumbed to rust and grime. Dubious establishments enticed one down a gaudy crimson tunnel. Our destination, by contrast, was marked by a sign of startling sapphire – The Blue Lotus.

Dillmore was clearly known here. He gestured Geraldine and I down a narrow corridor. Incense, smoke and the pulse of amplified music greeted us. The 'club' itself was simply a large room. It was in near darkness apart from the light of cabaret lamps on small circular tables. This must be one of the lowest dives in Cairo – the kind of place that British soldiers had been lured into, to be fleeced of their money in the last two world wars.

We selected a table, and a pubescent girl with bare brown midriff appeared to serve us. A group of musicians wearing fezzes and white suits was getting ready to play on one side of the room, although there was scarcely space for them.

I was squeezed into a cramped space next to Geraldine. Her accent had coarsened to pure Guildford under the influence of alcohol and she was now pawing at me. Dillmore brought his mouth to my ear. What was he saying? Something about a cocktail – the house drink. He grinned like an ape when it arrived. The colour of the liquid should have been warning enough. It was bright blue – a Blue Lotus.

The band struck up a tune and, to the popping rhythm of a tabla, the floor show, a dwarf, materialised. I was thirsty and had gulped down half my cocktail. The effect was instantaneous. The dwarf began to spin. As he did so, flakes of colour emanated from his white dress-like tunic and bounced into the corners of the room.

The conscious part of me knew that I had been drugged. Shimmying snakes of light lit up an array of ghastly faces. I noted, to my horror, that Dillmore's head had transformed into a skull. I could see through his skin, into his eye sockets and down to the roots of his yellow teeth. Geraldine had transformed into a carefully coloured anatomical model – her body was a delicate tracery of muscle and sinew.

My skin appeared to have turned to rubber. I had the unnerving ability to stretch my arms across the room. I could actually see, in slow motion, the notes the musicians were playing and *hear* the colours radiating from the dwarf's dress.

The dwarf bounced away. A gorgeous apparition now took the floor – a tall, amber-skinned beauty of the Nile. Her hair was coiled into tight black ringlets. Carefully drawn lines extended to the sides of her face in the pattern of the Eye of Horus. She was stunning. I could discern all of Egypt's greatest beauties in her shining face – Isis, Hathor, Nefertiti, Cleopatra.

To the sensuous rhythm of the tabla, she began to grind her hips. The voluptuous curve of her belly was the most alluring thing I'd ever seen. It was painful to tear my gaze from her writhing stomach, but I did – and looked at her face, which now appeared feline. It was that of the goddess Sekhmet, the lioness. And someone else. I was looking into the soul of Anita and Kitty. Her dark eyes invited me to plunge into them.

•••

I'm in a shuttered, stifling room, its air polluted by smoke from an oily lamp. Midsummer. Cairo. A baby lies in a wooden crib at the foot of a bed. The room is in darkness. It's empty, save for the baby. Most of the family's domestic life takes place here – a cramped space that serves as a combined living room, bedroom and workshop.

Here the baby's mother sews all day, close to his rocking cradle. He hears the reassuring click of the machine as she pushes the treadle with her feet. From time to time, she lifts him and clutches him to her bosom. She coos soft words and feeds him milk. He is a beautiful boy, her cherub. He gurgles with delight.

She sews for hour after hour as the sun tracks the sky, throwing shadows across the stuffy, closed-in room. The narrow side street where they live, close to a mosque, is always noisy. The prayers of the muezzin punctuate his days and the life and commerce of the busy street.

It is a world of smells. From the street come odours of drains, offal, putrid fish and rotting fruit. There are also the aromas of dust raised by the rain after a thunderstorm, of fresh pollen, of incense burning in the market and of his mother's lily of the valley perfume.

The apartment is permanently occupied by an army of brown, winged beetles. Sometimes, his mother must brush them from the baby's face. Bugs, too, live in mattresses and pillows, leaving spots of human blood on the wallpaper where they've been squashed. And flies. Millions of flies in thick, black swarms.

Above all, this locality is famous for its rats – armies of the creatures, bloated from the rich pickings in the street. Sometimes, his mother sees rats in the apartment. She chases them away. She says that there are holes in the wainscot and floorboard. His father must fill them in now that there is a baby. But he says there are no holes – they're merely in her imagination. Does he not have enough work to do?

Each night, his father snores. Mother and baby hear, from beneath the floor and behind the walls, the scratching of tiny rodent feet.

When evening falls, she places him in his homemade cot. A key turns in the door. It is his father. He does not like it when his father arrives.

Night after night, he hears their voices arguing. His mother is unhappy. Her voice picks at the man's. His deep voice responds. How dare she challenge him and say that he is not a man, she who is nothing but a needlewoman! Isn't it enough that he works like a dog, for a miserable pittance? Sometimes, he hears thumps and screams. His mother cries. When he is sad, his mother comes. She speaks to him in her own soft tongue, French. She sings him a lullaby, pulling him to her bosom.

Tonight, they are arguing again. Their discord invades the dark, stuffy room. He stirs. He is too hot beneath his woollen blanket. He hears a rustling sound. It is close to his head. He is afraid.

The rat jumps from the green eiderdown that covers the bed. The baby feels its soft, brown body move across his face, pressing on his mouth like his mother's breast. He sucks at the rat's matted belly. Something is wrong. No milk comes. The rat shifts. Its yellow teeth pick at the dried milk on the baby's lips. The baby breathes in a gulp of air. Its large, brown eyes flicker open, as wide as a full moon. The rat bites him.

The baby's scream is more piercing than any his mother has ever heard. She leaps from her bed and leans over the cot. In the dark, she detects a shape. It moves. She refuses to believe, for a moment, what she is seeing.

His mother's shriek fills the apartment. Later, she cries. She mops the baby's blood-spotted mouth, holding him close. His father watches, silently.

54

Bewitched

I was tied to a bed in a hot, airless room. My nostrils could detect the scent of Cairo – a bouquet of fruit, spices, tobacco and traffic fumes. From outside came the cries of vendors and hubbub of conversation – a street market. I could tell it was night-time. This was a nocturnal city. People liked to shop and socialise once the fearsome heat of the day had subsided.

I was gagged and my eyes blindfolded. I'd been trussed up tightly with cord, I could feel, and, from shaking my bonds, it appeared this in turn was attached to the bed frame with chains. Whoever had imprisoned me was taking no chances.

Was it my new friends, Gordon and Geraldine? No, this would not be their modus operandi. Their style would have been to trick me into a false romantic liaison – I would've woken up one morning in a hotel room and found that the faded blonde bombshell had vanished with my money and Rolex Oyster.

Using my special powers, I could have turned myself into the world's strongest man or any creature from the animal kingdom and freed myself in an instant. However, these means of escape were not available. Psychic as well as physical bonds had been placed on me. My mind was cloudy and sluggish. Under the wicked enchantment of Omar, I'd been turned into an automaton, a golem, as Kitty had been, appearing normal but deprived of human volition.

Hours passed, it seemed. The street market became silent. I heard muffled voices in a room below. The hours were punctuated by calls to prayer. My brain was pressing itself against my skull. I was tormented by thirst. My throat was like a cracked pipe.

I knew Omar would kill me soon. Why had he kept me alive for so long? Was it merely to enjoy my suffering? He enjoyed killing...What kind of torture would he use?

Hours or days later, as if from the depths of a dream, I felt the bed creak. This was it. I clenched my muscles.

'Bill?'

It was Kitty!

With infinite care, she untied me and removed the gag and blindfold. The light hurt my eyes. My body was aching in every conceivable place. She gave me a cool drink that tasted of lemons. We made love.

•••

'Thanks,' I said.

The act of love making had released me from Omar's spell.

'It was my pleasure. I was only returning the favour that you did me.'

Kitty lay next to me naked. It was far too hot for clothes.

This really was a miserable room, filthy and ill-furnished. Light barely struggled through a grimy window. The busy street that I'd heard as I'd drifted in and out of consciousness was two floors below.

'Where are we?'

'In Giza,' Kitty said. 'It is a poor part of Cairo, where the pyramids are. This is the quarter of the city that Omar grew up in. In fact, he lived with his parents in this room. He has retained the building to remind him of where he came from.'

'It's not exactly luxurious.'

'They lived in extreme poverty. Omar's mother was French. She was a seamstress. She used to sew in this room. His father was a poor labourer.'

'And a violent bully?'

'Oh yes, he beat both Omar and his mother regularly.'

'I know.'

I told Kitty about my dream. She nodded:

'That happened here, in this room. You travelled back in time on the astral plane. It is those experiences that made Omar what he is.'

'So, he's seeking vengeance on humanity because he was deprived of paternal affection and was abused by his brutish father.'

'Exactly.'

It was a familiar pattern, I thought, in the lives of bad guys. Should they still be considered evil?

•••

The door opened. An unshaven man in a stained brown djellaba and yellow slippers curved at the toes wandered into the room. He was very relaxed and still chewing his breakfast by the looks of it. In his hand was a vicious-looking knife.

He froze at the sight of a naked woman on the bed.

That gave us some time.

Presumably it was Omar's men who'd taken off my trousers and jacket and folded them on a chair. Why hadn't they taken my gun from my trouser pocket? Evidently so confident of the powerful spell under which I'd been placed, they didn't think it necessary.

By the time the man in the djellaba saw my Beretta, it was already in my hand. I fired. He looked down as an arc of blood scythed from his thigh. The sound must have alerted his partner in crime as we heard movement in the room below.

Kitty crossed to the window.

When the second man entered, he saw his stricken comrade on the floor. The threadbare carpet was now red.

The window was wide open.

•••

Kitty and I were flying high above the city through a bright, cloudless sky. I saw that Giza was attached to the southern side of Cairo. Its narrow streets were squeezed between the Nile and the desert.

To the west of the conurbation was a triangle of dust; rising from it, as if moulded from sand, were The Pyramids and The Great Sphinx. An army surrounded them on all sides. Parked around the perimeter were lorries and jeeps, some with white US army stars on their bonnets. Tanks had spilled from the road to the south onto the parched field. In front of them, hundreds of soldiers were standing in neat rows. They were all facing in one direction, their rifles and machine guns trained on the largest of the pyramids.

The men and machines seemed very still. When we flew closer, we saw that the men were frozen. Flies were crawling across their faces.

The largest structure, The Great Pyramid, was glowing. A bead of amber brilliance was pulsing from its core as if its stone walls were opaque. At its apex, fashioned from orange and yellow light, was something that amazed me – a perfectly formed outline of a familiar shape seen on any American dollar bill, the all-seeing eye.

What was going on? Well, I knew one thing. Only Omar could've turned his enemies into an army of dolls.

Kitty had assured me that an astral body had no mass in the physical realm and could pass through walls. Was this true? I asked myself. Now was the time to find out.

55

Black Aphrodite

I was standing in a passageway inside The Great Pyramid. It was lit by dim electric bulbs. The atmosphere was surprisingly cool – not clammy or claustrophobic, as I'd feared. The walls were formed of grey limestone blocks that had been meticulously cut by skilled artisans.

This reassuringly vast structure had been built to last. The stone-lined vault was a haven from the heat and confusion outside. The chamber was the height of four men but only about four feet wide. Its walls curved gracefully inwards meeting at the roof. It was about a hundred yards long, its floor sloping upwards. At the end of this stone gallery, a yellow light glowed faintly.

I made my way towards it. I only had one life left now – I had to be careful. Hearing a man's voice, I travelled the last few feet on my hands and knees. My heart was in my mouth. Kneeling on a stone step, I peered into a large room.

There were two men in there and one, in a stained khaki shirt, had his back to me. When he moved aside, I saw his companion. This fellow wore a pale brown suit. His hair was cropped close to his skull. His lips were moist and pink. The hazy glow around his head confirmed that this was an individual of enormous psychic power.

Behind the men was a crudely chiselled stone trough about seven feet long. It was glowing at the base as if it was red hot. Something of enormous power was held within. What could it be? No doubt it was The Arc of The Covenant or The Seventh Seal or The Spear of Destiny.

Close to them was a more mundane object, a wooden box with a T-shaped plunger – a detonator. A thick black wire trailed from it, leading through the doorway and into the passageway.

The man in the brown suit was staring into the other fellow's eyes, talking in a low monotone. He lifted the man's wrist and pointed at the dial of his watch. One hour, he was obviously saying to him. One hour. The glassy-eyed expression of his companion told me that he had been entranced. It was his job to push the plunger. This, I guessed, would activate a giant explosion that would reduce the pyramid to rubble. By that time, the man who had hypnotised him would be a long way off.

It was time to make my presence felt.

I had entered the room not wearing a suit but a long white robe and sandals. I carried a sword. The man in the khaki shirt screamed, released instantly from his spell. I had no ill intentions towards him. He scampered down the passageway.

Using my elevated powers, I caused fire to burn around the edges of the room. I spoke in a deep voice:

'I am Petosiris, the High Priest of Thoth, scribe and necromancer, answerer of the unanswerable.' I had no idea where these words had come from. 'Dost thou understand?'

'You are not Petosiris!'

The flames illuminated Omar's face. His dark eyes didn't blink.

I didn't speak but merely placed my hands around the pommel of my sword. Omar continued:

'It has been interesting watching your puny attempts to foil me!'

He spoke in Classical Arabic with no trace of a Cairo accent.

'I understand that you are a good lover. But Kitty is a whore. Her fires are easily lit.'

I didn't rise to the bait.

'Oh dear,' he continued, sneering. 'Your masquerade is wearing a little thin, don't you think? Kitty is a vulgar woman of the streets, nothing more. Once I have dealt with you, I will take pleasure in killing her and that pestilence, Culadar.'

He was staring at me, his dark eyes probing deep into my soul. His head glowed like the heart of a furnace, indicating his enormous powers. At the core of this man was an intense evil.

I tensed myself.

He must have sensed that my psychic defences were holding him at bay.

'Dost thou fear me, Omar?'

'Of course not.'

'You should. Before the sun rises, your soul will be weighed in the balance by Anubis. If it weighs more than a feather, you will be cast into the fiery pit.'

'Do you think that I am afraid?'

Our powers were matched, spell for spell.

'You are due for a reckoning, idolator,' I said.

'Really?'

Did I see a look of doubt in his face?

With a quick movement, he reached into his jacket and pulled out a pistol. I allowed him to discharge an entire magazine into my chest. The bullets passed through me and ricocheted away. Six cartridge cases clattered on the floor. I looked at them dismissively:

'Heed my words, killer of thine own father.'

He registered no surprise that I knew this fact from his biography. But I could only hold him for a moment. I must seize the initiative before he shape-shifted or summoned an evil spell. What was he most afraid of?

Rats. I summoned the creatures from the four cardinal points – lean, desert rats and slimy, bloated creatures, fat from the sewers of Cairo. In a thick, endless column, they flowed up the corridor and swarmed into the granite-lined chamber.

He showed an emotion now. Terror. The creatures clambered up his legs. A scream came from his lips.

'*Maman!*'

He fell backwards, obscured by a carpet of moving pelts.

I could tell, from the sucking, squelching sounds I could hear, that the rats were tearing into his face.

•••

Outside, the dusty brown landscape had come back to life. Kitty was standing at my side. For some reason, she was wearing her stage clothes – a clinging dress of shimmering red sequins.

The British army officer standing in front of us could not avoid glancing at her chest. He was a tall fellow with red hair and pale skin. He offered me a handshake. His grip was limp. He was one of the intellectual kind of army officers – not the square-jawed macho type.

'My name is Hall, Captain Tom Hall of The Royal Engineers,' he introduced himself. 'We really can't thank you enough.'

The British and American soldiers had woken from their soporific spell, smiling with relief and brushing sand from their uniforms. The air was filled with the smell of diesel as lorries and tanks fired up their engines.

The Great Pyramid was no longer glowing. It was 'merely' a vast stone edifice, casting an afternoon shadow across the world. Hall's men, a company of engineers, were on their way, threading through the pyramid's narrow passages. Their job was to defuse the bomb that Omar had placed in the lower chamber. It would take several hours. Other men, wearing white masks and overalls, would bring out his body.

'I still don't know how you did it,' Hall said in amazement. 'By the way, your girlfriend has been telling us all about you.'

I had reverted from robes to my shiny tight-fitting suit, with a touch of mohair.

'Can I offer you two a lift back to town?'

I looked at Kitty. She smiled.

'Staying at Shepheard's, I presume?'

I nodded.

'Tell you what,' Hall said, 'I'm sure we can get you and Kitty flown back to the UK by BOAC. It's the least they can do. After all, you've saved the western world haven't you? I've a feeling that you're going to be a bit of a hero when you get back home.'

He grinned, showing his crooked teeth. The British are not adapted to hot climates. His spindly white legs, exposed beneath his khaki shorts, looked absurd.

Soon, we were rattling down a rutted road in a jeep, heading into Cairo.

•••

Kitty dived gracefully from the deck and slid, like an arrow, through the crystal clear, turquoise water. She surfaced and swam around the boat. She seemed perfectly at home in the sun-soaked Mediterranean, a black Aphrodite.

'Come in, Bill!'

I squinted into the sun. Behind Kitty was the Bay of Mirabello. It was fringed by a crescent of yellow sand and the crisp white houses of a picturesque fishing village, Agios Nikolaos.

Britain's national airline, BOAC, had done just as Captain Hall had predicted. They'd flown us from Cairo to Crete in one of their Short S.45 flying boats. As one of their employees, I had the use of the company's villa and its yacht. We were staying here for a few days before returning to London.

'Are you coming in or not, lazy bones?'

She pretended to look cross.

'I'm thinking about it.'

She turned as if to swim away.

I knew that I loved her now. Since the business in Cairo, I hadn't wanted to be separated from her for a moment.

'Well, OK then.'

I stood up. My borrowed green trunks were too big and threatened to fall down. I glanced at the houses on the quay and the multi-coloured fishing boats. There was certain to be a restaurant there that sold locally caught fish. Tonight, we would stroll down from the villa and have a meal there.

I had made a decision: during the meal, I would ask Kitty to marry me.

'Here goes!' I announced.

Kitty frowned. She liked to mock how clumsy I was. I launched myself from the deck.

For a moment, the bay was upside down and the perfect white and blue world span around my head.

56

Arise, Sir William

'At a ceremony in Buckingham Palace yesterday, Her Majesty Queen Elizabeth conferred a knighthood upon London businessman William Wilkins. The ceremony was attended by the Prime Minister, The Right Honorable Sir Anthony Eden, members of his cabinet, the Privy Council and Sir William's fiancé, the jazz singer Kitty Simpson.

Sir William is an executive of the British Overseas Airways Corporation, responsible for the company's middle eastern routes. He was chosen for his knowledge of local customs and the Arabic language to be Britain's chief representative in crucial negotiations with Adbul Ismael Omar.

Mr Omar had threatened to destroy the Pyramid of Cheops in Giza unless his demands were met in full by the British, French and American governments by 11am last Friday. He was killed in a gunfight on Saturday.

A Foreign Office spokesman said: 'Omar was only seconds from detonating the bomb himself in the King's Chamber – the act of a desperate, cornered man. It was only Wilkins' bravery in entering the pyramid and his calmness and ingenuity whilst in grave danger that saved the day. It is a debt that cannot easily be repaid.'

The Times, 30th July 1956'

Bonus Task: Save Jimi Hendrix

You've already done more than could reasonably be expected of one person. So, thank you. Here, in appreciation, is my gift to you – look on it as a bonus track. You don't have to fight anyone. In fact, you have the opportunity to save someone's life.

You'll get to share a stage with one of the most gifted musicians and coolest human beings ever and to use your special powers to their full effect.

So here's the deal:

You are the drummer in a rising UK rock band in 1970. It's a four-piece – guitar, bass, keyboards and drums – called The Strollers. You are one of the hippest bands around. Your guitarist, Simon, combines a blistering attack with speed and fluency and is always melodic. Your rhythm section, drums and bass, delivers a bigger punch than Bonham and Jones but you are also soulful and psychedelic. Your music seems to contain hidden, secret harmonies. It hints at the truths of the universe. On a good night, no-one can follow you. That's why you have just played the Isle of Wight Festival and your first LP, Purley Way, is rising up the charts.

Tonight is the biggest and most high-risk challenge of your career. Your manager, Bernie Solomon, found you playing in a pub in South London. He looks like a hippie but he's an old-school Tin Pan Alley huckster. He's pushing your career as fast as he can – better clubs, gigs in rock venues, your first festival – not minding who gets hurt or pushed out of the way in the process.

This gig was his idea. Fill the Camden Hippodrome, an old variety theatre now a music venue, with your fans. Invite Jimi Hendrix to come and play with you. See who is better – Simon or Jimi? It's a challenge and a provocation. Simon hates the idea. He thinks it's a cheap, tawdry gimmick and he doesn't want to play. You are the peacemaker and diplomat in the band. You and Simon go back years. Usually, you can get him to change his mind.

On this particular night Jimi is with his German girlfriend, Monika Dannemann, in her apartment at the Samarkand Hotel in Notting Hill. He has been brooding over whether to accept the challenge and play in Camden for a week. His people have advised him not to and he's been sitting on the fence. However, he admires The Strollers and he wants to try something new. His girlfriend thinks it's the wrong choice. She has been urging him not to go out.

Just before eight o'clock, Jimi makes up his mind. He'll do it. He grabs his guitar, hails a black cab on the street and heads for Camden. It's a decision that will save him from dying from *asphyxiation after ingesting his own vomit in his sleep. Tonight's show is your chance to meet a unique human being who combines an amazing musical gift with spiritual enlightenment – and to rock your socks off. If it succeeds, you will give him a good night and open a new door that he can go through. Good luck dude.*

Time: 18th September 1970
Lives remaining: 1
Special powers: Level 4

The theatre balconies were quaking. The place was rammed from the stalls to the gods. From backstage, we could smell the dope and patchouli oil fumes wafting from the audience. Tribes of long-haired blokes and hippie chicks were expressing their allegiance to Simon or Jimi, like a football crowd. Some jokers were chanting 'Hank! Hank Marvin!'.

It was half past eight, thirty minutes after we were supposed to go on. Simon was clenching and unclenching his hands. Bernie was glancing at him every so often, like a nervous parent, not saying anything. I could see what was going to happen. Simon would refuse to play, and Bernie would explode.

•••

The chanting from the auditorium was growing louder. Tension was building. It was so thick you could taste it.

I crossed the dressing room to where Simon was sitting. My clothes were full-on hippie: tight purple trousers that ended in extravagant flares, black velvet jacket, cheese cloth shirt. I was bedecked with beads and bangles.

'Mate, I wanna talk to you,' I said, sidling up to him.
'What?'
Simon looked at me as if I'd just killed his pet rabbit.
'I know you don't want to play, why should you? I dig that. I just wanna tell you something, okay?'
'Right, okay, tell me then.'
'No, not here, we need to be somewhere private.'
Simon sighed. He brushed some ash from his flares and stood up. Bernie gave us a withering look and didn't say anything.

'It's cool,' I said to him. 'Just give us a minute.'

In the toilet, I placed my hands on Simon's shoulders.

'What the fuck are you doing?'

'Wait.'

I stared into his grey eyes now, seeing through the face that he presented to the world – that of a complex, troubled soul.

'Breathe out.'

A waft of cannabis resin filled the cubicle.

'You *are* good, you know. Very good. You make Clapton look like a beginner. He's a copyist. *You* are an original.'

He knew that already. I placed my hands at the sides of his head.

'I, servant of Hathor, High Priest of Thoth, pass to you my earthly and unearthly powers. They are yours to use until sunrise.'

Sparks seemed to crackle between my fingers and Simon's temples. His pupils swelled. I had temporarily transferred to him the full abilities of an Ipsissimus. They included sublime musical proficiency on any instrument.

•••

We walked back into the dressing room. It was twenty to nine. Ben was standing up, double-checking his bass. He was evidently anxious.

Bernie checked our expressions.

'It's OK,' I said. 'We're fine.'

'What about Simon?'

'He's good to go. He's looking forward to playing.'

Bernie must have thought that I'd slipped the Croydon guitarist some exotic powder.

There was a new intensity to the chanting. The long-haired guys in the balconies were stomping like wild animals. The whole building was shaking. It wasn't hard to guess the reason.

From the wings, we saw that Jimi, dressed in his famous Hussar's military jacket and red flares, was making his way through the audience. A white spotlight picked him out as one of our roadies took his guitar and helped him onto the stage. He looked at the Marshall stack and the Premier drumkit on its riser.

His favourite pedals had been attached to his amp. He smiled, acknowledging the awe that was flowing through the theatre.

He caught Simon's eye.

'Come on, man.'

A yellow silk bandana was tied round Jimi's head. A cigarette smouldered from the headstock of his guitar. Simon was terrified. He was stuck to the floor. After I'd pushed him on, a roar surged through the theatre. The chants for Simon were as loud as those for Jimi. Blinded by light, we took our positions.

There was a set list taped to the floor, but I barely glanced at it that night. Simon looked at me, then at Jimi. Jimi mouthed something – Third Stone from The Sun. Luckily, I knew the song quite well. I counted us in.

57

Reality

Only when we shall have reached the absolute Consciousness, and blended our own with it, shall we be free from the delusions produced by Maya [illusion].

H P Blavatsky

After a gig that's gone well, I always want to smoke. Anything. Perhaps it's because one has touched eternity and so drawing down a small portion of death doesn't matter. After this gig…well, as an Ipsissimus my mind had been neurologically connected to those of each member of the band, to Bernie, to Jimi's girlfriend watching him proprietorially from the wings, to every member of the audience, even to the theatre manager concerned about the Hippodrome being trashed tonight.

The music had been a pulsing, whirling lotus flower, both radiating and receiving energy. I had been at its centre, the heartbeat of a coruscating universe, expanding and contracting within an infinity of musical textures, colours and polyrhythms that I was reflecting and yet controlling.

Guitar, mellotron, synth, organ, bass and drums were an orchestra of infinitude. The call and response of slave ship chants were evoked by the curious, bewitching intervals of our interweaving guitar lines. Words that had never been written formed in our mouths as songs. They would've been captured on film and tape. But that did not matter. What mattered was in the present. Music was moksha, nirvana, shanti, the Holy Ghost. Music approximated and embodied an infinite and ineffable truth – the life spirit.

•••

'Chris?'
Anita was on the phone, calling from reception.

I had watched the TV screen in my hotel room, passively, as a blizzard of announcements embellished with golden stars had informed me that I had 'won' Get The Bad Guys and that a million dollars were now mine. I had listened to Strobe Kitson's louche Texan drawl congratulating me in a slippery manner, while watching slow motion films, in my head, of him collapsing and being manhandled into a lift and of a rocket exploding. The guy was a huckster. Why the hell had I trusted him?

'Chris. Are you OK?'

'Yeh. Christ, I need a smoke.'

'Well come to reception, darling.'

I walked down the staircase, which was lined with a pantheon of Freemasons – Louis Armstrong, Buzz Aldrin, Winston Churchill, Sir Christopher Wren.

I saw Anita behind the desk. Emotion welled through me. Our mouths touched in our first real-life kiss. We rushed to her room.

I was drawn into the plenitude of Anita – a drowning man being revived by the gift of breath...

Later, as we smoked, I could not find the words to describe what had just happened to me. Perhaps I never would. But it didn't matter. As we lay there, I felt completely at peace, fulfilled.

•••

'Have you seen this?!'

She handed me a copy of that morning's Daily Mail.

Two words – 'Death Cult!!' – were splashed across the width of the front page. Beneath was a blurry photograph: figures in white zip-up suits removing bodies from CloudCorp HQ:

> 'Eleven bodies have so far been recovered from a sealed vault which was discovered last night at the CloudCorp offices in City Road. Police and forensic officers raided the offices last night. The vault was sealed off behind a wall. The Daily Mail has learned that the bodies, stored on shelves, had been eviscerated and their brains removed.

A police spokesperson confirmed: 'These are not ancient bodies – paupers or plague victims. They're people who have only recently died. The worrying thing is that their organs have been removed, perhaps ritualistically, for reasons that are not yet clear. The victims are predominantly male. DNA samples are being taken.'

Strobe Kitson, CEO of CloudCorp, was not at his Holland Park home last night. The Metropolitan Police have issued a warrant for his arrest. They are searching for missing persons believed to have attended interviews with CloudCorp, a software and video game company based in Texas.

Last week, a coroner returned an open verdict on the death of backpacker Michael Mahoney, whose body was discovered at the chapel in June. It is likely that the investigation into his death will now be re-opened.'

'Fuck,' I said.

There were a few things in my room that I needed before we left for good, as we'd decided to do (especially after this). Anita had already packed. We walked to her Kia in the car park and drove away from the hotel. We looked back at the building and silently said our goodbyes.

At first, she seemed reluctant to talk on the drive back to her house. I was half apprehensive and half excited that a new chapter of my life was about to begin, but Anita wasn't responding to my questions. A heavy gloom settled over us. I couldn't focus on the china blue patches of sky over the sea. My mind seemed more in tune with the heavy, swollen clouds that were scudding across the South Downs.

Anita slowed down at a lay-by. She told me she needed to tell me something. There was a bus stop. Perhaps she was going to drop me off so that I could live my new life alone? *I'd been dumped at a bus stop before.*

'Chris.' She had turned in her seat to look me in the face.

In the next few minutes, she confessed that she was an actor and professional singer. She had been contracted to have her body digitised for gaming and to play the role of a hotel receptionist. It had been just another job, like a commercial or a voiceover. She had received monthly pay checks. Simon, Ben and Anya were also actors. The game had been real but in real life, there was no Strobe Kitson, no CloudCorp, no Texas Vampire. There was just this – the lay-by, the bus stop.

I just said 'oh', then nothing.

'Say something.'

'So, everything thing you told me in the hotel was a lie.'

'Well not everything. But it was in my contract to stay in character, or I wouldn't get paid.'

'Is that the most important thing to you?'

'It's my job, I'm an actor.'

'Is this in character?'

'No, it's me, Chris.'

'How do I know it's you?'

'Oh, Chris, it's me, of course it's me.'

She began to cry.

I looked out of the window. Behind a wire fence on the other side of flat green fields dotted with withered bushes would be a strip of shingle and the English Channel. Ahead of us, the looping coils of the River Cuckmere glinted like silver horseshoes.

After a while, once I'd smoked two more cigarettes, I put my arm around her. I'd decided I believed her, that she was being the real *her* now. We pledged our love for each other and continued our journey. Life had resumed. Soon, we would drive through Seaford, where new-looking houses and blocks of flats longingly face the ocean. Peacehaven and Saltdean are the same – lonely places for lonely people – dog walkers and people pushing walking frames, looking out at their final horizon. In Kemptown, at the edge of Brighton, the white buildings are taller and grander. It adds a few more revs to the seafront. Once you've reached the Palace Pier, you are in proper, full-on English seaside. We were talking now, excitedly speculating and making plans.

The next time we parked, it was in front of a terraced house, identical to all the others in this street where Anita lived. This was Preston Park, close to The Lanes, Brighton's mini Covent Garden. She'd bought a flat here a couple of years before with her ex-husband.

Now it was *our* home.

Brighton is a magnet for performers – those who are, those who want to be, those who were. The town, which is half of a city, invites you to loosen your tie and walk around with a smile, even if you're not on holiday. Its colours are wave turquoise, acid yellow and candy pink. Chip shops and Indian restaurants provide its olfactory palette. Its purposes are the bracing health of the sea, scary rides in the fairground on the pier and illicit sex. They're written into the by-laws.

It's not a challenge to find a means of expression in Brighton – many people express themselves simply by walking down the street. Music and theatre are in its bloodstream.

•••

Time passed in our new life together. With the help of her agent, Anita often worked professionally, sometimes in London. It had fallen to me to provide a steady income. I chose to do so by working in a garden centre. Three or four nights a week I was playing the drums for small amounts of money. At the weekends, we would drive along the coast and walk by the sea or on the South Downs. Often on Saturday nights I had gigs and, soon, Anita began to sing with one of the bands I was in. People loved us, because the music was unusual, and she was sensational. Being big in the bubble of Brighton and Hove is no indication of wider success but, even so, we were starting to get bigger gigs in the book. We were getting noticed. The life we led suited us. We were happy. But everything was soon to change.

Early the following year, in February 2019, I was driving our car to go shopping at a local retail park. That was what my life was like then. Anita had just been cast in a minor TV soap. As far as I was aware, she was in Manchester. My phone bleeped. It was an unknown number and I was curious, so I pulled over to read the text properly. Normally, it would have been Anita, reminding me to buy some essential item that I, as a man, was incapable of remembering.

It was an unknown number. The text said, 'Hi. I need to see you'.

I decided to play along, so I texted back: 'Where are you?'

They replied immediately: 'At The White Lodge.'

Well, that was intriguing. The hotel was about 30 minutes' drive away. Anita and I had driven past a few times out of curiosity to check it out – although these days its entrance was blocked by locked gates guarded by a private security company. I had noticed the name of the company because it was not familiar to me – Carson Utilities.

What should I do?

'Okay,' I texted, 'when do you want to meet?'

The response came back instantly: 'Now'.

58

The Job

The security barrier at the gate lifted as I approached it. The front door of the hotel was open. In the lobby, I saw step ladders and dustsheets. The whole place was midway through being redecorated. The fish tank in the bar was gone, so was the pool table and the picture of George Washington.

A man walked towards me. He was tall and wore a black t-shirt and blue jeans. His hair was cut midway between insurance salesman and rock star. He had a wide, uncomplicated smile and a firm handshake.

'Hi,' he said.

It was Strobe Kitson.

'Wanna drink?'

Miraculously, the bar pumps were plugged in and there was a barman, the same one as before. He greeted me as if I had never gone away.

'Yes, I am your buddy without the Stetson and the white duds,' said the man. 'You don't hate me, do you? You have no reason to. I'm not a vampire, honestly. Please, have a drink with me.'

We sat and I listened.

'Look, deception is easy, even in your country,' he drawled. 'A little makeup and some coloured lights is all it takes. There were no mummies. There were no Daily Mail stories, except on the fake website we made and the fake copies we had printed.'

I went along with his story, not telling him that I already knew the truth – or at least part of it.

'What about the demonstration at CloudCorp?' I asked pointedly.

'Rented building. Actors.'

'Mick Mahoney, the tragic backpacker?'

'Pure invention.'

'And the ranch in Brazil?'

'What about it?'

'Is that yours?'

'I rented it.'

'And the rocket launch pad?'

'I'm not investing in space. Not yet. I'm no Elon Musk. It's too fricking dangerous.'

'So, the rocket explosion…'

'…was fake news.'

'What about this place?'

'I own it. I'm turning it into a mind gym, as you can see.'

'A mind gym?' I looked at him blankly.

'We're flying in kids from developing countries and turning them into software engineers, coders, using gaming as incentive. It will be a kind of university. Look, as of this moment, I'm one of the richest people in the world, richer than Dave Grohl – he's my friend by the way – although I'm *not* richer than Elon or Jeff Bezos or the sainted Bill Gates. I like the fact that you've never heard of me. That's because I keep a low profile and because what I do is extremely dull. Well, most of what I do.'

'Which is what?'

'I own Carson Utilities, the company guarding this place. Security and facilities management are one of my businesses. But we don't just do that. We build schools, hospitals, roads, whole towns in some cases. We create physical and digital infrastructure.'

'Digital infrastructure?'

'Our cities are smart, Chris. Very smart. The digital side is mainly Chuck Tyler's baby.'

'Chuck Tyler? Isn't he dead?'

'Where did you read that?'

'In the Daily Mail.'

'And you believed it? He *is* my business partner but that's not his real name. Strobe Kitson is not my real name either. I'm not from Texas but Idaho, which is known as the potato state.'

'What's your name?'

He told me. It was very ordinary.

I looked at the door. Simon had just walked in. He was wearing a leather coat and carrying an overnight bag and a guitar case.

We greeted each other, although Simon held back.

'I hope that you two will do me the honour of playing a gig for me when we get to Nevada,' 'Kitson' commented.

'Nevada?'

'Yeh, we're going there. That's the plan. Simon and I were hoping you'd want to come – to accept your position.'

'My position?'

'At Carson Utilities.'

'My position as what?'

'Oh, I don't know. Job titles are bullshit. Pick a name. How about "Thought Leader" or "Imagineer", if one of those floats your boat. I told you there'd be a job for you if you finished the game, didn't I? I wasn't lying, Chris. Think of the game as a very elaborate and expensive job interview. That's what it was. And it worked. I got my man. And I got my own house band. Anya and Ben are coming to Nevada too by the way. Ah, here's Anita.'

She crossed the room and stood in front of me. I kissed her. Her cheeks were cold.

'I thought you were in Manchester.'

She opened her mouth to speak.

'You were lying to me *again* weren't you.'

'Chris...'

For a moment, I was annoyed. How many times had we agreed that we had to trust each other?

'For fuck's sake.'

Kitson broke the silence:

'To be honest, Chris, we're pretty confident that you'll say yes to your new job. It's better paid than what you're doing. Not that there's anything wrong with working in retail of course. Anita has packed your cases, ready for the journey.'

'The journey?'

'Yes, to Carson City, Nevada. That's where my company is based. We can leave whenever you're ready. There's a helicopter on standby. Oh, and by the way?'

'What?'

'You know I promised you a million dollars if you got to the end of the game?'

I nodded, suspiciously.

'The money was transferred this morning to your account – that is, your joint account. I hope that's okay.'

'Right. Well, thank you,' I stuttered, by now totally flabbergasted.

'My pleasure. So, would you like the job?'

I had no idea what the job was, but I said yes anyway.

I looked at my nearest and dearest who was now standing next to me. She smiled and I instantly forgave her.

59

The Ape Roared

We flew by helicopter to Northolt Airport that afternoon. Wheeling over the green fields and chalk cliffs, Anita and I said goodbye, not just to the hotel this time, but to England. A private jet – a white Boeing 747 with 'Carson Utilities' written on the side – was about to fly us to America.

When we finally arrived in Nevada, we saw that the company's global HQ was set in a hollowed-out mountain in the Sierra Nevada. Since it was a civil engineering company that had branched out into other areas, this massive project wouldn't have been too much of a problem. Most of the HQ was inside the mountain.

We took the company's cable car up to the main entrance. From here, those with the correct credentials could descend into a world made up of multiple floors and mezzanine levels with white walls and lots of glass and polished chrome. Busy people carried water bottles from meeting to meeting, continuing their conversations in break-out areas enlivened by pool tables and cushions in primary colours.

Some of them must have been doing dull stuff connected to designing buildings and motorway junctions, I imagined, it was hard to tell. That was the whole point. At Carson work was never boring. It was all fun.

Chuck Tyler (not his real name) had his own area within the complex – his 'play pen'. His wild hair gave him the distinctive look of a genius. It was said that he kept a well-stocked armoury in his office.

It was Tyler – I have persisted in using his fake name – who had come up with a new concept for Carson Utilities – the molecular web. It would not require giant servers or data centres sucking up half the electricity of the world. But it would connect every person and intelligent device on the planet like a nervous system – a biological metaverse. He'd come up with another idea – or some bright spark in marketing had – ClickMonkey.

As soon as the molecular web was switched on, this smiling creature would appear as an icon on every internet-connected device with a user interface on earth, announcing that nothing would ever be the same again. This was Web ∞ (infinity). ClickMonkey could be used for every transaction and communication and sharing platform. It would not carry advertising and extract no profit from its services. The cheeky little chap would be ubiquitous. Amazon, Meta and X would be toast. That was the theory.

As the digital giants wasted away, Tyler predicted, they would move in for the kill, with the full might of the data military complex behind them. At some point, their drones would arrive and bomb the mountain.

But no-one would be here. The joke would be that most of what the complex contained was air. Carson Securities didn't have a gigantic server cooled by water drawn from the depths of the mountain. It didn't need one.

The masters of the universe would not understand that – nor that, once the molecular web had been switched on, it could never be switched off. Ha ha. *Ever felt cheated?*

•••

Anita and I had moved into a spacious lakeside house with a steeply pitched roof and dormer windows, made from wood. It was decorated with Native American artefacts. A wooden platform at the front of the house projected directly onto the water – perfect for canoeing trips, fishing and playing the guitar.

From here, in the far distance on a clear day, you could see light reflecting from the glass panels on Mount Carson. At sunset, the sky over the mountains was like a blood orange cut in two.

At night, we would burn pinyon and juniper wood. Their smoke, mingling with that of our pleasantly mellow weed, was like the sweet breath of the land. You could hear coyotes call. If you echoed their sound with an owl hoot from your cupped hands, they would call back.

What is my job? I still don't know. It says 'Global Thought Leader' on my business card. I suppose my job is, indeed, thinking – that's what most jobs are now – and talking. And some writing.

First this story, relating what has happened in the last two years: 'The Texas Vampire'.

My next task, as we wait for the great switch-on, when ClickMonkey will be set loose on the world, is to write a creation myth – a parable. It will be a new Bible, Quran, Bhagavad Gita and Gilgamesh rolled into one, as humans begin a new journey and spread their seed through the universe. (It turns out that the company *is* into space travel and has invented a new deep space drive.) The Bible thing was Strobe's idea. Yes, I still call him that – not his 'real' name, it's too boring.

So I began writing it last night. The main thing is writing short, numbered paragraphs and the wacky baccy imagery. The local weed helps. It starts like this:

1:1 In the 2000s, as well as computers and smartphones, we began to acquire 'intelligent' fridges, ovens and cars and, hidden in gizmos, little digital friends that we could apparently talk to and appeared to do our bidding. Actually, they were not separate but part of one entity – a planetary nervous system.

1:2 We did not become aware of this until the decade was reaching its close but these innocent and useful machines were able to read our minds – indeed, that was an essential part of their purpose. Soon, using secret algorithms devised by the alchemists of 'information technology', they could predict our desires.

1:3 Initially, this appeared to be harmless. After all, the screens were merely dangling before our eyes the things that we wanted. We clicked and they became manifest. Physical goods arrived more and more quickly – at first by motorised vehicle and then by drone – delivered efficiently to us in fleets of neat silver capsules that darkened the skies.

1:4 The new masters of the universe were extracting from our brains and life signs the most precious commodity of the 21st Century: data. Data was the new oil – the stuff of life itself. It allowed the masters of the world to manipulate and influence our decisions – not just in shopping but in politics and the public realm.

1:5 Billionaires, millionaires, trillionaires, zillionaires – humans ran out of words to describe the wealth that they were acquiring. They knew everything about us, we knew almost nothing about them. Some people could glimpse the future, in the flickering shadows on the wall of Plato's cave. But human senses were dulled by consumption – the immediate fulfilment of their wants.

1:6 By the first quarter of the 21st Century, three entities came to dominate what was known, ontologically, as the digital world. One beast, with razor-sharp teeth, resembled a tyrannosaurus. It had become the largest animal on earth by constantly gratifying its hunger. Another, a marine armadillo, had slid onto the land from the depths of the darkest oceans, issuing a corrosive bile from its mouth. Its back was covered with scales that could deflect any weapon. The third was a giant worm. It grew larger by gorging on the excrement of the two other beasts.

1:7 A fourth creature jumped down from a tree – a giant ape. The ape roared. Its countenance was like thunder. It clambered onto the backs of the two beasts. Its razor talons rent into their flesh. Initially, the armoured hides of the creatures protected them. But not for long. Soon their bodies began to disintegrate.

1:8 The ape tugged at the head of the worm. It pulled the creature from the earth and slashed it to fragments, link by link. Emboldened, the ape gave a roar of triumph. It could feel itself growing stronger. Smiling, it skipped across the world.

Thanks and acknowledgements

Writing a book is a long, solitary road. I am so grateful that I have a loving family, especially AJ, who tolerates my lack of cleanliness, because my thoughts are generally elsewhere. And Karina.

My mother set me on the path of fiction because she asked questions, as did my father, because he failed to answer them. Thanks both.

I have some brilliant and highly supportive friends. Chief among these, for the purpose of The Texas Vampire, have been the peerless Pippa Lang, metal queen, who passed the MS through a second pair of eyes and cleaned up some of my numerous mistakes and grammatical, linguistic and cultural solecisms, graphic design maestro, Jon Heal, who designed the cover and Adam, my coffee companion and touchstone.

I must acknowledge here my departed and much-missed south-east London buddy, the amazing Peter Gentle, who beat me at pool, made me laugh, always, and with whom I had many long and illuminating conversations.

To my other friends, some of whom are in this book in thinly-disguised form – thank you too. You know who you are. Thanks are also due to Rod and Paul at Wild Wolf, who made this book possible.

Printed in Great Britain
by Amazon